ANNA SAYBURN LANE

Murder On The White Cliffs

A 1920s murder mystery

**STARLING
STREET BOOKS**

To my parents David and Brenda, with love, thanks, and memories of childhood holidays in Broadstairs

Foreword

Murder On The White Cliffs is the sixth in a series of 1920s murder mystery adventures featuring assistant private investigator Marjorie Swallow.

A word about spelling: I'm a British author, so I use British spelling and grammar.

You can find out more about the books, get free short stories and a prequel novella when you sign up to my Readers Club newsletter on my website, annasayburnlane.com.

Chapter 1

'Oi, Marge! There's a nun in the office,' Frankie called.

I paused on my way up the stairs.

Frankie, Mrs Jameson's chauffeur, was lounging in the hall in her smart uniform. She'd removed her peaked cap and was using it to fan herself. The day was already hot and sticky. I felt warm from my trip out to the Post Office, even though I was wearing my lightest cotton frock.

'Really?' We'd never had a nun as a client before. 'When did she get here?'

I'd heard Frankie's opinion of religion – 'the opium of the people' – and hoped she hadn't felt the need to share it with the poor nun.

'About half an hour ago. I picked her up from Victoria station, off the morning boat train. She'd been on the overnight sailing from Calais and looked pretty ropey. She's Italian.'

Well, that was interesting. Ever since I'd started working for Mrs Jameson's detective agency, almost two years ago, my employer had been getting regular letters with Italian stamps, post-marked in Rome, which she never spoke about. I dealt with the rest of her correspondence but had been taught on

1

pain of extreme disapproval not to open anything from Italy.

Eagerly, I ran up the rest of the steps, tapped on the door of the agency and opened it. Was I finally going to discover the secret that Mrs Jameson had been keeping all this time?

'Good morning.' I crossed the big room with windows onto Bedford Square, where the July sun was dappling the dusty plane trees with gold. I reached for the pad on my desk to take down my usual shorthand notes of proceedings, and smiled at our visitor. 'I'm Miss Swallow, Mrs Jameson's secretary.'

The nun wore a brown habit and white wimple, all traces of hair scraped away from her face. She appeared to be of middle age, and returned my smile with warm brown eyes, the same colour as her habit. I wondered why she wasn't wearing black, like the few nuns I'd seen in London. She was sitting in one of the green leather armchairs, tucking into a coffee éclair. My mouth watered and I checked the tray to see if Mrs Smithson, the cook, had put out enough for all of us.

Mrs Jameson looked up and I saw at once that she was annoyed. That was never a good start to the day. Her pale lips were pressed thinly together, and her grey eyes had a hooded aspect, like an eagle pausing before it pounced on some unwary rodent.

'Marjorie, please wait downstairs. I wish to speak to Sister Agnese privately.' Her American accent was sharper than normal.

Bother. It looked like I wasn't going to crack the mystery that day.

'Of course.' I set my things down and made a hasty retreat.

\#

Downstairs in the big kitchen, Mrs Smithson was chopping

vegetables for lunch and Graham the butler was polishing the silver.

'Get chucked out, did you?' asked Frankie. She'd stripped off her jacket and was sitting by the open back door in her shirtsleeves, tinkering with something that looked like it belonged under the bonnet of the Lagonda.

I nodded, ruefully. 'She said she wanted to talk to her in private. I didn't even get one of Mrs Smithson's éclairs.'

I made a big pot of tea and handed around the cups.

'Thank you, Marjorie. I've not had one all morning,' said Graham, his perspiring face creasing into a smile. 'I'm parched.'

'You only had to ask,' said Mrs Smithson, a little peevish.

'I don't like to trouble you,' he told her. 'We've all got enough on our plates.'

Everyone in Mrs Jameson's household was a little fretful, probably because of the heat. June had been a wash-out, but July was promising to be a scorcher, and London was never at its best when the temperature rose. Mrs Jameson had been talking for ages about taking a trip to the seaside. I had the impression the staff would be happy to see her go, so they could get on with the annual deep clean that happened in most of the big houses when their owners were away for the summer.

I took my tea to the open doorway to get a breath of air. A few sparrows hopped around, hoping for crumbs.

'Here you go, girls,' said Mrs Smithson, setting down a plate with an eclair each for me and Frankie. 'I kept a couple back for you.'

We fell on them joyfully, Frankie giving her hands a perfunctory wipe on an oil-stained rag. The choux pastry was light, the cream whipped to perfection and the coffee glaze sweet.

'They're delicious,' I said, as soon as my mouth was empty enough.

Frankie gave Mrs Smithson a thumbs-up. 'Blooming lovely,' she announced.

'Tell me more about the nun,' I said to Frankie. 'What did you find out when you picked her up?' Although Frankie's official role was chauffeur, she took an active part in our investigations. She also made a handy bodyguard, being skilled in the martial art of jiu-jitsu, which I too had been learning. If I couldn't find out directly, I'd see what I could glean from Frankie.

'Her name's Sister Agnese. She's from a convent in Rome, but she speaks decent English,' reported Frankie. 'And she's known Mrs J for donkey's years.'

'From when she lived there, I suppose,' I said. Mrs Jameson had lived in Rome for many years before her husband's death, and since then in other cities on the Continent. She spoke casually of sojourns in Paris, Geneva, and Vienna. However, I'd never heard her mention a convent before. As far as I knew, she wasn't a Roman Catholic. Indeed, I had never heard her express any religious faith at all.

As a young woman, my employer had married a famous artist, Julian Jameson, who was notorious as a womaniser, drinker and gambler. During a stint working undercover at a newspaper, I'd discovered a clipping about her husband's death in Rome. He'd died twenty years ago from a gunshot wound, inflicted accidentally while he was cleaning the gun. The police had ruled out any suspicious circumstances, the report had said.

However, I'd wondered about his death ever since. I'd seen

Mrs Jameson wield a pistol. She was an excellent shot. The thought made me more than a little uneasy.

'I didn't find out much else,' said Frankie. 'She's staying at a convent in London tonight, then going back tomorrow. So, she must have only come to see Mrs J. Unless the business is with the convent, and she just dropped in to say hello.'

It hadn't looked to me like a purely social visit. If it had been, would I have been banished so summarily? What could have happened that required the woman to travel all the way from Rome for one night? Why could she not have written instead? I wondered if all the letters Mrs Jameson received from Rome had come from the nuns.

'Sister Agnese didn't tell you the name of the convent in Rome, did she?' I asked. I could examine the envelopes that Mrs Jameson threw away, to see if they had the convent's return address.

Frankie grabbed the last piece of éclair that I'd been saving and ate it.

'You rotter!' I protested.

She grinned. 'Payment for information. She did, actually. The Convento... Something, sounded like Hospital – of Santa Francesca Romana. She says they're Franciscans. That's why they wear those brown robes, instead of the black ones the Sisters of Mercy wear.'

'You seem to know quite a bit about nuns.'

She nodded. 'Went to a convent school in Shoreditch for a while, run by the Sisters. They were all right. Taught me to read and write, anyway.'

I laughed. I couldn't imagine Frankie as a dutiful convent schoolgirl. 'They must have been rather puzzled by you.'

She looked up, unusually serious. 'They took me as they

found me. They were more interested in what was inside my head than how short my hair was cut. They were the only ones who actually cared about what happened to us kids, excepting my Auntie Clara.'

I digested this. Although my shop-keeper parents weren't rich, they'd made sure I got a good education and were proud as anything when I won a scholarship to Sydenham High School. I hadn't even thought before about where a girl like Frankie might have learned her letters. She never mentioned her parents; from what I could gather she'd been brought up by her aunt – a formidable suffragette – and cousins, when she wasn't roaming the streets of the East End on her own.

The bell rang. Graham set down his cleaning cloth. 'I'll go,' he said.

He was back a few minutes later with Mrs Jameson's tray, empty coffee cups and plates.

'You're to bring the car around to take Sister Agnese to her accommodation, Frankie,' he reported. 'And Marjorie, Mrs Jameson says she wants you in the office straight away.'

Chapter 2

To my relief, Mrs Jameson's fit of annoyance seemed to have passed. Perhaps the éclairs had cheered her up.

'Ah, Marjorie, there you are. May I introduce you to Sister Agnese Giuseppina, a dear friend from my time in Rome? Sister Agnese, Marjorie is my secretary, a complete treasure. I can't begin to tell you how much of an asset she is to the detective agency. Nothing gets past her sharp eyes, I can assure you.'

I glanced at my employer suspiciously, wondering a little at this unusual gush of praise. She looked quite serious, although she was fidgeting with her fountain pen. Something had made her nervous.

Sister Agnese rose and took my hands between her own warm, smooth fingers. She looked steadily at me. Up close, I could see the fine network of lines that spread across her tranquil face. She was older than I had realised at first; more than fifty years old, I thought now.

'That is apparent,' she said, her Italian accent soft. 'Marjorie, I am happy to see you. You must take very great care of our dear Iris. You will do that, won't you?'

Puzzled, I smiled my agreement. 'Of course. That's what

I'm here for.' But what was Sister Agnese here for?

'Bene. That is good. Blessings upon you,' she said, making the sign of the cross with a swift gesture. I imagined what my mother would say if she could see me being blessed by a Catholic nun. Mum fought an ongoing battle with the rather High Anglican vicar at our local church against any signs of what she called Papism.

Sister Agnese turned back to Mrs Jameson. 'I am so happy to see you again, Iris,' she said. 'I am sure you will do what is best.'

She glided to the door and Mrs Jameson saw her down the stairs to the hall. I crossed to the window and watched Sister Agnese climb into the back seat of the Lagonda, assisted by an unusually deferential Frankie. They drove off.

My eyes fell on a small pile of books on the low table before the armchairs. All were bound in red cloth. I turned my head sideways. They were travel guides, but not to Rome or the Continent. *'Ward Lock Pictorial and Descriptive Guide to Brighton and Hove,'* read the top one. The second offered a guide to Windsor and its castle, the third to Eastbourne and the fourth to Broadstairs. Was Mrs Jameson planning a summer tour?

My employer came back in.

'It's time I saw more of England,' she said, briskly. 'High summer is no time to be in London, especially as the newspaper weather forecasts are predicting a heatwave. Where shall we go? The seaside, I think, don't you? Sea breezes, perhaps a chance to bathe. I wish to go at once. Tomorrow, or Friday at the latest.'

'That would be lovely, Mrs Jameson.'

I wondered why she had decided it was so urgent to leave

London. The weather was perfect for a trip to the coast, it was true. But she'd been talking about it for ages. Was her sudden desire to get out of town linked to Sister Agnese's visit, and whatever news she had brought?

However, I wasn't going to look a gift horse in the mouth. How glorious it would be to visit the coast, get away from the stale dust of London and plunge into the sea. I'd learned to swim on our trip to the south of France the previous year and was keen to practise again.

I picked up the books and flicked through. 'Have you been to any of these places before?'

She shook her head. 'I leave the choice of destination to you, Marjorie. What would you recommend?'

Goodness, what a responsibility. I'd been on day trips to Brighton and Margate, both of which were fun but rather crowded and full of noisy Londoners out for cheap entertainment. I wasn't sure they would suit Mrs Jameson.

I remembered one of my school teachers used to spend a fortnight every summer at Broadstairs, playing golf on the links. We'd all been rather keen on Miss Levitt, with her masculine stride and brisk air of authority. Perhaps that would do.

'Broadstairs is nice,' I ventured. I picked up the guidebook and handed it to Mrs Jameson. She flicked through.

'Charles Dickens used to go there on his holidays,' I remembered. Miss Levitt had told us that every September. 'He wrote *Bleak House* there.'

Mrs Jameson laughed. 'Well, if it's good enough for Dickens, I guess it's good enough for me.' She turned the page, then smiled and waved the book at me.

'This looks most suitable. A castle on the white cliffs,

overlooking the sea. Give them a call, Marjorie, and book us in for two weeks. Remember, I want to leave as soon as possible. I'll go and speak to Jenny about the packing.'

She swept out of the room. I read the description in the guidebook. Kingsgate Castle, two miles from Broadstairs, had recently been converted into a smart hotel. The book reproduced a photograph of a proper castle, with crenellations, battlements and towers, set against a backdrop of sea.

'A magnificent building equipped with every modern luxury – Golf at the famous North Foreland Club, dancing, tennis and putting course – Unique situation perched on the top of the white cliffs – Private baths in every room...'

It did sound rather wonderful. However, it was already July. I suspected such a desirable hotel would be booked up early. Mrs Jameson was not always patient if her sudden whims were not accommodated. On the other side of Kingsgate Bay was the Captain Digby tavern, which looked nice but had the ominous phrase 'perfect for families' in its description. Mrs Jameson had low tolerance for screaming babies or boisterous children.

I put a call through and waited. A young woman, sounding rather superior, said that they were usually fully booked for the summer.

'However,' she said, making it sound as if she was doing me a tremendous favour, 'we have had a late cancellation for Friday. You're very lucky. Now, how many rooms, and do you require servants' accommodation and garaging for a motor car?'

Triumphantly, I made the booking for a fortnight and went to share the good news with Mrs Jameson.

Chapter 3

Kingsgate Castle certainly lived up to its billing. After a pleasant drive through Kentish orchards and hop-fields, we arrived at the hotel with its battlements and towers, sitting atop the sheer white chalk cliffs. The sea sparkled as if sprinkled with diamonds and the sun blazed overhead.

Frankie turned in at the gate, went down a straight gravel drive through smooth lawns and right up to a gatehouse complete with portcullis. A man in an immaculate charcoal-grey morning suit glided out to greet us, followed by uniformed porters.

'This is a bit of all right,' remarked Frankie, pulling up by the gatehouse. She wasn't wrong. I craned my neck to take in the fluttering flag that rose from a turret.

Mrs Jameson and I climbed out, then Frankie parked alongside the other cars lined up to the left of the gatehouse. The motors suggested a high-class clientele – a Rolls Royce, a Hispano Suiza and a dashing little royal blue sports car.

'Mrs Jameson? And Miss Swallow. I am delighted to welcome you to Kingsgate Castle,' said the man in the morning suit. 'I am Mr Ashcroft, the manager. Please don't hesitate to ask if I can be of any help during your stay.'

Mrs Jameson was gracious and generous as always, ensuring that the staff would vie to look after her. She expressed herself delighted with the hotel's situation.

'Tell me, Mr Ashcroft, what is the history of the castle? Have archers with bows and arrows repelled invaders from the battlements since Roman times?' she asked, a hint of tease in her voice. She was actually very well versed in British history.

He smiled with a hint of pleased superiority. 'Ah, I'm afraid the castle is much more recent than that,' he said. 'It was built in the eighteenth century, more or less as a folly, in imitation of a medieval castle. It was a private residence until two years ago, when Lord Avebury sold the estate and it was converted into an hotel. Do come this way. The porters will help your chauffeur with the trunks and see him to his quarters.'

I grinned. Frankie was used to being taken for a man. No doubt she'd put the porters right.

We crossed beyond the portcullis and into the courtyard. A brisk woman in a black and white uniform with a bunch of keys at her waist approached.

'Excuse me, Mr Ashcroft, might I have a word about the advertisement for the new kitchen staff?'

Mr Ashcroft waved her off. 'Later, Mrs Heath. I'm with guests,' he said, his smooth voice betraying barely a hint of irritation. 'The main restaurant is through here,' he said to Mrs Jameson, gesturing towards a long room with French windows opening onto the courtyard and a glimpse of blue sea through the windows on the other side. 'We will be serving luncheon from half past twelve. And if you would like an aperitif, the terrace bar is open now.'

'I'll go to my room and wash up first,' said Mrs Jameson. 'Marjorie, I shall see you on the terrace shortly.' She disappeared with Mr Ashcroft. The brisk Mrs Heath followed on his heels.

I couldn't wait to see the sea. I followed the glimmer of blue through the dining room and out onto a wide paved terrace which ended abruptly at a low wall. Beyond was the sea, cornflower-blue and alive with white sails. I took a great lungful of salty air, enjoying the tang of seaweed on the breeze and the mewing of gulls. I shook out the skirt of my cotton frock, hoping the breeze would smooth the creases from the long drive.

Someone called my name and I squinted in the dazzling sun as I turned towards the bar set up on the terrace. Jaunty red and white beach umbrellas shaded the wicker tables.

'Marjorie!' Sarah Post wriggled down from a bar stool and clasped her hands together, her lovely face flushed with sun. 'How marvellous! Look, Bertie, see who's here. Oh, do say you're going to stay. Are you with Mrs Jameson?'

I laughed with pleasure. I liked Sarah and Bertie. They were actors, both tremendously good-looking, and had married the previous year. The photographs in the illustrated papers had been lovely. I had met them at a fateful party in Bloomsbury, during what became my first case with Mrs Jameson. Bertie, I remembered, was the owner of the blue sports car I'd admired outside.

'Oh, good show. How d'you do, Marjorie?' Bertie beamed. He wore a striped blazer and straw boater, and his smooth Grecian profile was tanned.

Sarah embraced me, her platinum-blonde curls squashed up against my cheek. 'I thought I'd die of boredom,' she murmured. 'Everyone else here is ancient. Heavenly to see you.' Her pretty silk dress, a becoming shade of blue to match her eyes, had probably cost ten times the price of my crumpled cotton frock. Their fortunes had clearly improved since their marriage. Perhaps I should change before luncheon.

But in a trice I was installed on a bar stool alongside them, a glass of champagne in my hand.

'We're celebrating,' announced Sarah. 'The first night of Pimpernel was a sell-out last night, and everyone loved it. You will come to see it, won't you?'

'Pimpernel?'

'Our new play,' explained Bertie. '*The Scarlet Pimpernel*. Based on the novel. You know: "They seek him here, they seek him there!" I'm playing Sir Percy, and Sarah is Marguerite. We're performing at the Hippodrome in Margate for the rest of the month, then it transfers to Brighton.'

'How lovely! I read the book at school,' I said. 'I fell madly in love with the Pimpernel when I was fifteen. You'll have to watch out, Sarah.'

A man with a stick walked through the dining room and crossed the terrace, screwing up his eyes against the sun. I realised from his gait that he had an artificial leg. He propped himself against the bar and ordered a whisky and soda, then turned to smile at my companions. He wasn't ancient, at any rate, although he was rather thin and pale, with dark hair swept back from his face.

'Hullo, you two. Congratulations again, on last night. Tremendous fun. Can I get you anything?'

Bertie introduced me. 'Marjorie, this is James Lockwood. James, meet our friend Marjorie Swallow. Are you here on business, Marjorie?'

'Heavens, no,' I said. 'Thank goodness.'

I turned to smile at Mr Lockwood. He looked like he could

do with a bit of sun and sea air. 'I'm here with my employer, an American lady, on holiday. I expect she'll be joining us soon. I'm her secretary.'

Sarah squealed. 'Are you sure you're not investigating something? Marjorie is a private detective, James. We met her when that horrid old woman was killed after the party in Mecklenburgh Square. And she solved it all!'

'Mrs Jameson solved it,' I corrected her. Although I had uncovered a few secrets on my own, including a rather important one about Sarah herself. I wondered if she'd shared it with Bertie yet.

'How exciting,' said Mr Lockwood, raising a dark eyebrow. 'Isn't that a bit of a dangerous game?'

In the past two years, I'd been kidnapped by gangsters, threatened by a blackmailer, driven off the road by a murderer and forced at gunpoint to dig my own grave. This last in particular still made me shudder.

'Oh, you know,' I said. 'It has its moments. What about you, Mr Lockwood? What's your profession?'

He shrugged and looked embarrassed. 'I'm not much use for anything now, I'm afraid.' He put his hand to his knee and shifted his leg. 'I was training to be a solicitor, before the War. But now I write, you know. Stories.'

'I love to read,' I said. 'What sort of books do you write?' I did hope it wouldn't be highbrow stuff that I'd have to admit to not knowing. I liked a good detective story, although that had become a bit of a busman's holiday.

'James writes romances,' interjected Sarah. 'They're marvellous. But not under his own name, you know. It's all very hush-hush. What do you say, James, shall we let Marjorie in on the secret?'

15

Chapter 4

Mrs Jameson arrived at that promising moment, and I had to curb my curiosity while Mr Lockwood was introduced again. Then it was time for luncheon, and we trooped into the restaurant, where Sarah begged the staff to rearrange the furniture so we could all eat together.

'Terribly good grub here,' said Bertie. 'We usually have a big luncheon, then just a bite to eat in the afternoon. They're very good about rustling up some supper when we get back late after the show.'

Mrs Jameson smiled approval. 'I do hope so. My cook is so good that I'm spoiled for eating anywhere else.'

I fell greedily on the menu card. We'd had breakfast early before motoring down, and I was famished.

'What's a Caesar Salad?' I asked.

'Oh, it's quite delicious,' said Sarah. 'American, you know. Lettuce with eggs and anchovies and croutons. I'd have it every day, but the dressing is quite garlicky, and I don't want to knock out the front row when I sing.'

Feeling daring, I decided to give it a go, with chicken escalope to follow. The important business of ordering out of the way, I looked around at the other tables.

'Who is everyone?' I asked.

An elderly couple in the corner bickered gently over their food, while two brisk-looking women in their thirties strode across the dining room wearing golfing plus-fours and diamond-patterned sweaters. One was tall, dark and athletic, the other wiry but shorter, with tousled fair hair like a terrier.

Sarah glanced around. 'Those little tabbies in the corner are Mr and Mrs Goldsmith,' she said. 'Sweet, but ancient. They've been married forever, and I don't think they go a day without an argument. The golfing women are Scottish, Jean McDonald and Helen Fraser. Miss McDonald's a schoolteacher and rather brusque in manner: "Though she be but little, she is fierce." Helen's the one with the money. Fraser's of Dundee, you know, the ones who make the marmalade. She doesn't talk much; probably can't get a word in.'

The women were followed across the room by a couple also in golfing attire. They too appeared to be in their thirties, despite Sarah's complaint that everyone at the hotel was 'ancient'. The woman, who was tall and icily elegant with sleek dark hair, stopped halfway across the room and made a sign of displeasure. Her companion summoned the waiter, and before long a team of staff were moving a table out of the sun and repositioning it until it met the lady's satisfaction.

Sarah threw a disparaging glance at the new arrivals. 'The Treadwells are awful. He works in the City and likes to make sure everyone knows how much money he has. Mildred Treadwell's a dreadful snob, although she really has no cause to be.'

Mr Lockwood laughed. 'I'd hate to hear what you say about me when I'm not here, Sarah.'

'You're a dear, and I wouldn't say anything different.' She

patted his hand, and his pale face flushed. I did hope he wasn't enamoured of her. Sarah loved to flirt, but she was devoted to Bertie.

'What about those two by the French windows?' I asked. Sarah followed my gaze. A morose-looking man in his forties with a big military moustache sat opposite an older woman who kept up a stream of chatter to which he made occasional brief responses.

'Major Redfern and his mother, Mrs Redfern.' Sarah's face became serious. 'He's rather frightening. They've just come back from India or somewhere else hot, and he gets these fits. Drinks too much and shouts at the waiters. I feel sorry for his mother. You can see she hates it.'

'The major's not so bad,' said Mr Lockwood. 'Had a rotten time of it during the War. He was in the Indian Army, took part in the Mesopotamian campaign, then the disaster of the Dardanelles.

'He's recovering from a bout of malaria,' he told me. 'Poor fellow. There are a lot of us about, you know, Miss Swallow. War damage.'

'Of course.' I'd met plenty of them during my time nursing soldiers at the Maudsley Hospital. 'We must make allowances.'

Mr Lockwood pushed back his plate impatiently. 'Not at all. We don't want allowances. Nor do we want pity, or gratitude. We just want to get on with our lives. D'you see?'

#

In the afternoon, Frankie and I explored the hotel and beach with the Posts, although I drew the line at taking the tunnel from the basement through the chalk cliff. It emerged partway down onto a set of precarious-looking metal steps direct to the beach.

'It's by far the best way,' Sarah urged me. 'You can run straight down in your bathing costume and robe, without having to go out and along the road.'

Even so, I decided I'd prefer the longer trek. I wasn't keen on tunnels. But the beach itself was delightful; soft white sand which sloped gently into the sea. The height of the cliffs meant you couldn't see it from the road, and it was only overlooked by the hotel and another crenellated building at the far end of the bay, which Bertie said was the Captain Digby tavern. Frankie and I dived into the sea, squealing in the chilly water, washing away the dust of London.

After his prickly outburst, I was a little wary of Mr Lockwood. He dined with Major Redfern and his mother in the evening, then played bridge with them and Mrs Jameson. As I didn't play, I read a book in the lounge until Sarah and Bertie returned from the theatre.

'What's Mr Lockwood's secret?' I whispered to Sarah, as Bertie ordered drinks and the staff set out a light supper for the actors on a low table. 'You were going to tell me, then we got interrupted.'

She laughed gaily and called him over. 'James! Come and confess your alias.'

He made his way over to the sofa. Although he was trying to look severe, he had a half-pleased expression that suggested he was glad to be asked.

'Don't tell everyone. Blissful anonymity is the whole point of having a pen-name.'

'James Lockwood is Selina Summerville,' announced Sarah. 'Isn't that the best thing you've ever heard?'

'No!' Selina Summerville was a literary sensation, the author of wildly popular romance novels set in Regency times. I'd read two and thought they were great fun. I would never have guessed they were written by a man.

'I'm afraid so.' Mr Lockwood gave an embarrassed chuckle and took the seat next to me. He had begun writing stories while in the trenches, to cheer himself up and entertain the men, he said. Then he'd continued in hospital after his leg was taken off, and a friend of his father who worked for a publishing company had seen them.

'The men used to laugh their heads off when I read them aloud, but the publisher said the general public would love them. Turned out he was right. Apparently women are all for romance, so long as reality doesn't intrude.'

Jean McDonald, playing chess with Helen Fraser nearby, looked up. 'You write those dreadful Regency romances?' she asked, her tone disapproving. 'Then I have a bone to pick with you. They're all my girls will read. I've been trying to wean them off onto Jane Austen, or at least Sir Walter Scott.'

'You have daughters?' asked Sarah. She gave the upright Miss Macdonald a wide-eyed look.

'My pupils,' said Miss McDonald. She shot a glance of dislike at Sarah, before returning her focus to Mr Lockwood. 'I'm trying to instil a sustaining love of good literature, but all they want is to read about handsome dukes and swooning servant girls. Utterly historically inaccurate, I hope you realise.'

Mr Lockwood sighed and sank down into the sofa. 'Fortunately, I'm not a history teacher,' he said. 'I write stuff that sells. That's all.'

Miss McDonald's mouth twisted in something that looked very like contempt, and she turned away.

'Shall we go up now?' Miss Fraser packed away the chess

pieces with an anxious glance at her friend. 'It's getting late.'

'Well, I think they are perfectly lovely,' said Sarah, flashing James a bright smile. She rolled her eyes at me. 'I wouldn't want Miss McDonald as a teacher, would you?' she whispered.

Miss McDonald rather reminded me of my own head teacher at Sydenham High School, who had been high-minded and hadn't approved of our enthusiasm for detective and adventure stories. However, she had ensured we all left with the ability to use our brains and make our ways in the world as independent young women. And for that, I continued to feel grateful.

Chapter 5

During the next four days, we settled into a happy routine at Kingsgate Bay: swimming, walking on the cliffs or reading on the terrace, taking trips into Broadstairs and to see the North Foreland lighthouse. I'd all but forgotten the visit by Sister Agnese which had preceded Mrs Jameson's sudden decision to decamp to the coast.

Frankie and I played tennis with Bertie and Sarah on the hotel's brand-new courts, finding to our pleasure that we were quite evenly matched. The Treadwells, playing on the neighbouring court, threw us a disapproving glance as we walked out onto the grass. I wasn't sure whether it was Frankie's cobbled-together outfit of rolled-up trousers and shirtsleeves that offended them, or the fact that the chauffeur was playing tennis at all.

However, most of the residents seemed to accept Mrs Jameson's unconventional household, perhaps putting her informal relations with her staff down to her American nationality. Miss McDonald and Miss Fraser tried to teach us to play golf on the North Foreland links across the road from the hotel, albeit without much success. I was too clumsy and Mrs Jameson annoyed Miss McDonald by not taking it seriously enough.

'You have a most promising swing,' she exclaimed. 'But you need to keep your mind on the game.'

It was unlike Mrs Jameson not to concentrate. But as we walked back to the hotel, I realised her attention had been on something else. 'Miss McDonald is a good player,' she said, with a feline smile. 'But nothing like as good as her friend. Miss Fraser lets her win, and so tactfully that Miss McDonald doesn't even realise.'

The evenings were a little dull: the older guests played interminable games of contract bridge after dinner, and although the house band was good, there weren't enough people dancing to make it really jolly. Frankie said it was more fun in the servants' quarters, and tended to spend her evenings there. I was looking forward to our outing to see *The Scarlet Pimpernel* at Margate on Friday night.

Most mornings, Mrs Jameson, Frankie and I went down to the beach for a bathe before breakfast. They used the tunnel from the hotel basement, but I carried my towel and bathing costume through the garden and around the road to the public steps.

By the time I reached the beach on the Wednesday morning, Mrs Jameson and Frankie were already in the water. I unstrapped my sandals and wriggled my toes in the soft, warm sand, changed quickly in one of the red-and-white bathing tents and went to join them. That's when I noticed the woman.

She was tall, dark-haired and wore a plain white cotton frock, belted around the waist. She'd taken off her white sun hat and was swinging it in her hand, her dark curls blowing in the breeze. She stood by the edge of the water, looking out to sea where my companions swam.

As I approached the little waves lapping on the beach, she turned. She was pretty and quite young; perhaps just twenty, with an upturned nose and olive complexion. There was something sharp, almost calculating, in the way she looked at me.

'Are you from the hotel?' she asked. Her voice had a foreign accent, lilting like Sister Agnese. Was she Italian?

'I'm staying there, yes.'

'Who is that lady?' she asked, pointing at Mrs Jameson.

Something made me pause before giving her a name. 'She's one of the guests,' I said. 'Why do you want to know?'

'Mrs Jameson,' she said. 'I think it is Mrs Iris Jameson.' She gave me a sly smile.

'Then why did you ask me?' I felt a prickling of unease. Perhaps I should warn Mrs Jameson that someone was looking for her. I flung down my towel on the sand and ran quickly into the surf, before the woman could question me further.

The water was cold, even in July, and I thrashed through it with the front crawl that Frankie had been teaching me, until I'd acclimatised. When I reached the others and turned to look at the beach, I couldn't see the woman. Mrs Jameson floated serenely, her face blissful. I'd tell her later.

'You're getting better at this swimming lark.' Frankie dived beneath us, then surfaced and splashed me. 'Race you to the arch.'

The soft chalk cliffs that surrounded the bay on all sides had left a picturesque archway at the far end, which you could swim through at high tide. It wasn't much of a race; Frankie pulled away quickly in her striped costume, slicing through the water like an eel. When I finally caught up with her, she was circling in and out of the arch.

'It'll come down one day,' she predicted. 'It's already quite worn away by the waves, see?' She pointed to the eroded chalk stack. I shivered and turned back to shore. I wouldn't want to be there when the arch collapsed.

We swam back to shore in a leisurely way. Mrs Jameson was out of the water before us, her beach towel wrapped around her and a towelling turban on her head.

'Very bracing,' she said. 'Perhaps I should find a house by the coast and come every summer. It feels much healthier than London in July.'

I scanned the beach. 'Someone was asking about you,' I said. 'A woman. But I can't see her now.'

Mrs Jameson looked around sharply. 'What sort of woman?'

'Young. She had a foreign accent.'

'Hmm.' Her look darkened. 'Tell me if you see her again. Now, I'm ready for my breakfast.'

Mrs Jameson and Frankie walked across the sands to the foot of the cliff, where the iron steps started. Shading my eyes to watch them go, I saw with a start the young woman in white step out from behind the rocks.

They paused. The woman spoke to them, although I was too far away to hear what she said. Then Mrs Jameson jerked back and put out a hand, as if in self-defence.

I ran across the sand towards them. As I panted my way over, Frankie gave the young woman a shove, pushing her off-balance. Mrs Jameson disappeared up the steps and into the tunnel. Frankie stood firmly at the foot of the stairs, blocking the way.

'What happened?' I asked, breathless.

'This woman wanted to talk to Mrs J,' said Frankie, glowering. 'But Mrs J doesn't want to talk to her. Dunno what they

25

said, it was all in Italian.'

'I need to ask her something,' insisted the woman. 'It is important. I come all the way from Italy. My mother is dead. She give me a message for her.'

Frankie and I exchanged glances. 'You've had your chance,' said Frankie. 'You'll have to write to her or something. Come on, Marge. Time for breakfast.'

I gave the woman a brief smile. 'That's probably best,' I said. 'We're on holiday.'

I wasn't surprised when I came out of the bathing tent to see the woman still hanging about on the beach. She walked up to the road with me, while my curiosity fought with my conscience. I knew Mrs Jameson would not approve of me pumping the woman for information.

'I'm sorry about your mother,' I said. 'Was it a recent loss?'

She looked confused for a moment, then grinned, small white teeth in her tanned face. 'When I am having my last birthday,' she said, 'I am twenty-one years old. She told me everything and said I can come to England to get what I am owed. Then she died, so I am here.'

I wondered how she had found us. Mrs Jameson had left strict instructions with Graham that no-one inquiring at Bedford Square should be given our address, but that important messages could be passed on by telephone or post. A few letters had been forwarded, but none from Italy.

'Will you give her a letter, if I write it down?' the young woman asked, as we approached the hotel gate. 'So that I know she will get it?'

'Give it to the hotel,' I said, briskly. I hurried in through the gates.

Chapter 6

When I joined her for breakfast, Mrs Jameson seemed out of sorts. She drank black coffee and restricted herself to toast and marmalade, eschewing her usual appetite for a cooked breakfast. She laid down the newspaper as I took my seat.

'There you are, Marjorie. What are your plans for the morning?' she asked.

I glanced out of the window. The day was heating up and it might be too hot to do anything much in the afternoon. I'd finished my book and knew that Frankie planned to replace the fan belt on the car, so I couldn't suggest a drive. Sarah and Bertie slept in late and didn't usually surface until just before lunch. I was at a bit of a loose end.

'I might go for a walk along the cliffs towards Margate,' I said. 'As far as Botany Bay, anyhow. Do you want to come?' The picturesque long bay was only a couple of miles away, and it had a lively little cafe serving delicious ice-cream.

Mrs Jameson's grey eyes were clouded in thought and she seemed barely to listen to my reply.

'Hmm? Oh, no. I don't think so. I have a headache. I shall spend the morning on my balcony, resting.'

That was unlike her. Mrs Jameson usually enjoyed excellent

health and had little patience for those who did not. The en-
counter on the beach had clearly upset her. I wondered again
who the woman was, and whether her sudden appearance was
connected to the visit of Sister Agnese.

'That Italian woman who tried to talk to you,' I began,
tentatively.

She lifted her eyes to me, lips compressed. I knew the
warning signs but ploughed on.

'She said she had a message for you from her mother. That
she was owed something. Who is she?'

Mrs Jameson gathered up the newspaper, her face paler than
usual. 'I have no idea. She wanted me to investigate something,
some legacy that she says her mother was owed, or something.
I wasn't really listening,' she said.

She rose, not waiting for me to finish my bacon. 'I'm not
taking on cases while we're on vacation. It's ludicrous. I need
a proper break, and I intend to have one.' She beckoned to Mr
Ashcroft, who broke off from an intense conversation with
Mrs Heath, the housekeeper, and hurried over.

'How can I help, Mrs Jameson?'

'I will be keeping to my rooms this morning, and I do not
wish to be disturbed by housekeeping,' she informed him. 'I
was approached by a woman outside the hotel earlier, who
wished to engage my services. However, I am here for a
complete rest. Please ensure that nobody from outside the
hotel is permitted to enter and approach me. Is that clear?'

'Of course.' Mr Ashcroft was smoothly efficient as always.
'I shall speak to Mrs Heath at once, and to the reception desk.
Can I send anything up to your suite?'

'I will take coffee at eleven o'clock,' she said. 'That will be
all.'

She left, and I finished the last of my bacon, chewing thoughtfully. Mrs Jameson usually either told me exactly what she thought, or didn't feel the need to tell me anything at all. She was never vague, and she always listened when people talked about business. I was left with the uneasy feeling that she hadn't been telling the truth.

Who was the Italian woman? It seemed too much of a coincidence that two people had come from Italy to see Mrs Jameson as a matter of urgency in the past week. The visits had to be connected. And why wouldn't Mrs Jameson tell me what it was all about? She had always told clients that I was completely trustworthy, and that they could speak freely before me.

So why didn't she trust me herself?

#

As I crossed the reception hall to begin my walk, I saw Mrs Jameson in the glass-walled telephone booth. She stood with her back to me, clutching the receiver to her ear and speaking into the mouthpiece.

Shamelessly, I lurked behind the bookshelves which held leaflets and travel guides to the surrounding attractions. After a moment, the door of the booth opened.

'Thank you, Graham. That will be all.' Mrs Jameson's clear tones carried across the hall. She set the receiver down and walked quickly upstairs. I waited a moment, then darted into the booth.

'Operator? Can you put me through to a number in Bedford Square? I was just talking to them, but we got cut off,' I said.

'Good morning,' Graham answered at once. 'Mrs Jameson's residence.'

'Graham, it's me. Marjorie. Were you just talking to Mrs Jameson?' I asked.

'I was,' he said, surprised. 'Why, is something the matter?'

'Not exactly. It's just… what did she want?'

There was a disapproving pause. 'Why don't you ask her yourself?' he said, reasonably.

'I would, but she's in one of her moods. Someone turned up here wanting to see her this morning, and I'm worried. I mean, how did they know she was here? I thought you were to tell everyone she wasn't available. Has anyone been given our address here?'

He sighed. 'She asked me the same thing. There was a young Italian woman who came calling on Saturday. Of course, she got nothing out of me. But I'll talk to the rest of the staff and make sure. I'm sorry to hear she's been bothering you.'

'Frankie made it very clear that she should leave Mrs Jameson alone,' I said. 'Don't worry, Graham. We'll look after her.'

Slowly, I headed out for my walk. So, the woman had come looking for us in Bedford Square, just a day after we'd left London. Now I was more convinced than ever that our trip to the seaside had been prompted by Sister Agnese's visit. But how had she found us in Broadstairs?

'You look very bright and breezy.' Mr Lockwood smiled from behind his newspaper as I crossed the courtyard. 'Off somewhere nice?'

Out of boredom with the gingham check cotton dress I'd been wearing half the week, I'd put on my new red linen frock with the sailor collar, which I had been saving for best. I wore my favourite straw hat with a scarlet ribbon around the brim.

I smiled back. 'Not particularly. I just felt like wearing something different.' I was seized with an impulse for company. 'Do you want to come for a walk to Botany Bay?'

He hesitated, then threw aside the newspaper. 'Why not? I'll come some of the way, anyhow. I'm skiving off work. I've got stuck on a plot point, the muddle in the middle. Maybe a walk will help.'

He grasped his stick, and we walked out into the gardens.

'Tell me about the book,' I said, intrigued by the idea of this former soldier writing romantic fiction in his room every morning. 'I liked *The Stolen Heart*, especially the character of Lizzie, the governess who married the marquis.'

'Oh, it's the usual tosh,' he said, with a self-deprecating grin. 'This one will be called *The Heart Always Knows*. The last one was *Listen To Your Heart*, and I expect the next one will be *Her Faithful Heart* or something.'

'You know the title already?' I asked. I'd always assumed writers struggled for ages to think up a title that summed up the essence of their novel.

'The publisher comes up with them. The stories are more or less the same, anyway, so it doesn't much matter. It's either a chambermaid falls in love with a lord, or a stable boy falls in love with a lady,' he explained. 'Everyone disapproves so they carry on in secret. They get caught and punished, then a hidden letter proves that the chambermaid or stable boy is really a lady or lord, so they can get married after all.'

That was pretty much the plot of the two I'd read, I realised. I felt a little disappointed to know they were written to a formula.

'This time it's the turn of the chambermaid,' said Mr Lockwood. 'She's the long-lost daughter of a French marquis who got his head lopped off in the French Revolution.'

31

'Golly. You should come with us to see *The Scarlet Pimpernel* on Friday,' I suggested.

'Saw it last week, on the first night. Very useful. It saved me having to do proper research.'

'I'd love to write a book one day,' I said. 'I think it's very impressive to be an author.' I had thought about writing up my adventures with Mrs Jameson, although I wasn't sure anyone would believe them.

He shrugged. 'It gives me a decent income. I don't have to live with my mother and sisters in Edinburgh. I've got a flat in London, so at least I'm independent.'

The road dipped down as we rounded the bay past the grand Holland House, once the seat of the lord who had built the castle, then rose again on the other side of the bay towards the Captain Digby tavern, another mini-castle with crenellations on the roof.

'Does your leg hurt?' I asked, noticing Mr Lockwood's grimace on the slope, and the way his knuckle whitened over his stick.

'No,' he said, curtly. He walked fast enough, although it clearly cost him some effort. I remembered what he'd said the day I met him. I should leave him to get on with it, not draw attention to his struggles.

He looked at his pocket watch as we passed the pub. 'Bit early, or I'd suggest a drink,' he said. 'I often join Major Redfern here for a quick snifter before luncheon. He likes it here, and he can get away from his mother for a while.'

He gave an apologetic smile. 'Sorry I was short with you, Miss Swallow. We men don't like to admit our limitations. I can't walk very far without pain, unfortunately. I'll leave you here, but enjoy your walk to Botany Bay.'

'Thank you. Call me Marjorie, won't you?'

He took a seat in the garden of the public house and pulled out a notebook from his pocket. 'And I'm James. Thank you for the walk. Maybe the change of scenery will help me to dash off the next chapter.'

Chapter 7

I liked Botany Bay. I ate a strawberry ice-cream on the long curved beach crowded with families and day-trippers. Children splashed joyfully in the shallow water and built sandcastles with buckets and spades, while young mothers unwrapped sandwiches and men with trousers rolled up to the knee opened bottles of beer. I preferred the hubbub to our secluded bay, where few people came unless they were guests at the hotel.

On my way back, I paused to inspect a miniature fort on the edge of the golf course, known locally as Neptune's Tower. Mr Ashcroft had told us that, like the castle and the Captain Digby tavern, it had been built by the eccentric Lord Holland to add interest to the view from his manor house. The fort was just four stone walls with towers at each corner, barely twenty yards across and overgrown with brambles. The structure had begun to disintegrate.

I stepped through the doorway into the weed-choked interior.

'Oh!'

I jumped. A man sitting in one of the window arches sprang eagerly to his feet. It was Major Redfern. For a moment he beamed, then his face dropped and he looked guilty as a schoolboy.

'I'm so sorry,' I began.

He flushed red, and removed his Panama hat. 'Miss Swallow. My apologies, I didn't mean to startle you. I thought…'

'Not at all. I didn't realise there was anyone here,' I said.

His eyes slid around me to the entrance, and he took a hasty glance at his watch. He was waiting for someone, I realised, and for a moment he'd thought I was that person. Who was he expecting?

'It's a shame they've let the fort deteriorate so much, isn't it?' I said. 'It makes rather a romantic ruin, though.'

'Hmm? Oh. Yes, I suppose so.' He glanced cursorily around. 'Do you, er…'

'Do I come here often?' I asked brightly. 'This is the first time I've looked in. I was walking back from Botany Bay for lunch at the hotel. Are you heading that way too?'

He rubbed sweat from his forehead and put his hat back on. 'No, I'll just… I'll just rest here a moment longer, then have my lunch at the Captain Digby,' he said. 'Don't wait for me.'

I relented and left him to it. The tavern was only a short walk away and I paused to see if James Lockwood was still in the garden, but he'd gone.

'Wait, Miss!' I spun around at the Italian voice. The woman I'd seen on the beach that morning rushed out of the doorway to the inn, pulling on her white sun hat over her dark curls. 'I wrote a letter, like you said. Will you give it to her? To Mrs Jameson?' Her accent stretched the name, Meesees Jame-ee-son. She held out a cheap white envelope, addressed in an untidy schoolgirl scrawl.

I shook my head. I knew how annoyed Mrs Jameson would

be if I ignored her express wishes and brought her a message from the woman who had followed us from London.

'You will have to put it in the post-box at the gate,' I told her. 'I'm not acting as your post-boy.'

She gave a glance back towards the fort and hesitated, as if uncertain what to do. A suspicion formed in my mind. Was this the woman that Major Redfern had been waiting for?

But she quickly fell into step alongside me. 'Is Mrs Jameson your mother?' she asked, unexpectedly.

'No. And if you really knew her, you'd know that perfectly well,' I said.

She smiled. 'Good. That makes it easier, then.' I didn't much care for her smile, or her tone of voice.

I stopped and turned to face her. 'Who are you, anyway?' I asked, bluntly. 'What do you want with Mrs Jameson? You followed us here from London, didn't you? How did you know where we were?'

She gave a half-shrug. 'You take the letter, and I will tell you, maybe. I'm called Julia. Julia…' she hesitated for a second, 'Julia Donatello.'

'Donatello.' I allowed my disbelief to sound in my voice. 'Like the artist.'

She laughed, a delighted cackle. 'Yes, like the artist! You are clever, I think. You should call me Julia. What is your name?'

I wasn't going to give it to her, but as we rounded the corner to the hotel entrance, Mr and Mrs Treadwell crossed the road from the golf course. She looked cool and superior in a crisp white blouse and yellow linen skirt, while his tweeds were both too loud and too warm for the day.

Mrs Treadwell would have walked on without speaking, but her husband raised a hand in greeting, and I was forced out of politeness to stop and wait for them.

'Miss Swallow,' said Geoffrey Treadwell, tipping his golfing cap. I saw him glance with interest at the Italian woman. 'Are you on your way to luncheon? Who's your friend?'

'I have only just met Miss Donatello,' I said, coldly. 'She has something she wishes to deliver to the hotel. She's not staying here.'

Mrs Treadwell gave Julia a cursory glance, her nostrils pinching with distaste at the woman's cheap clothes. She nodded briskly. 'I see. Well, we've earned our luncheon, Miss Swallow. Eighteen holes, and I never lost my lead once. Did I, Geoffrey?'

He glanced in irritation at his wife. 'You played well. Those lessons are paying off,' he said. 'Lucky that you can spend so much time on them. Some of us have business to attend to.'

His eyes strayed back to Julia. 'Are you coming in, Miss Donatello? Perhaps we could all have lunch together,' he said.

'Unfortunately that won't be possible.' I jumped in before Julia could answer, noticing the look of horror on Mrs Treadwell's face. 'Miss Donatello is not stopping. She just wanted to deliver a letter.'

Mr Treadwell grinned. 'No need to walk all the way up the drive, then, is there? I'll take it for you, Miss Donatello.'

Relieved, I walked ahead with Mildred Treadwell. Her husband took rather a long time taking possession of the letter and bidding Julia Donatello farewell at the gate.

I thought back to Major Redfern, waiting patiently in the fort for someone. Was I putting two and two together and making five?

Chapter 8

The next morning, I persuaded Frankie to drive into Margate with me. I was getting tired of the seclusion of the hotel and wanted to be somewhere a bit livelier. Frankie too was missing London life, and jumped at my suggestion.

Mrs Jameson had remained closeted in her room during the previous afternoon, and had been silent and moody over dinner. If she'd received the letter from Julia Donatello, she didn't tell me about it. Today she had said she had letters to write, and would do so in the hotel's library.

'I needed to get out, and so did the Lagonda,' said Frankie, pulling the car through the hotel gate and onto the cliff-top road. 'I love driving out here, where there's plenty of space. Beats the London traffic.'

As we passed the Neptune Fort, I saw Mildred Treadwell putting on the green, looking rather fed up. She was alone. Perhaps her husband had got tired of being beaten.

Frankie put her foot down and we whizzed along the coast road. I sat up front next to her, enjoying the breeze and the vista of sparkling sea to our right. We swung around the headland at Foreness Point and were soon driving due west. The road dropped down into Margate, with its jetty sticking out into the long bay. Wherries and other craft criss-crossed the shallow water, crowded with pleasure-seekers.

Frankie parked on the busy seafront, and we clambered out.

'This is more like it,' she pronounced. 'Where do we start? Down on the sands for a donkey ride, or shall we go straight to Dreamland?'

We had a riotous morning, recklessly spending our pennies on swing boats, riding a carousel, laughing at a Punch and Judy show, and trotting up and down the sands on a weary-looking donkey in a straw hat.

Then we entered Dreamland, the new pleasure park, and queued for the unforgettable thrill of rattling along the Scenic Railway, leaving our stomachs behind as the cars clattered to the top of the wooden track and plunged down again, the whole ride shrieking with excitement.

'That's enough,' I said faintly, staggering off the ride feeling rather green. 'I need a sit down and a cup of tea.'

'I need a bottle of beer and a bag of winkles,' said Frankie. 'It's not the seaside without winkles.' We compromised with a table in the tea garden, which advertised both tea and beer, seafood and scones. Frankie went to order at the kiosk while I watched the crowds go by: children in Sunday best ruffles; rows of girls with newly washed hair, swinging past in cheap summer frocks with their arms linked; men with open collars laughing loudly and pretending not to notice the girls.

Frankie slid back into her seat. 'Here, Marge. That Italian woman is over there, on the other side of the flower beds.' I turned to look, but she grabbed my arm. 'Don't turn round. She's with one of the guests from the hotel. That bloke that plays golf and likes to flash his cash about. Very cosy, they look.'

'Mr Treadwell? Where?' I picked up my handbag and took out my powder compact. Under cover of checking my make-up, I scanned the tables behind us on the lawn.

They were under the shade of a big, leafy tree. Julia Donatello was tearing hungrily into a plate of scones with jam and cream. Geoffrey Treadwell was laughing at something, and I saw him slide his arm around her shoulders. She wore a striking set of jade and coral beads over her white dress, flashing green and orange in the sun.

'Bet that horsey wife of his doesn't know he's here,' said Frankie. 'She gets about, that Italian girl, doesn't she? She was hanging around the back of the hotel yesterday flirting with one of the waiters. Alfred, the good-looking one with dark hair.'

'Really? Mrs Jameson won't like that. She told Mr Ashcroft to make sure she didn't get into the hotel.'

'Yeah. Well, she won't be back.' Frankie grinned. 'Etta – that's one of the chambermaids – reckons Alfred's her bloke. They had a right ding-dong about it. Then Etta told Mrs Heath that Julia was distracting Alfie from his work, and Mrs Heath told Julia to sling her hook and not come back. I tell you, it's all go behind the scenes.'

She stretched lazily and took another look at them. 'Shall we go and say hello? See what Treadwell's got to say for himself.'

I wasn't sure that was a good idea. I had no desire to be pulled into whatever the Italian woman wanted with Mrs Jameson, and I didn't much like Mr Treadwell.

'Let's leave them be. It'll only get complicated. Look, here's our food.'

We were famished after our morning's fun, and for a few minutes all conversation was abandoned.

Frankie polished off the last of her winkles and began to pick her teeth with the pin. 'Nice here, ain't it? My Auntie Clara used to bring us kids down to Margate for a day in September, after the hop-picking was finished. They kept lions and bear cubs from the circus here then, a whole menagerie. I wanted to be a lion tamer and keep a pet cub.'

I laughed. I could imagine Frankie leading a bear cub around on a leash. 'My dad brought us to Margate once, on August bank holiday when the shop was closed. But I don't think Mum liked it much. She worries about looking common if she's having fun. She sat on the sands with her shoes on and wouldn't take off her coat.'

Frankie grinned. 'Potty. How can you enjoy yourself if you worry about what other people think?'

I glanced at her, shirtsleeves rolled to the elbow, waistcoat unbuttoned and cloth cap pushed back on her cropped hair, her ankle resting on one knee. 'Have you never worried what people think, Frankie? About the way you dress. Wearing men's clothes, I mean.'

She gave a lazy smile. 'They're not men's clothes, they're my clothes. I've dressed like this since I was a kid, soon as I could get away with it.

'I hated being trussed up in petticoats and stuff, so I borrowed my cousins' clothes. The other kids... well, I had a few fights, but I learned to fight properly. Auntie Clara took me to the suffragettes' jiu-jitsu classes, and everyone left me alone after that. I do my own thing, and leave other people to do theirs.'

I wished I was as brave as Frankie, but my mother's training ran deep.

'What'd you do if you didn't care what people thought?' she

asked. 'Go on. Tell me.'

'Ride a motorcycle again,' I said, promptly. I'd learned during the War, when the hospital had needed people to take urgent messages. It had been terrifying, and also exhilarating. And I'd worn breeches to ride in, too.

'Do it!' Frankie laughed. 'What are you waiting for?'

I shrugged. It was hard to explain to Frankie, who had chosen to live outside of the expectations placed on women. I wanted a career, and excitement, and independence. But I hadn't given up hope of romance, either.

My thoughts went involuntarily to Hugh, the artist who had bruised my heart during our adventures on the Riviera the previous year. He hadn't followed up on his promise to take me out when we were home again, and I was far too proud to write to him. Besides, I knew he wasn't trustworthy.

'I'm happy as I am,' I said firmly. 'Life's quite exciting enough.'

'Not pining after Freddie?' The jazz pianist, a good friend, had left for America, touring with his band. I'd refused his proposal of marriage at Christmas, although I was fond of him. My heart didn't give a leap in my chest when I saw him, the way it did for Hugh.

'Not at all.' Although I did miss his company, rather.

'Hugh, then? You're better off without him, Marge. You'd never know where you were with Hugh.'

I blushed and said nothing. Frankie knew me too well. I finished off my tea.

'Drop it. I haven't seen him for ages. Can't we just enjoy ourselves, like you said?'

'Course we can.' She pulled me up from the deckchair. 'Come on, let's have a paddle in the sea before we go. It's getting too hot to sit in the sun.'

As we passed, Geoffrey Treadwell was whispering something in Julia Donatello's ear, his hand pressed on her knee. They didn't look up as we walked by.

Chapter 9

The next morning was uneventful: bathing, a stroll along the cliffs and lunch with the Posts before they set off to the theatre in Margate. In the afternoon I went to the hotel library to borrow a book to take into the gardens. A pleasant, quiet room, done out in a modern style, it looked a bit like the big new cruise liners, all sleek lines and chrome.

Miss Fraser was sitting at a teak desk, frowning over a letter which she covered quickly with her arm as I came in. Sheets of hotel writing paper and envelopes were strewn about her. She leaned back, as if frustrated by the interruption.

'Good afternoon. Are you looking for anything in particular?' she asked.

'Just something light to read.' I browsed the open shelves, relieved that she wasn't Miss McDonald, who might have tried to steer me towards improving literature. I found a book of Chesterton's Father Brown stories.

'Miss Swallow?'

I paused on my way to the door and smiled. The woman's dark eyes were troubled, and she'd been gnawing at the skin around her thumb. Her brown hair was rumpled and shedding hairpins, as if she'd been running her hands through it.

She had turned over the page so that her letter was face down. But there was a white envelope beside her elbow, addressed to her and Miss McDonald in large, untidy handwriting. It was torn open and crumpled, as if it had been retrieved from the waste-paper basket.

Miss Fraser didn't seem to know how to begin.

'How can I help?'

She gave me an uncertain smile. 'Your employer, Mrs Jameson. I believe she investigates things? I mean… I've seen her in the newspapers.'

I nodded. 'She runs a private detective agency, yes.'

'Do you think… would she… I have something I'd like to ask her about. Her professional opinion, I mean.' The woman's face was flushed, her cheeks a dark pink.

'I'm sure…' I began. Then I remembered Mrs Jameson's displeasure at being approached by the Italian woman, and her instructions to Mr Ashcroft. 'I could ask. But I'm afraid she isn't taking on any cases at the moment. She needs a rest.'

Miss Fraser looked down, her mouth set unhappily. 'Of course. Never mind. Please don't bother her. Perhaps… do you have a card? I might consult her after her holiday.'

I reached into my handbag and extracted a business card. I wondered what business Miss Fraser might have in mind. 'Is there anything I can help you with in the meantime?' I asked.

She hesitated a moment. 'Everything she investigates… it's all very private, I suppose?'

'Of course. Client confidentiality is most important to us.' I hesitated, burning with curiosity. 'Perhaps you'd like to tell me what it's about?'

She looked at me speculatively for a moment. 'No, I don't think so. Not yet. But thank you.' She put the card in her pocket.

Wondering, I took *The Innocence of Father Brown* into the gardens and lounged on a deckchair until it was time to eat.

#

Mrs Jameson had ordered an early supper on the terrace before our trip to the theatre to see Sarah and Bertie's play. She looked much more cheerful this afternoon, quizzing Frankie and me about our previous day's jaunt to Margate and promising to come with us next time.

'My headache is gone. I must have needed the rest,' she said. 'But I absolutely want a ride on that Scenic Railway before we return to London. It sounds like the one at Coney Island. I love a good rollercoaster.'

Mrs Treadwell came through from the bar clutching a gin and tonic. She glanced around and scowled when she saw the three of us eating together, then took a seat alone, looking out to sea. Frankie had heard from the staff that Mrs Treadwell had complained to the manager about Mrs Jameson's cross-dressing chauffeur being allowed to socialise in the guest areas. Apparently Mr Ashcroft had told her that Mrs Jameson was a valued guest and could invite whoever she wished to eat with her – by which I guessed that my employer was more generous than the Treadwells in tipping the staff.

'Hullo, ladies.' James came over to our table. He'd never been snobbish about our unconventional party. 'You're eating early. Mind if I join you?'

Mrs Jameson smiled hospitably. 'Not at all. Have a sandwich, or a piece of asparagus quiche. We'll miss dinner tonight, because we're going to the theatre.'

'Ah, you're Pimpernelling today? It's great fun. You'll enjoy it.' He took a piece of quiche. 'I rather wish I was going with you. I've had enough of sitting around in the hotel. And I'm bored to tears with my book.'

'Mr Lockwood is writing about the French Revolution,' I said. 'In his new novel.'

'Indeed? A dreadful time,' said Mrs Jameson. 'So interesting, the way a hunger for bread can tip quickly into thirst for blood.'

'Yes, well,' James gave a sardonic chuckle, 'I'm afraid my novel doesn't exactly go into the politics. It's just a light-hearted romance. I'm not an intellectual, Mrs Jameson.'

She laughed. 'How very English. Even the writers deny being intellectuals,' she observed. 'No wonder you don't get on with the French. However, anyone who can write a novel has my admiration. I simply don't think I could sit still for that long.'

I saw a flicker of irritation cross his face. I supposed sitting still wasn't something he had much choice about.

'Now, I must go and get changed. Don't be late, Marjorie. Frankie, will you bring the car around for six?' Mrs Jameson swept away.

Up in my room, I changed into my lavender crepe de chine evening frock and strapped on new silver shoes with high heels. They were an extravagance, but one I felt I'd earned. Pretty clothes gave me such pleasure, and it was rare to have an occasion to wear them.

It was half past five, but I was too restless to sit around in my room. I went down and strolled onto the terrace, but James had gone. Mr Treadwell had arrived and was sitting in silence with his wife. He'd caught the sun on his nose, and was looking rather smug. I resisted an impulse to tell him we'd seen him in the tea garden at Dreamland yesterday, just to see what he said.

Miss Fraser and Miss McDonald were taking tea; Jean McDonald chatting happily about her lesson with the golf pro that afternoon, and how he had admired her drive. I wondered if I should have told Mrs Jameson about Miss Fraser's approach. She'd been so adamant that she didn't want to take on cases, however, and she surely deserved a rest. Perhaps I'd tell her in the morning.

I followed the wall around, peeping over to the sheer drop of chalk cliffs. Below, the sands were almost deserted; the Goldsmiths were standing hand in hand at the water's edge enjoying the late afternoon sun. I wandered around to the garden, keeping to the gravel path so as not to get grass stains on my silver shoes.

Raised voices caught my attention. I recognised at once Mrs Jameson's voice, sharp and clear. Peering around a clump of bushes, I saw she was speaking to Julia Donatello.

I hesitated, but only for a moment. I edged closer, careful to keep myself out of sight.

They were speaking in Italian. Frustrated, I tried to pick out a few recognisable words from the rapid stream.

Now Julia was talking. I clutched at the word 'convento' and something that sounded like hospital, ospedale. Santa Francesca Romana. Wasn't that the convent that Sister Agnese had come from? I'd ask Frankie later. Mio padre, mia madre... my father and mother? She'd told me she wanted Mrs Jameson to investigate something her mother had told her she was owed. But what did that have to do with the convent in Rome?

Mrs Jameson snapped something in return, repeating the word 'madre'. Then another rapid stream, concluding with the word 'polizia'. Police. I didn't need a translator to know what she was threatening.

Mrs Jameson turned on her heel and strode back to the hotel, her face thunderous.

Chapter 10

The Hippodrome was an impressive building on a big square near the sea front. Theatre-goers milled around its grand colonnade outside in the evening sunshine. Mrs Jameson had been quiet on the drive to Margate, but seemed to recover her humour as Frankie pulled up at the kerb.

'Well, this is splendid!' she exclaimed. We stepped out to join the crowd. I was pleased to see complimentary reviews from the newspapers pasted across the billboards advertising the play. 'Sarah Post is ravishing… The dashing Bertie Post… A rip-roaring tale of adventure!' I felt a tingle of proprietorial pride for my friends.

I loved the theatre, but it was so expensive in London that I hardly ever went. This outing was a real treat. Mrs Jameson took the tickets from her handbag and gave them to me. Frankie hurried back from parking the car on the square, and we went through into the grand cream-and-gilt foyer, already full of people.

I handed the tickets to the smartly uniformed usher, who had so much gold braid on his jacket he looked like a general on parade. He glanced in surprise from Mrs Jameson to Frankie, who gave him a cheerful wink.

It was hot, the hottest day of our holiday so far. Perspiration broke out on my forehead as we made our way through the throng up the stairs to the Grand Circle.

I got a childish thrill from being ushered into a private box, and leaned eagerly over the edge to take in the splendid surroundings – plush crimson curtains with gold tassels, an ornately painted panelled ceiling in cream and gold, lamps with gilt fittings sparkling from the walls. The stage, which was right next to our box, was wide. Sarah had said there was a large company, with a whole troupe of dancers who performed in the big numbers.

I settled back in anticipation for the curtain to rise.

#

The show was a triumph. I loved a musical, and even more so when it was such an exciting story. Sarah sang affectingly and looked beautiful in her blue satin gown and magnificent towering wig. Bertie made a swashbuckling hero, and I was in danger of falling in love with the Scarlet Pimpernel all over again. The dancers showed their versatility, one minute performing as guests at a high society English ball, the next as rioting French peasants wielding pitchforks. When the curtain fell after the final call, the palms of my hands stung with clapping.

'What fun!' said Mrs Jameson, who seemed to have enjoyed it as much as I had. 'And Mr Post was terribly good. Sarah too, of course.'

'She did well to sing without that wig falling off,' said Frankie. 'But it was all a bit ridiculous, wasn't it?'

Mrs Jameson gave a mischievous smile. 'I suppose you sympathised with the revolting peasants, Frankie. Remind me not to trust you with a pitchfork.'

An usher tapped at the door of our box. 'Compliments of Mr and Mrs Post, and would Mrs Jameson and party like to step down to the dressing room?' he asked.

We followed him through a doorway and down a set of back stairs. I was thrilled to be behind the scenes of a theatre. Dancers squeezed past, their heavily made-up faces glistening, much less glamorous without the stage lights. There was a pungent smell of sweat.

But inside Sarah and Bertie's dressing room, it was masked by the scent of lilies. Sarah had whipped off her wig and was sitting at a dressing table, wiping away her makeup with handfuls of cold-cream. She swung around on her stool, a radiant smile on her face.

'Darlings! You did enjoy it, didn't you? Say you did! I thought it went pretty well tonight, didn't you, Bertie?'

Bertie wiped his face with a towel. His mask was gone, and he was once more a handsome but modern man, an actor. 'Pretty well,' he said. 'Good of you to come, Mrs Jameson. Hope you had a good time.' He poured us each a glass of champagne from the ice bucket on the side table.

We assured them of how much we had loved it. I knew that Sarah in particular needed the reassurance. She might seem confident, but she said she was always waiting for something terrible to happen and all her success to disappear overnight.

I noticed a photograph tucked into the mirror. A studio portrait of a small boy, his cherubic blond curls framing a wide-eyed gaze.

Sarah saw me looking and bit her lip. 'Pretty, isn't he? Our nephew, Kenny.' Bertie glanced over, and I saw a look of understanding pass between them.

'Jolly little chap,' he said, heartily. 'We often have him to stay with us, when we're in London. He and Sarah are very fond of each other. We're thinking of adopting him, actually, because her sister has a houseful already.' He smiled at Sarah tenderly.

I breathed deeply. So that was all right, then. She'd told Bertie about her illegitimate son, and he'd accepted the child.

'That's wonderful,' I told Sarah. 'I'm so glad.' She ducked her head with a smile.

Mrs Jameson had been watching benignly. 'There's room in the car if you'd like us to drive you back,' she told them. 'We don't mind waiting until you're ready.' She finished off her glass of champagne and looked hopefully at the bottle.

'No, that's fine. I've got the motor,' said Bertie. 'We'll be a while finishing up. There's a producer from London in tonight, and I'd like to have a word with him before we leave.'

We took the hint and departed. Outside, the crowds had melted away and the sun had finally set. A bright moon had risen, almost full. It painted a silver path across the sea as we rejoined the coast road back to Kingsgate.

'I do like a happy ending,' said Mrs Jameson, who hadn't missed a thing in the dressing room.

'Not very happy for the peasants,' called Frankie from the driver's seat.

Mrs Jameson smiled at me. 'I wasn't talking about the show.'

A huge yawn overcame me as we rounded the headland by Neptune's Tower and swung south to Kingsgate Bay. I thought of Major Redfern, and how startled he'd looked to see me in the tower. Had whoever he was meeting kept the appointment in the end? The Captain Digby tavern sounded lively when we passed it, with gramophone music blaring out from the bar and people spilling into the garden to dance. I wondered if the Major was inside, drowning his sorrows.

'Here we are,' said Mrs Jameson with satisfaction, as we slowed to turn into the hotel driveway.

Then she let out an exclamation of annoyance. 'Oh, really. Drive on, Frankie. The gate's open. Don't stop.'

Beside the gatepost was a tall figure in a white sun hat and dress, gleaming in the moonlight like a ghost. Julia Donatello, watching for our return. I shivered at a sudden chill. Someone walking over my grave. What was she doing, lurking out there in the dark?

Chapter 11

Frankie dropped us at the portcullis gate. I wondered if Mrs Jameson would insist that Mr Ashcroft have it lowered, with pots of boiling oil prepared to repel invaders.

I could see by the clench of Mrs Jameson's jaw that her benign mood of a few minutes ago had evaporated.

'Shall we have a drink in the lounge?' I asked, tentatively.

She shook her head. 'I'll take a turn around the terrace, then go to bed. It's been a tiring evening.'

Mrs Jameson wasn't usually one for an early night. 'Would you like me to fetch you anything? A shawl, or your cane?' She had broken her ankle two years ago and it sometimes pained her after a long day.

'I'm not an invalid, Marjorie. Don't fuss. I would prefer to walk alone,' she said.

I winced. 'Sorry, Mrs Jameson.'

She stalked through the empty dining room and out to the terrace.

My head was too full to sleep. I glanced into the lounge. A card game was in full swing: Major Redfern was paired with his mother, James with Geoffrey Treadwell. More interminable bridge.

James glanced up and saw me. 'Hullo, Marjorie. Can I get you a drink?'

I hesitated. I wasn't wild about the idea of joining the bridge players, when the night was so lovely outside. Also, I wanted to know what Julia Donatello was doing at the gate.

'In a while. I'm just going out for a stroll.'

He looked a little anxious. 'Don't be too long. The bar closes at eleven.'

I smiled. 'I won't. I just… I thought I saw someone I knew.'

Mildred Treadwell crossed the room to join the card players, a glass in her hand.

'Why did you bid no trumps, Geoffrey?' she asked sharply, looking at his hand. 'You could have…'

Her husband glanced up in irritation. 'Why don't you take over, if you're so much better than me?'

'Quiet,' muttered the Major. 'Can't bloody concentrate with all this chatter.' From his belligerent tone, it seemed the whisky by his elbow was far from his first of the evening.

I went back through the courtyard and out onto the drive. I glanced around, not wishing to run into Mrs Jameson, but saw no-one. I walked up the driveway to the gate, but Julia Donatello was gone.

\#

Back in the lounge, I was just in time to accept a glass of lemonade before the bar closed. I settled down to watch the game. Contract bridge seemed to be terribly complicated. I failed to understand the attraction of throwing away money on a game of cards, when there were so many more interesting things one could spend it on.

'Major and Mrs Redfern are one rubber up,' James told me.

'So, we need to win the next game, if we're to recoup our losses before the end of the evening.'

Mrs Redfern smiled mildly over her spectacles and turned over a card. 'Hearts are trumps,' she said.

James sighed. 'Oh well. Your turn, Major.'

Geoffrey Treadwell and James lost the next trick, and the one after that.

'Maybe we should call it a night,' said James, stretching out his leg. 'You're too good for us, Mrs Redfern.'

She gave a little chuckle and looked nervously at her son.

'Let's walk out onto the terrace, Marjorie,' James suggested. 'The moon's so bright this evening.' I looked up in alarm. Was he suggesting a romantic interlude? I liked James, and he was quite attractive, I had to admit. But I was wary of holiday romance, after my chastening experience with Hugh in Nice. I hesitated, wondering how to put him off without hurting his feelings.

To my relief, Major Redfern broke in. 'Not until we've finished this game. You can't break off halfway through, man.' He dealt another hand, shoving the cards aggressively over the table. James picked up the cards with a sigh.

Geoffrey Treadwell, who also seemed to have had more than his share of whisky, wiped away perspiration from his brow.

'Well, I've had enough of this, Redfern,' he growled. 'You've taken enough money off me for one night.'

'Maybe we should take a break,' said Mrs Redfern, her voice quavering. 'Everyone's getting tired, Cedric.'

'I'm not,' he stated. 'What's the matter, Treadwell? Don't you like losing?'

I glanced up quickly at his belligerent tone. The two men were staring at each other with frank dislike. I began to wish

I'd gone straight to bed after our return, rather than walking into someone else's quarrel.

'That's the trouble with playing people who know each other. You and your mother have got some system going, haven't you?' said Mr Treadwell. 'Scratch your nose to bid high, put your glass down on the left or right side – I know the sort of thing. Well, it might pass muster in India, but it looks rather shabby here.'

Major Redfern went very red and closed his hand tightly around his glass.

'Those of us in India saw active service. Unlike those of you with so-called reserved occupations, sitting around at home making money out of the War. What exactly are you accusing us of, Treadwell? You want to watch out. You can say what you like about me, but don't you dare accuse my mother of being a cheat.'

The word hung in the air, glinting with danger.

Oh, goodness. I looked around for the hotel manager. This could all get rather nasty.

Mrs Redfern put down her cards and laid a hand on her son's arm, her face filled with dismay. 'Now, Cedric. I'm sure that's not what Mr Treadwell meant.'

'Course it isn't,' said James, looking with alarm at his partner. 'You beat us fair and square, Major. Luck of the draw and all that.'

Mr Treadwell threw down his cards. 'You know exactly what I meant. You two have been fleecing me all week. I suppose that's what you do, is it? Go round the hotels swindling decent people who actually make their own money, rather than waiting for hand-outs from the government. I suppose you think you're better than me?'

Major Redfern was on his feet. 'Well, that wouldn't be difficult, would it? Come on, then. Let's settle this.'

'Oh, for crying out loud,' exclaimed Mildred Treadwell. 'You're both drunk. Don't be ridiculous – you're not school-boys. I've had enough of this nonsense.'

She took her drink and went through the French windows to the terrace.

To my relief Mr Ashcroft, alerted by the noise, glided through the room.

'Now, gentlemen. Let's all calm down. Perhaps it's time to call it a night?'

But the two antagonists were squaring up to each other, their faces very red. I felt sorry for poor Mrs Redfern, who looked really distressed.

'Outside,' snarled Major Redfern. 'Not in front of the women.' He grabbed Geoffrey Treadwell by the lapels of his blazer.

'No violence,' said Mr Ashcroft, panic in his voice. 'Please, gentlemen. Not in here. I don't want to have to call the police.'

Major Redfern dragged his opponent to the French windows and out onto the terrace, followed by a frantic Mr Ashcroft. James shook his head and got to his feet. Just then, Sarah and Bertie burst through the door.

'What's happening?' asked Sarah, taking in the scene at once.

'Oh, my dear. I do wish someone would stop them,' said Mrs Redfern.

'A fight?' asked Sarah, her eyes lighting up. 'Come on, Bertie. Do let's see what's happening.'

Chapter 12

My curiosity won over my distaste, and I followed Sarah and Bertie through to the terrace. Major Redfern and Mr Treadwell circled each other warily, their faces set in ugly masks. Mr Ashcroft stood to one side like a referee, his ineffectual pleas for restraint ignored by the combatants.

The major struck out first, but Treadwell stepped back and avoided the blow. Both of them were slow, lumbering heavily around. With a little light jiu-jitsu, Frankie and I could have had them on their backs begging for mercy in moments.

Mrs Treadwell leaned on the terrace wall smoking a cigarette, gazing out to sea. She seemed thoroughly indifferent to whether her husband took a pasting. But he landed the first blow. His rather wild punch made a lucky connection with Major Redfern's jaw. The major's head snapped back, and he let out an angry bellow.

Mrs Redfern clutched my hand. 'Oh, I do wish they wouldn't,' she said, helplessly. 'Cedric has been so unwell. Mr Ashcroft, Mr Post, can't you do anything?'

'Stop this at once,' called Mr Ashcroft. 'Or I shall call the police.' He didn't want to have to do any such thing, I realised. The police turning up at the hotel would be awfully bad publicity.

Bertie, having left the daredevil character of the Scarlet Pimpernel firmly behind in the dressing room of the Hippodrome, was standing well back.

'Can't risk getting a black eye, I'm afraid,' he said. 'Not really my line of business, fighting.'

I remembered his swash-buckling sword-play on the stage, and bit back a smile.

Sarah stood beside him, clutching his hand and watching avidly. James stood at a distance, looking out to sea. His hand gripped his stick and his face was grim. I supposed he hated feeling helpless in this sort of situation.

The wind was getting up and I shivered, hearing the waves breaking against the base of the cliffs. Major Redfern shoved his opponent backwards, and Treadwell stumbled.

'Oh, do stop,' I cried. They were getting too close to the wall surrounding the terrace. 'This is silly. Mrs Treadwell, can't you help?'

She turned and looked at me in surprise. 'I don't get involved,' she said. 'I should advise you to take the same course, Miss Swallow.'

I walked over to the wall, hoping she would change her mind. 'Mrs Redfern is really worried,' I said. 'Major Redfern has been unwell. Malaria. She says it makes him do silly things.'

Mrs Treadwell didn't answer. She was gazing down to the beach, her cigarette held halfway to her lips, a frown on her face.

'What's that?' she asked. 'Down on the sands, where the waves are breaking on the beach. A sort of white thing.'

I peered down through the dark. The moonlight shimmered on the sea, caught the white chalk of the cliffs. The waves were lapping closer, covering the expanse of sand and seaweed. As Mrs Treadwell had said, there was something on the beach, halfway along the shore near the caves. A white bundle, the glare of the almost-full moon reflecting off it.

I was seized with dread. For a moment I found it hard to speak. I'd seen too much violent death not to recognise what this might be. I wished Mrs Jameson was with me.

I turned to the tussling men. 'Stop it,' I shouted. 'Mr Ashcroft, come quickly. There's someone down on the beach, where the tide's coming in. They're… I don't think they're conscious. We need to go and get them, before they get washed away.'

My shout had the desired effect. Major Redfern let go of his opponent and lumbered over, reeking of whisky. 'Where?'

I pointed. The white bundle was rolling slightly in the tide. My throat tightened and fear closed a cold hand around my heart.

'Good grief,' said Mr Ashcroft. 'We'd better go down.' He glanced to the bottom of the cliff where the iron steps met the beach. 'The steps are just about passable at this tide, although you might get your feet wet. Major, Mr Treadwell, will you come and help? I might not be able to manage alone.'

Suddenly sober, the two men ran back with the manager into the hotel towards the basement.

'I'll go around the road way,' I called. 'I won't be much longer. But get her out of the water.'

'Her?' Bertie turned a puzzled glance at me, as Mr Ashcroft, Major Redfern and Mr Treadwell disappeared.

Sarah was gazing at the beach in horror, her earlier excitement drained away. She clutched Bertie's hand. 'Marjorie… is that a dead body?'

'I don't know. I think so,' I said, turning to go. 'Would one of you see if you can find Frankie? I'll get Mrs Jameson.'

But there was no answer when I tapped on the door of Mrs Jameson's suite, and the door was locked. I supposed she was sleeping, and after her sharpness when we'd arrived back at the hotel, I didn't have the nerve to wake her.

My silver sandals had high heels and would be no use on the sand. I slipped into my adjoining room, kicked them off and quickly laced up my tennis shoes, before running through the hotel corridors and across the courtyard to the garden.

I dashed down the drive. To my relief, I saw Mrs Jameson at the gate, looking up and down the road. But as I watched, she turned aside and walked away through the hotel garden into the trees, darkness swallowing her up.

My mouth was open to call to her, tell her what was happening. But something stopped me. Why was she prowling around the garden in the dark?

A worm of suspicion uncoiled in my brain. I wasn't sure I wanted to know the answer to that question.

I hesitated. Perhaps I should see what was happening on the beach first.

Chapter 13

By the time I reached the beach, the three men had dragged the bundle up onto dry sand, above the tidemark of seaweed. I took a deep, trembling breath. I'd been right. The Italian woman, her cheap white dress soaked with sea-water, her dark hair matted with sand. I knelt and checked for the non-existent pulse. I frowned. It was hard to tell in the moonlight, but I thought I could see marks on her neck.

'I recognise her,' I told Mr Ashcroft, who was also kneeling by her body. 'Her name's Julia Donatello. She's been hanging around the hotel these past few days. I think she was staying in the tavern across the bay.'

He got to his feet. 'I'll go for the police,' he said. 'I've seen her, too. She came around earlier this week asking for work.' He glanced at the others. 'You'd better wait here with her, if you don't mind. I shan't be long.'

I heard a choked sob. I looked up in surprise. Geoffrey Treadwell didn't seem the sentimental type. But the noise hadn't come from him.

Major Redfern crouched beside me and took the dead woman's hand. 'They got to her,' he said. 'Poor, poor Bianca.'

'Bianca?' I asked, startled. 'What do you mean? Who got to

her?'

He turned desperate eyes on me. 'She was in hiding. But those damned dogs got her.' He stifled another sob. 'I should have been there. I should have taken her away, protected her.'

'Protected her from what?' I asked, trying to make sense of this outburst.

'The mafia, of course,' he said. 'The Italian mafia.' He took out a large white handkerchief and blew his nose noisily. 'Bianca Colomba. The little white dove.'

Goodness. Whatever had she been telling the man? I glanced up at Mr Treadwell, wanting to see his reaction. He was mopping his face and began to sway a little. I hoped he wasn't going to faint.

'Are you all right?' I asked.

'Hell of a thing,' he muttered, sitting down on a rock. He looked rather sick.

'Oi, Marge! What's happened?' To my relief, I saw Frankie sprinting across the sands from the base of the iron steps, feet bare and trousers rolled up. She held an electric torch, the light bobbing across the bay as she ran.

'It's her,' I said, taking the torch. 'The Italian woman.'

Julia's face was ghastly in the artificial light of the torch. Wet sand had settled around her nostrils and smeared across her cheek. I shone the beam on her neck. Four slight half-moon scrapes, and one small oval-shaped mark in the centre of her throat. A bruise?

I thought of the medical pathology text books Mrs Jameson had given me to study, their gruesome yet fascinating diagrams. The scrapes were probably from Julia's own nails, as she tried to prise something, or someone, away from her neck. The oval mark most likely from an assailant's thumb, pressing down on her windpipe. I shone the light on her face and looked carefully. There was a speckling of red pinpoints on the thin skin around her eyes. Petechiae, a possible sign of asphyxiation.

I shuddered. Unless I was badly mistaken, Julia Donatello – or Bianca Colomba – had been strangled.

'Shall I get Mrs J?' asked Frankie.

I hesitated, thinking of the locked door, of Mrs Jameson in the garden. I didn't know what to make of it. But perhaps I should wait until I could speak to her privately. There was no reason to involve anyone else before then.

'No,' I said. 'Not yet. I'll call her when the police get here.'

Frankie looked surprised. 'If you say so. Now, what've we got? Where are her shoes? What about a handbag?'

Good point. Julia Donatello was barefoot, and had no bag with her. I had to ignore my fears about Mrs Jameson and focus on the job at hand. I needed to assess the crime scene, note the evidence and record it as soon as I could.

'She was found down there,' I said, pointing towards the lapping waves. 'That's where we saw her from the terrace.' If she'd been killed there, any signs of struggle would have been swept clean by the sea.

'We should look for her stuff, before it gets washed away,' said Frankie. 'You stay with her, Marge. I'll search the beach.'

The two men went with her, systematically walking up and down as the torch beam criss-crossed the sands.

Left alone with the body in the dark, I felt a sudden surge of fear. What if the killer was still lurking on the beach, hiding in one of the caves? And yet… I laid a finger on her neck. The body was cold. She had been dead for some time.

I frowned. What time exactly had we arrived back at the hotel and seen her waiting outside the gate? We'd left the theatre just after ten, and it wasn't a long drive from Margate to Broadstairs. Say twenty minutes past ten o'clock. It couldn't be more than an hour later now, surely?

I crouched again to examine the body by the moonlight. One arm was flung out. Her hands were small with short fingers, like little paws, and her fingernails were filed to a point. One nail was broken. I imagined her struggling against her assailant, scrabbling with her nails to free herself, and swallowed hard. Whoever had done this might have marks on their hands, perhaps their face. That was something to look out for.

Her dress was ripped at the shoulder, the seams giving around the bodice. Had that happened before or after her death? I felt immensely sad. The woman was so young. She seemed to have led a complicated life – aliases, stories of mafia, a lost inheritance. What had brought her from Italy to this little strip of peaceful English seaside, and who had brought that life to a brutal end?

I heard a bell ringing as a car engine droned around the bay and stopped. Moments later two figures started down the steps from the road, both holding torches. Thank goodness – the police.

I stood and waved. 'Over here!'

Chapter 14

Before the policemen reached me, Frankie came bounding back over the sand. There was something in her hands.

'Here! We found them over by the base of the cliffs, at the mouth of that cave. They were lying on the sand, as if she'd kicked them off in a hurry.'

She held out a pair of silver sandals. They were similar to mine, and it gave me a queer feeling to see them.

'Treadwell and the Major are searching the cave to see if they can find anything else.'

Bother. I realised too late that I should have told them not to disturb anything. Any footprints or signs of struggle in the cave would be kicked away. And now Frankie's fingerprints would be on the shoes. I'd been too distracted to do my job properly.

The two policemen reached us.

'What's happened here?' The older of the two crouched down to examine the body. 'I'm Sergeant Cox. Did you find her, Miss? What's your name?'

The younger man pulled out a notebook.

'I didn't find her, but I saw the body from the terrace.' I pointed to the hotel. 'Up there. Although I didn't know what it was for sure. I'm Miss Swallow. I'm staying at the hotel. Mr Ashcroft, the manager, came down first with the others. He's the one who telephoned you.'

'The others?'

Just then Geoffrey Treadwell and Major Redfern came puffing up. 'We didn't find anything else in the cave,' said Mr Treadwell. 'Perhaps the handbag was stolen. Maybe she was killed in a robbery.'

'It was the mafia, I tell you,' said Major Redfern. 'Just as she warned.'

Sergeant Cox looked from one to the other of us, eyebrows raised. 'I'd like you all to go to the hotel lounge with Constable Perks here, and give him your names and addresses,' he said. His voice was calm and slow. 'I'll come and take your statements after the inspector arrives.'

He looked at the sandals in Frankie's hands, and then doubtfully at her breeches and shirtsleeves. 'Are those yours, Miss?'

She snorted. 'Don't look like it, does it? They're hers, I reckon. We found them in that cave in the cliffs.'

He sighed. 'Please put them down. I suppose you've been trampling all over the beach?'

'I'm sorry,' I told him. 'I should have thought of that.'

He gave me a surprised look. 'No reason for you to think of it, Miss. But it's better for us if people leave it to the professionals. We're trained not to disturb the crime scene, see.'

I nodded humbly, thinking in embarrassment of what Mrs Jameson would have to say about the matter. I glanced up at the hotel again. Would she have heard from Sarah and the others about what was happening on the beach? If so, surely she would have come down herself to investigate.

'Right, then,' said Constable Perks. 'Come with me, if you would.'

'There's a tunnel up to the hotel,' Mr Treadwell began.

'No!' I called. I couldn't bear the thought of it. I looked over, and saw that the base of the steps down from the tunnel was already awash. 'The tide's too high,' I said. 'We'll have to go around by the road.'

#

The constable led us to the hotel. Nobody by the gate, nobody in the gardens – unless they were lurking in the dark. I was glad of the constable's company, and of Frankie's reassuring presence beside me.

The manager was waiting for us in the lounge, his usual calm demeanour ruffled. I supposed the discovery of a body on the hotel beach was not the sort of publicity he'd hope for. He'd reopened the bar and was dishing out drinks to the shocked guests. Mrs Redfern was drinking brandy and seemed to have been weeping. She jumped up and ran to her son.

'Cedric! What's been happening?'

He sat down heavily. 'I need a drink,' he said.

'Are you all right, Marjorie?' James hurried forward with the cardigan I'd left on my seat. I slipped it around my shoulders with a weak smile, glad of the warmth. I'd begun to shiver.

Mildred Treadwell leaned against the bar, smoking, her cool gaze taking in the party, and the policeman. 'It was a body, then, I take it?' she asked.

Sarah sprang up from her armchair and clutched Bertie's arm. 'Not another murder!' she cried, with unnecessary drama.

Constable Perks, a rather stolid youth with cropped fair hair, was not one to have his head turned by a pretty face.

'If I could ask everyone who was not on the beach to leave us, we've police business to attend to,' he said. 'Unless you know something about the incident, Miss?'

'Oh, golly, no.' Sarah tried a winsome smile. 'I just want to know what happened.'

'We all do,' said Mr Treadwell. 'Ashcroft, I want a whisky.'

'Come on, Sarah. It's late. Time for bed,' said Bertie. 'We'll hear all about it tomorrow.' He ushered her gently away. James offered his arm to Mrs Redfern, and Mrs Treadwell stubbed out her cigarette and followed them out of the door.

'May I go and call my employer?' I asked Constable Perks. 'Mrs Iris Jameson. She's had a lot of experience at investigating things. She often works with Scotland Yard.'

He gave me a sharp glance. 'Please wait here until the inspector says you can go, Miss. I'll take your details first, shall I?'

He noted down my name, address and employment, raising his eyebrows when I told him I worked as a secretary for a private detective agency. But he said nothing, merely moving on to take down the particulars of the rest of the party.

I refused Mr Ashcroft's offer of a glass of brandy. I felt I needed to keep my head clear. The night was sultry for England, but I'd begun to shiver, despite the cardigan. Delayed shock, I knew. I'd have liked a glass of milk and to sit by the Bedford Square kitchen fire.

Instead, I sat on an over-stuffed sofa with Frankie, wishing we were alone so we could speak freely. I wanted to tell her what I'd seen when I ran through the gardens to the road. I wanted her to tell me I'd been wrong, or to come up with an obvious explanation for why Mrs Jameson had been lurking around the gate. Most of all, I wanted her reassurance that Mrs Jameson had absolutely nothing at all to do with the dead body on the beach.

'What do you reckon, Marge?' she asked in a low voice. 'It's got to be a bloke, hasn't it? Strangulation, after all. You need strong hands for that.'

Female killers were not unknown, and we'd met a few whose coldness had terrified me. But their weapons had been poison, or other indirect means. Frankie was right that the violent death of a young woman was usually down to a man. And usually a man she knew.

Both Major Redfern and Geoffrey Treadwell had known Julia, although only one of them was admitting it to the police. But they had been in the lounge playing cards at the time of her death.

'What about that waiter?' I asked. 'The one you said she was flirting with. What did you say his name was?'

'What about him?' Frankie gave me a sharp look. 'You should have let me get Mrs J. She'll be fed up to have missed it.'

'I did try to call her before I went down to the beach,' I admitted. 'But there wasn't any answer from her room.'

'All right, everyone.' A middle-aged man with an officious air walked into the room. He wore a poorly fitting navy-blue suit. His heavily stubbled jawline and baggy eyes suggested he had recently been called from his bed. Even so, I thought, he might have tried to look professional.

'I'm Detective Inspector Dyson, of the Kent Constabulary. I want to speak to each of you separately. Which of you is the manager?'

Mr Ashcroft stepped forward. 'That's me, sir. How can I help?'

'I want a private room to work from. And a pot of strong coffee.' He exchanged a word with Constable Perks. 'Which of you is Miss Swallow?'

I stood up.

'Right, then. Let's start with you.'

Chapter 15

Inspector Dyson sat at a writing desk in the library. He pointed to a leather club chair, and I sat down. One of the bar staff brought in a pot of coffee with two cups, and began to pour.

'Leave it, man,' snapped the inspector.

He didn't offer me any coffee, although I would have welcomed some. He poured a cup for himself and rubbed his tired eyes, then tipped back in his upright chair. Constable Perks sat beside him, notebook at the ready.

'Detective agency, hey? Fancy yourself as a sleuth?' Inspector Dyson asked.

'I work as a secretary for a private detective,' I said. 'Mrs Iris Jameson. You may have heard of her.'

He ignored this. I wasn't boasting, but our recent cases had hit the newspaper headlines, especially our investigation of the death of *Daily Post* proprietor Lord Ravensbourne. However, Inspector Dyson was not going to give me the satisfaction of telling me he knew about Mrs Jameson.

'I want to make one thing clear,' he snapped. 'This is my investigation. I don't want any repeat of that nonsense on the beach. If you were a trained detective, you'd know to preserve the crime scene, not clod-hop all over it moving the evidence around.'

I winced. 'We were worried Miss Donatello's things would be washed away. The tide was coming in.'

'That's what I mean. Worrying. Interfering. You're a pretty girl, Miss Swallow. Leave the thinking to those of us with more brains than beauty, won't you?' He set his cup down and glared at me.

I bristled, but said nothing. Mrs Jameson would make short work of Inspector Dyson in the morning, I felt sure. She particularly enjoyed besting a policeman who thought that women lacked analytical thinking skills.

'Now, you called the woman Miss Donatello. How do you know her, and when did you last see her?'

The man's rude manner brought out my stubbornness. I would answer his questions truthfully, but offer no further information.

'I don't know her. She was hanging around the hotel, and she told me her name when she walked along the cliff with me. She had a letter to post in the hotel letter-box. That was two days ago, just before luncheon. Wednesday.'

I didn't know what had happened to the letter, I realised. Mrs Jameson had not mentioned receiving it.

'And that was the last time you saw her?'

I shook my head. 'I saw her this evening, at the gate of the hotel. I returned from the theatre with my employer, and Miss Donatello was standing under the trees. About twenty past ten, I think, although I can't be exact.'

He looked up sharply. 'You're sure of that? Who was with you?'

I gave him Frankie and Mrs Jameson's names.

He wrote them down, and frowned. 'And then? Sergeant Cox says you saw the body from the terrace.'

'I'd been in the lounge bar, where there was a group playing bridge. I went outside and stood by the terrace wall, talking to Mrs Treadwell.' I saw no need to go into the details of the silly fight. Mr Ashcroft or one of the others could give him that information.

'She pointed to something on the beach. I looked down, and realised it could be a body. I told Mr Ashcroft, and he went down through the tunnel with Mr Treadwell and Major Redfern. I...' I hesitated a moment.

'Go on.'

'I don't like using the tunnel. I went around the road way and joined them on the beach. They'd dragged her body up and out of the water. I checked for a pulse, but Miss Donatello was dead. So, I told Mr Ashcroft to go and call the police.'

I knew I should have mentioned knocking on Mrs Jameson's door. I knew I should have told him about seeing her in the garden. But I was still hoping there would be an innocent, simple explanation. I'd talk to Mrs Jameson before I told the police, I decided. Especially this policeman.

'You knew she was dead?' he asked.

'Yes.' He waited, so I added: 'I worked in a hospital, during the War, with the Voluntary Aid Detachment.' I'd also seen more than my fair share of murdered corpses, in the past two years.

He tipped back his chair again, teetering precariously on the back two legs. 'So, you saw this woman once on the cliffs, then recognised her again tonight, in the dark, from a moving car. Is that right?' His tone was frankly disbelieving.

I flushed. 'Actually, I'd seen her several times,' I said. 'On the beach, on Wednesday morning. And in Margate, yesterday afternoon.'

He raised his eyebrows. 'You seem to be following her around, Miss Swallow. What were you doing with her in Margate?'

'Oh, she wasn't with me,' I said. 'She was with Mr Treadwell. They were having afternoon tea together in the Dreamland tea garden. I just happened to see them.'

His eyebrows shot up. I smiled to myself. Let him find out what Treadwell was doing with her.

He kept me a few minutes longer, then told me to go to bed. 'No more sleuthing, do you hear?'

I nodded politely, and ran up the stairs to Mrs Jameson's room.

She answered my rap on the door this time, wearing a buttoned-up floral dressing gown and with her hair wrapped in a silk scarf. She looked tired and irritated.

'Marjorie, it's gone midnight. What's the matter?'

'The Italian woman, Julia Donatello. She's dead. We found her body on the beach. And the police are here now, interviewing everyone. I thought you'd want to know.' I was gabbling, stumbling over my words in my anxiety.

Mrs Jameson, whose posture was always upright if not imperious, seemed to sag. Her face suddenly looked much older than her fifty-one years. She beckoned me into her room, shut the door firmly and sat on the stool by the dressing table. I hovered, unsure whether to take a seat myself.

'Dead?' she repeated. 'How?'

Quickly, I explained what I'd seen. 'It looked like strangulation. She had marks on her neck, from her nails. And petechiae around her eyes.'

Mrs Jameson's hand flew to her own neck. The overhead lighting threw shadows over her pale face, hollowing her cheeks and making dark caverns of her eye sockets. Her pale mouth was a thin line, her lips almost disappearing as she pressed them together.

She thought for a moment, then asked me to tell her what I'd seen of the crime scene, and who had been there. She watched me closely, her hooded eyes hawkish, and drummed her fingers lightly on the dressing table. Large, capable hands, with short nails buffed to a sheen. I looked away.

To my surprise, Mrs Jameson didn't chide me about the disturbance of the evidence on the beach, or my failure to call her earlier. She turned away, caught sight of her reflection in the mirror and frowned, tucking a stray lock of grey hair under her scarf.

'Stupid,' she muttered. 'Stupid girl.'

I hoped she didn't mean me. 'The inspector's downstairs in the library,' I said. 'Inspector Dyson. He's one of those policemen who don't think women should get involved in investigations. I don't think you'll get on.'

Mrs Jameson nodded, but did not smile. She had abstracted herself, in the way she did sometimes when deep in thought. One index finger tapped on her chin, and her grey eyes took on a glazed look in the lamplight. I waited, knowing not to interrupt her.

A minute later, she'd made a decision. She stood, and her features seemed to snap back into focus.

'The inspector is right, Marjorie. We're on vacation. It's very sad, but this is nothing to do with us. Go to bed, and try to forget about it. Let the police investigate. No doubt they will find the culprit.'

I stared at her in surprise. 'But Mrs Jameson...'

She sighed. 'I'm very tired. I came here for a rest. I won't have you tangling us up in a random crime. You must learn to curb your curiosity. You can't investigate everything.'

'But you were...' I caught her eye and quailed.

'I was what?' Her voice warned me to be careful with what I said next. You were there, I wanted to say. You were in the gardens, when I went down to the beach.

'Nothing.'

She moved to the door and held it open. 'Good night, Marjorie.'

Wondering, I retired to my bed. It had been a long day, and I was weary. As I switched off the bedside light and pulled the sheet over me, I wondered if I should have told her that I'd seen her in the gardens. I imagined myself demanding to know what she'd been doing, why she had been hanging around at the hotel gate. But she was my employer. I'd never demanded anything of Mrs Jameson.

And there was another thing. Julia Donatello had come to Kingsgate to see Mrs Jameson, to ask for her help. Mrs Jameson had seemed threatened by her, refused to meet her and pretended not to know what she wanted. Now the woman was dead. Why didn't Mrs Jameson want to investigate that death?

I squeezed my eyes tightly shut. The worm of suspicion wriggled again. I remembered a conversation we'd had during our very first investigation. We'd talked about motives for murder, and Mrs Jameson had said I'd missed one.

'I think the main motive is fear,' she'd said. 'Fear of losing something, fear of discovery. Fear of what the other person will do to you.' I'd wondered at the time if she was speaking from personal experience.

Had Mrs Jameson feared Julia Donatello, and if so, what had

she done about it?

Chapter 16

Mrs Jameson was quiet at breakfast, reading a newspaper and sipping her coffee. She wished me good morning when I joined her, but made no mention of the events of the night before. I wasn't in the mood for chatter either. It was too hot for bacon and eggs, so I settled for toast and marmalade.

However, the topic of Julia Donatello's death was hard to avoid. Old Mr and Mrs Goldsmith paused by our table and wanted to know all about it.

'I hear you went down to the beach yourself, Miss Swallow,' said Mrs Goldsmith, in the shocked yet fascinated tone I recognised. She wanted to demonstrate disapproval, but also hear all the gory details. I glanced at Mrs Jameson, noting the way she'd pressed her lips together.

'I'm afraid I can't really talk about it,' I said, not wishing to irritate my employer further. 'The police don't want me telling people what I saw.'

'You see, Mary?' said Mr Goldsmith. 'I told you we should mind our own business.' They retreated to their corner table, arguing as usual.

But Major Redfern was less easy to put off. He strode across the breakfast room towards us, his mother trailing behind him, pulled out a chair and sat down at our table.

'See here, Mrs Jameson,' he began, bluntly. 'That damned fool policeman isn't up to the job. Anyone can see that. Hey, Miss Swallow? You heard what I said about the mafia. Well, he's a provincial policeman, isn't he? He's probably never travelled beyond Margate. Anyway, I don't think he's taking it seriously. The mafia link, I mean. There's an Italian chap over at Broadstairs, you know, selling ice-cream. Seen him with my own eyes.'

Mrs Jameson laid down her newspaper. 'I'm not clear what you want from me, Major.'

'I'm so sorry,' said Mrs Redfern. 'I said we shouldn't trouble you, Mrs Jameson. I know you're on holiday.'

'We've read about your investigations,' the major continued. 'You're a detective, aren't you? I want you to investigate, Mrs Jameson. On my behalf. Bianca looked to me for protection, and I failed her. Well, I won't fail her now.'

He thumped the table and Mrs Jameson recoiled.

'Who is Bianca?' she asked, with restraint.

'Major Redfern knew Julia Donatello as Bianca Colomba,' I interjected. 'He says she was hiding down here from the Italian mafia.'

Mrs Jameson sighed and folded her newspaper. 'I hate to disappoint you, Major Redfern, but as your mother says, I am on vacation. I am not taking on any cases at this time. I'm sure the police will investigate thoroughly.'

Major Redfern had gone rather red. 'I loved her, you see,' he muttered. 'I was going to ask her to marry me. Girl like that needs looking after. Anyone could see that. And I may not be much use to the army, but I could have offered her a home. A safe English haven, away from those foreign gangsters.'

Mrs Redfern looked as startled by this as the rest of us.

'Cedric, my dear. You barely knew the girl.'

He stood up, his fists balled. 'I knew enough. I should have known something was wrong when she didn't meet me last night. I waited an hour. If only I'd known.' He choked on his words and pulled out his handkerchief. 'Sorry. Damn fool that I am.'

He strode away, his mother skipping behind him to keep up.

'Goodness,' I said. 'What do you think, Mrs Jameson? Shall I see if I can find out where he was going to meet her last night, and what time?'

She pushed away her coffee cup, her lips compressed. 'No, Marjorie. I think you should finish your breakfast and take your detective stories to the beach, if you're determined to solve crimes. I plan to take a walk into Broadstairs, alone. I don't wish to be cross-questioned by every guest wanting to know about Miss Donatello's death.'

However, the police had other ideas about our plans to leave the hotel. Before we could speak further, Inspector Dyson entered the room, accompanied by Mr Ashcroft and Constable Perks.

'I want everyone who was in the hotel last night from ten o'clock onwards to stay within the grounds, until I tell you otherwise,' said the inspector. 'The beach is, of course, out of bounds until the police have finished with it.'

There was a collective groan, and immediate protests from one of the golfing ladies.

'Helen and I went to bed at ten,' exclaimed Miss McDonald. 'We had nothing to do with it. And we want to get a full eighteen holes in before lunch.'

Her friend looked uneasy. 'It's all right, Jean,' she said quickly. 'We can practise our putting. Don't make a fuss.'

Inspector Dyson turned to Constable Perks. 'Nobody leaves until I say so. Is that clear?'

The constable nodded. 'Yes, sir.'

'We will, of course, be doing all we can to make everyone as comfortable as possible,' said the harassed manager. 'Please don't hesitate to ask me, or any of the staff, if you need anything. The tennis courts and putting green are at your service. Refreshments will be served on the terrace all morning.'

Mrs Jameson sighed in irritation. 'I shall go to my balcony and read,' she said.

'Later, Mrs Jameson,' said Inspector Dyson. 'I want to talk to you first, about your relationship with the deceased. And your assistant, too.'

#

'What relationship?' asked Mrs Jameson, sharply. 'I barely knew the woman.'

We'd been ushered into the library, which was hazy and smelled strongly of Virginia Shag, the same pipe tobacco my father smoked. A briar pipe lay on the side of the ash-tray next to a heap of expired matches, and the blotter was covered with scribbled doodles. I wondered what time the inspector had got to bed. If, indeed, he had slept at all: he was wearing the same shapeless suit, and his chin was patchily shaved.

'We found this in the room where she'd been staying at the Captain Digby,' he said. He held up a white envelope, addressed to Mrs Jameson in an untidy scrawl. It had been slit open.

She held out her hand to take it. The inspector put the letter back on the pile of documents on the blotter.

'Why was she writing to you, Mrs Jameson?'

She raised her eyebrows. 'As I have not read the letter, I have no idea. Perhaps you can enlighten me.'

'It was not the first time she had written to you. Was it, Miss Swallow?'

I remembered the letter she'd carried to the hotel. How had he known about that? I thought back. We had met the Treadwells, and Geoffrey Treadwell had offered to take the letter for her. He must have seen it was addressed to Mrs Jameson, and told the police. I wondered if he'd also told them about his trip to Margate.

'She asked me to take a letter to Mrs Jameson, but I told her to post it in the hotel's letter box,' I said. 'I didn't want to get involved.'

He turned to me, eyes sharp. 'Involved in what?'

Mrs Jameson sighed and tapped the table. 'The woman calling herself Julia Donatello had asked me to investigate something for her. I don't know the details, because I told her I had no wish to take on the case. I imagine that letter was a further attempt to persuade me. If you let me read it, I can confirm that.'

'What was in the first letter she sent, Mrs Jameson? And where is it?'

My employer returned his gaze coolly. 'I threw it away. It was a request for me to investigate an inheritance that her mother said she was owed. I am here on vacation, not on business, so I took no notice of it.'

Her gaze flickered back to the envelope with her name on it, in large, childish letters. I could tell she was itching to take it from him.

'And when was the last time you spoke to Miss Donatello?'

My employer paused for a moment, frowning. 'I believe I have only spoken to her once. Wednesday morning, after an early swim. She accosted me as I came back to the hotel. I told her I had no interest in her case. That's all.'

I glanced at her quickly. Had she forgotten? Or was she deliberately not telling the inspector about her argument with Miss Donatello just before we left for the theatre? I waited to see if she would remember.

'And was that the last time you saw her, Mrs Jameson?' Inspector Dyson leaned forward, scrutinising her face. She wore a bland expression of mild serenity, which I knew in no way reflected the workings of her mind.

'No. I saw her outside the gate of the hotel, yesterday evening, when we returned from the theatre in Margate. However, we did not speak. The gate was open, so I told my chauffeur to drive straight past without stopping.'

The inspector nodded slowly, checking against a sheet of notes. 'And what time would you say this was?'

'Approximately twenty past ten.' She didn't hesitate. 'I took a turn around the terrace, checked my wristwatch and saw it was almost half past ten. I went to my room and slept until after midnight, when Marjorie woke me and informed me of the discovery of the body.'

I swallowed, glancing at her again. That was the second lie. I'd seen her in the hotel garden, on my way down to the beach. Both times, I realised, she had not known I had seen her. She'd thought herself alone. And now she was lying to the police, deliberately. What possible reason could she have?

Chapter 17

Mrs Jameson went straight to her room after Inspector Dyson waved us away. I dithered, then ran along to my room to fetch my sun hat. Whatever I decided to do with my morning, the sun was already too hot to go bare-headed.

The straw hat with a red ribbon always made me think of Hugh, who had helped me choose it at the market in Nice. Hugh, it had turned out, was a charming companion, but untrustworthy. He'd lied to me, then abandoned me without explanation, putting me in danger to save his own skin.

I picked up the hat and walked slowly down the corridor. Was that what was happening again? Mrs Jameson had lied to the police, twice. Once might have been an oversight. Twice suggested she had something to hide.

I'd thought I would trust Mrs Jameson with my life. Indeed, she had saved my life on more than one occasion. I'd lived and worked with her for almost two years, and never known her to be anything other than honest. She guarded her secrets closely, and I knew there were many things she didn't tell me, but I'd never known her to lie before.

My musings were interrupted by Geoffrey and Mildred Treadwell, dressed in tennis whites, swinging their rackets.

'We might as well get in some practice at the tennis court, if we can't cross the road to the golf course,' said Mrs Treadwell. 'Nonsense, of course. As if it would make the slightest bit of difference to the police.'

Her husband was looking glum. Perhaps he'd hoped for a snooze on the terrace after the late night. I was seized by an impulse for mischief.

'Lucky you managed that trip to Margate on Thursday, Mr Treadwell,' I said. 'I don't suppose there'll be much chance to take tea at the Dreamland gardens today.'

He stared at me, and his face turned beetroot. Mrs Treadwell turned to him with a quizzical look. 'You went to Margate, Geoffrey? I thought you had a business meeting.'

'I did,' he stated, wiping his hand across his mouth. 'In Margate. Went to see a fellow about some investments. Someone has to pay for your golf lessons. We finished earlier than expected, so I went for a look around the town afterwards. Why shouldn't I? I'm on holiday too, aren't I?'

She threw a withering look in his direction. 'I see.' She stalked off down the corridor.

Mr Treadwell turned his sweating face to me. 'I say, Miss Swallow. I have told the police, you know. I just happened to bump into Miss Donatello in Margate, you see. After we'd met the two of you on the cliffs the day before, I thought I'd treat her to a spot of tea. Best not to say anything to Mildred, do you see?'

Hmm. I nodded brightly and he trotted after his wife.

I followed more slowly. I decided to look for Frankie, as I hadn't seen her at breakfast. She took her meals in the servants' dining room, which she said was preferable to the guests' quarters.

'You get as much grub as you can eat, and don't have to worry about your table manners,' she reported. 'The gossip's better, too.'

At the bottom of the stairs, poor Mr Ashcroft was besieged. Jean McDonald was insisting she should be allowed to see the inspector, then go to the golf course. Mrs Goldsmith wanted to borrow a book from the library, currently occupied by the police. Mrs Heath hovered, brandishing a laundry list.

'I've checked the inventory twice, and there's a sheet missing,' Mrs Heath was saying in her insistent voice. 'It has to be right before it goes to the laundry, or the whole system will go to pieces.'

I gave Mr Ashcroft a sympathetic smile as I passed. Constable Perks came out of the library and both Miss Macdonald and Mrs Goldsmith pounced on him.

'Do let me pop in and see if there are any more like this Georgette Heyer novel,' implored Mrs Goldsmith. 'It's terribly good. Perfect for reading on the terrace.'

'Can we go next?' asked Miss McDonald. 'It's too bad, all this waiting around.'

The policeman ignored her and turned to her friend. 'The inspector would like to speak to you next, Miss Fraser.'

Helen Fraser flushed a dark pink and nodded. 'Of course.' Her fingernails were bitten down and the skin by her thumb was raw with her picking at it. Her nerves had not improved since the previous day.

Miss McDonald immediately began to insist that they should be seen together. Miss Fraser caught her arm. 'Leave it to me, Jean,' she said, her voice betraying unusual frustration. 'I'll sort it out.'

I frowned. What needed sorting out? In all that had happened since, I had almost forgotten about Miss Fraser's request for Mrs Jameson's professional services. I thought back to the scene in the library. She'd had a letter, an envelope. Cheap paper, a scrawled address. Hmm. I tried to remember the handwriting on the letter Julia Donatello had sent to Mrs Jameson.

'Miss Swallow?' called the girl on the reception desk. 'There's a message for you. Can you call a Mr Graham Hargreaves, of Bedford Square?'

Mr Ashcroft took the opportunity to depart with Mrs Heath, presumably to investigate the laundry. I slipped into the telephone booth and asked to be put through.

'Hello, Marjorie. You wanted to know about that young Italian woman who called around asking for Mrs Jameson?' said Graham. His gruff tones were reassuring, and I wished for the first time that we were back at home.

'I think I know what happened. Jenny's been taking the letters to forward onto Mrs Jameson at the hotel. This woman apparently got into conversation with her, and walked with her to the Post Office on Saturday.

'Jenny's very sorry, but she says the woman told her she'd got a shoe-lace loose, and she gave her the letters to hold while she tied it. Turns out there was nothing wrong with the lace, but I suppose that's how she got the forwarding address from the letters. I do hope she's not caused you any trouble.'

I sighed. 'Tell Jenny she's not to worry about it,' I said. 'The woman won't be causing any more trouble now, I don't suppose.'

I replaced the mouthpiece. There was no reason to worry Graham or Jenny with what had transpired. I only hoped my words would not be proven overly optimistic.

Chapter 18

I made my way to the terrace, hoping to find Frankie, but she was nowhere to be seen.

'Hullo! Come and tell me all about it,' said James, waving from a shaded deckchair where he lounged with his notebook. 'What happened after the police arrived? My leg was playing up last night, or I'd have come down to the beach with you.'

'I was just looking for Frankie,' I said. I didn't want to go through it all again.

'Haven't seen her, I'm afraid. Come on, sit down and spill the beans.'

I adjusted my hat and sat down next to him. The sun was high, dazzling in a sky of cloudless blue. We could almost be on the Riviera.

I closed my eyes and remembered Julia Donatello's face, the sand encrusting her nostrils and eyebrows. In all the busy activity that a sudden death prompted, it was easy to forget the person at the heart of it. The young Italian woman, whose real name I didn't even know.

'It was horrible, actually. And the police just asked a lot of questions, about who she was and when I'd seen her before.'

'I'm sorry. I was being insensitive,' said James. I opened my eyes. He was looking at me kindly, his hazel eyes shaded by his Panama hat. 'I suppose I thought you'd be busy hunting for clues or something.'

I smiled. 'That's all right. I thought I would, too. But Mrs Jameson doesn't want us getting involved.' My smile faded as my suspicions about her reasons flooded back. But surely not. I was being silly.

'Probably best,' said James. 'But I bet you're tempted. Would you like an iced coffee?'

During our stay I'd become very fond of this American concoction of coffee, milk, ice and sugar, although Mrs Jameson sniffed and said it was nothing more than a milkshake, fit only for children.

'That'd be lovely,' I admitted. 'Thank you.' James waved to the waiter and placed the order.

'Go on then, tell me what you think. Do you believe this story that Major Redfern's been hawking around about the Italian mafia?' he asked.

I sighed. 'I'm sure he believes it. Poor man, he seemed very upset. He said at breakfast that he was going to propose to her.'

James nodded. 'He told me as much. He's not such a bad fellow, you know. Doesn't have much experience of women. He was in the Indian army for ten years. He says the English women out in Jaipur were a poor lot. And he's not had much luck since he got home.'

He laughed. 'Funny, isn't it? Everyone says there's a shortage of men and England's crawling with girls desperate for a chap. But they're not interested in the ones with shell-shock, or bad lungs, or bits of us missing.'

I flushed. 'That's a bit unfair.' I'd always been understanding about Freddie's bouts of neurasthenia. It wasn't that which had put me off marriage to him. But then I realised James was talking about himself, and I looked at him more kindly. 'I'm sure there are plenty of nice girls around who'd like to meet a successful author.'

He snorted. 'A writer of pot-boiling romances?'

I laughed. 'Well, you can't have it both ways. Some women might like the idea of a man who hasn't given up on romance.'

The waiter arrived, and I took a slurp of iced coffee. It was delicious.

Major Redfern stomped across the terrace to join us, looking determined. He wore a battered straw Panama and a khaki safari jacket, every inch the retired Colonial officer. He sat down and clasped his big freckled hands between his knees.

'Miss Swallow, can't you persuade that boss of yours to get involved? The police haven't asked me anything about Bianca's story, you know.'

I sighed. 'I'm afraid I've never been able to make Mrs Jameson do anything she doesn't want to do. But why don't you tell us, Major?' I half-hoped the mafia story would turn out to be true. Perhaps that would explain her many aliases, her flight from London. Maybe she was being menaced by an Italian ice-cream seller in Broadstairs, after all.

He settled in and began his story eagerly.

'I met her in the Captain Digby, you see, on Tuesday. I've got into the habit of taking my lunch there. It's more my sort of place than the hotel.

'Anyway, there was some sort of misunderstanding. A chap staying with his family had lost his wallet, and accused Bianca of having taken it. All very unpleasant. Anyway, I had to get involved, and he soon backed down.' The major jutted his chin aggressively. 'He found it later, outside in the garden.

No doubt it was one of the children. He had eight, you know. Noisy little blighters.'

Goodness. Was there a man in the whole of Kent who the mysterious Italian woman had not been involved with?

'She was very upset, so of course I asked her to have lunch with me and tell me what had happened. She said she'd come to Britain because her brother in Naples had got on the wrong side of some of these mafia chaps, and they'd threatened to kidnap her in revenge. Dreadful, Miss Swallow, you wouldn't believe the savagery of these gangsters.'

He glared fiercely at us. 'She'd been in London, but she'd seen one of the beasts on the street, so she'd run into the train station and taken the next train – which happened to be going to Broadstairs. She was short of funds, of course, but the people at the Captain Digby had said she could stay there in return for helping out in the kitchen. And that's what she'd been doing, poor girl. Skivvying away, while the rest of us were enjoying ourselves.'

He scratched the back of his hand. I narrowed my eyes. He seemed to have some kind of lesion on it. He saw me looking.

'Eczema,' he said, roughly. 'Gets worse in hot weather.'

Interesting. I hoped the police had taken note of the marks on Julia Donatello's neck. Also, I hoped they were talking to the manager of the Captain Digby. I hadn't seen Julia skivvying at any point during our stay.

'So, you took her under your wing,' said James, sympathetically. 'That was kind of you, Major.'

'Well, obviously I said I'd pay for her to stay there, so she could rest and recover from her ordeal. She told me how frightened she was that the gangsters might find her. She'd seen someone in Broadstairs, you see, an Italian chap, and she wondered if he might tell them where she was staying. They all know each other, these mafia people.'

The major shook his head heavily. 'I told her not to worry; that I would look after her. I blame myself, Miss Swallow. I should have known something was wrong. I'd planned to propose to her last night, d'you see? I waited an hour, but she didn't arrive.'

'In the Neptune Fort?' I asked. 'Were you waiting for her there before, when I saw you on Wednesday morning?'

He nodded. 'I know it's silly, but it became our special place. She did arrive, you know, on Wednesday. A bit late, but she said she'd had to deliver a letter. Anyway, we were to meet there after dinner last night, at half-past eight. I waited until half-past nine, and then I went into the Captain Digby, but she wasn't there either, and the manager said he hadn't seen her since seven o'clock.'

Where had Miss Donatello been from seven o'clock until we'd seen her at the gate? Despite Mrs Jameson's instructions not to get involved, I was starting to construct a timeline in my head. I reached into my handbag for pencil and paper to note down what the major had said.

'You are going to investigate, aren't you?' James observed. 'Do let me help. I'm so bored with my book.'

'Would you really?' asked Major Redfern, eagerly. 'We could do it together. Three musketeers, you know.'

Oh, goodness. What had I started?

Chapter 19

Lunch with Mrs Jameson was not a success. I tried to tell her what I'd learned that morning about Julia, or Bianca, or whatever her real name was. I rather hoped she would be interested enough to get involved in the investigation – in which case my suspicions of her could be laid to rest.

'Major Redfern said Julia Donatello had been accused of stealing a man's wallet at the Captain Digby, and that he'd intervened on her behalf. He was paying for her bed and board, because she didn't have any money.

'But Geoffrey Treadwell looked very friendly with her when Frankie and I saw them having tea together on Thursday afternoon in Margate. He hadn't told his wife about it, and asked me not to say anything. Frankie said she'd seen her flirting with one of the waiters, too. Alfred, I think his name was.'

No comment from Mrs Jameson. I paused to fork up some delicious poached salmon and cucumber, and pressed on.

'Then, Major Redfern was supposed to meet her last night after dinner at the Neptune Fort, but he says she didn't show up. What if she did, and he'd proposed marriage, and she'd turned him down? Or maybe he saw her with another man – Mr Treadwell, perhaps, or the waiter. The major would feel an awful fool, and we know he has a sharp temper. He was terribly belligerent about being accused of cheating at cards last night. And he has a mark on the back of his hand.'

Mrs Jameson, who had been listening to my chatter in silence while she ate her grilled Dover sole, finally laid down her knife and fork.

'Marjorie, you know I don't like gossip.'

That wasn't true; she loved it. The first time I'd met her, she'd been eavesdropping shamelessly on the conversation at the next table in the Ritz hotel's Palm Court. Gossip was an important part of our business.

'This is all most distasteful. I don't wish to hear any more about the unfortunate woman's romantic entanglements. Anyway, you're forgetting that Major Redfern and Mr Treadwell both have an alibi. They were in the lounge when we returned to the hotel,' she said.

I hadn't forgotten, actually. But I had hoped to draw her into a discussion of the case.

'Of course,' I said. 'How silly of me. Who else do you think, then? Who didn't have an alibi?'

She glared at me, although I could see a twist of amusement in her lips. She'd seen straight through my ploy.

'Really, Marjorie. I thought you had a higher opinion of my intellect than that. As I have made abundantly clear, I don't wish to be involved in this case.'

She pushed her plate away and took a sip of water. Her tone was serious again.

'I understand that you want to test your skills. But there are some affairs which are better left to the authorities, I promise you. The less you know about Julia Donatello, or whatever her real name was, the better for both of us. Let us just hope

97

that the police do their work efficiently.'

I gazed at her in despair. 'But how can I be of any use, if you won't tell me anything about it? I know there's something wrong, Mrs Jameson. It's to do with Rome, isn't it? Sister Agnese's visit.'

She wavered. She pressed her napkin to her lips, eyes cast down towards her lap. Her habitual expression of alert amusement had vanished, leaving lines etched by trouble and sorrow.

I waited, holding my breath. Would she let me in on the secret? We had worked together so closely in the past. If she would not tell me, I wondered how long our working relationship could last. Everything I loved – my exciting job, my financial independence, my home and my best friends – had flowed from my position as Mrs Jameson's secretary. But if we could not trust one another, that position seemed doomed.

Mrs Jameson stood, abruptly. 'I won't be cross-questioned like this, Marjorie.' Her voice was sharp. 'I warn you not to test my patience further. It will not go well, for either of us.'

She turned and strode away, leaving me in dismay.

Chapter 20

Mrs Jameson did not get far. As I watched her retreat, she was halted at the restaurant door by Inspector Dyson. She gave a gesture of annoyance, and tried to pass, but he put a hand on her arm. I jumped up, but he led her away before I had a chance to follow.

I ran across the room, just in time to see them disappear into the library. Oh, goodness. Had someone else reported having seen Mrs Jameson at the gate, or arguing with Julia? Or perhaps something had come to light which explained what Julia wanted with her.

Disconsolate, I went in search of Frankie again. I finally tracked her down sitting perilously on the wall behind the hotel, smoking a Woodbine as she looked out to sea, her legs dangling over the cliff.

'They've been crawling over that beach for hours,' she observed. 'Dunno if they've found anything yet.'

I leaned against the flint wall, hot to the touch in the midday sun. A line of five policemen was literally crawling across the sands, along the tideline where the seaweed was deposited in malodorous clumps. At least they were being thorough.

'The inspector is questioning Mrs Jameson again,' I said. I

told her about my morning's discoveries, and how I'd tried to draw Mrs Jameson on what she thought about the case and been rebuffed.

'It's rum, no mistake,' said Frankie, flicking her cigarette ash. 'But don't worry. I'm sure Mrs J will come around. She's proper fond of you, you know that.'

Perhaps. But she didn't trust me.

'What's the gossip among the staff?' I asked. 'Anything interesting?'

Frankie grinned. 'I might have heard a few snippets.' She got to her feet. 'Come and say hello to Etta. She can tell you herself.'

She led me through to a cool whitewashed room at the back of the hotel, its shelves stacked with starched white bedlinen. A gangly young woman with tawny hair was reaching up to the top shelf, sorting through pillowcases and folded sheets.

'Hullo, Frankie. Got a tab?' She wiped her forehead with the back of her hand. 'Blooming hot, ain't it?'

Frankie introduced us, and Etta came to sit with us on the wall while they smoked. She had a wide smile, and freckles scattered across her face.

'Tell Marge about that Italian woman coming here for work,' said Frankie. 'The one that got killed.'

Etta's pale skin flushed pink. 'I don't like to, now that she's dead,' she said.

'Go on,' said Frankie. 'Not your fault, is it?'

Etta gazed out to sea, then took another drag of tobacco. 'I just feel bad about her, that's all. She came round on Monday, you see. She called herself Bianca, said she needed work and would be happy with bed and board in exchange. Well, that's all very nice for her, but if everyone did that then those of us what does this for a living would be out on our ears, wouldn't we? And you could see she was a bit of a madam.

'So I told Mrs Heath I didn't like the look of her. And then Mrs Heath asked for her references, and she didn't have any, so that was that.'

She ground out the cigarette with her heel.

'Didn't see her again until Wednesday morning. I came out for a smoke, and she was here with Alfie.'

'She'd got a cheek,' observed Frankie.

'Well, that's what I thought! And you know what men are like. She was laughing at whatever he said, and giving him looks from under that stupid sun hat, and I could see he liked it, the daft ha'p'orth.'

She stood and clenched her fists. 'So I says to her she'll have me to deal with if she's not careful, and Alfie says to me not to be daft, and I says to him not to be daft himself, and then Mrs Heath hears and comes running.

'And I says to her that this Bianca woman was distracting the waiting staff from their work, and Alfie storms off, and Mrs Heath tells Bianca that she was to leave the premises immediately and not come back.'

She came to a halt, her colour up and her green eyes flashing.

'Etta!' Mrs Heath rounded the corner with a clip-board. 'Have you found it yet?' She saw us and halted, uncertain. She never seemed to be sure whether to treat Frankie and me as guests or servants.

The maid subsided. 'Sorry, Mrs Heath. Still looking,' she muttered. 'Just having a quick ciggie break.' She trotted back to the laundry room.

Mrs Heath looked at me in irritation. 'Please don't distract our staff more than necessary, Miss Swallow. It's hard enough to keep an operation of this size running at the best of times.'

We tried to look penitent until she too had retreated indoors.

'Oh dear,' I said. 'Poor Etta. We'll get her into trouble. What's he like, this Alfred?'

Frankie put away her tobacco tin. 'He's all right. A bit moody. He's used to all the maids making eyes at him. He didn't know what to make of me, I don't think.' She laughed. 'Then I helped him fix the puncture on his bike and he's been nice as pie since.'

I thought about what Etta had told us. 'Does he have an alibi for after we got back from the theatre?' I was grasping at any explanation that would mean Mrs Jameson wasn't involved. 'Have the police interviewed the staff?'

Frankie nodded.

'They talked to all the staff after breakfast. The waiters finished serving dinner at ten, and Alfie cycled straight home to his mother at their cottage in St Peters. He reckons he was home at quarter past ten, because he heard the church bell. He says he stopped to talk to his old school teacher, who was on his way home from the village pub.'

'Oh dear,' I sighed. 'So it can't have been him. It's all so difficult.'

She shrugged. 'Why? None of our business, is it?'

'That's the thing,' I said. 'I'm rather afraid it might be.'

Checking that we were alone and couldn't be overheard, I told her about seeing Mrs Jameson in the garden, before I ran down to the beach.

'I haven't said anything to her, because she's been in such a bad mood. But she lied about it to the police. She said she walked on the terrace for ten minutes, then went to bed and slept until I woke her.'

Frankie's face was serious, but she shook her head.

'Mrs J must have her reasons,' she said. 'It's not for us to worry about, Marge. There's no reason to tell the police everything, is there? You're too law-abiding, that's your problem. Growing up in Limehouse, you learn that quickly enough. Only tell the police what you have to. No sense looking for trouble. They didn't get much out of me this morning, I can tell you.'

'I'll remember that,' I said. I nodded behind her, to where Sergeant Cox was puffing across the lawn, his face shiny with heat. 'Here they come now.'

Unlike his boss, Sergeant Cox had a kindly manner and a weathered face. He looked like a gardener or gamekeeper, someone who'd lived their whole life outdoors and knew about wildflowers and birdsong. That may have been why his demand took me unawares.

'Miss Swallow, isn't it?' he said. 'I'm afraid I need to ask you to come with me to the police station in Broadstairs. Inspector Dyson's orders.'

I jumped up. 'To the police station? Can't he talk to me here?'

Frankie swung her legs over the wall and stood beside me. 'What's going on? You can't just take her away.'

The man looked uneasy. 'I'm very sorry, Miss. I know it's an inconvenience. But the inspector says he wants to talk to you at the station. He says new information has come to light.'

'Wait.' I began to feel panicky. 'I don't understand. Are you arresting me, sergeant? What if I don't want to go?'

'I'll get Mrs Jameson,' said Frankie.

'No!' The word burst out of me. New information. Inspector Dyson had been talking to Mrs Jameson just half an hour earlier. Now I was being marched off to the police station.

103

Where would that new information have come from, if not Mrs Jameson herself?

'Well, Miss, you're not under arrest, and I don't want to arrest you,' said Sergeant Cox in his slow, measured voice. 'But I might have to, if you refused to come to the station with me. That would be obstructing the course of an investigation, you see. I think it would be better if you came along willingly, all things considered.'

I clutched my handbag. Everything felt unreal: the shimmering heat haze over the sea, the dizzying drop from the cliffs, Sergeant Cox himself, sweating slightly in his uniform.

I tried to smile at Frankie. 'I'll be all right,' I said. 'I expect I'll be back soon. Don't worry.'

I turned and walked through the garden to where the police car was parked in front of the hotel.

Chapter 21

Sergeant Cox escorted me into a small, hot room with no windows. An electric lamp buzzed overhead. I sat on a hard-backed wooden chair drawn up to a table.

'I'll bring you a cuppa, Miss,' he said. 'The inspector will be here soon.'

I sat while my tea got cold, and wished I had a book with me. Police stations always seemed to involve an enormous amount of waiting around. At least at the doctor's office, the receptionist offered you an illustrated magazine to read while you waited, to distract you from your nerves. What did the inspector want from me?

My handbag had been searched and returned to me when I arrived, but there was nothing of any entertainment value in it: a handkerchief, a pot of pink lip tint, a comb and half a bag of mint imperials, left over from our trip to the theatre. I crunched a couple of these, before starting to feel a little sick. I had no intention of primping myself up for the police, so left my hair uncombed and my lips in their natural state.

My mind was all over the place. If the police had simply wanted more information, the inspector would have spoken to me at the hotel. Could it be that they actually suspected me of carrying out the murder? I went back in my mind over everything I'd told them in my first interview, and again with Mrs Jameson. I couldn't remember saying anything incriminating.

Our friend in the Metropolitan Police, Inspector Peter Chadwick, said asking people to attend the police station was a good way to get them off-guard. They became nervous, and sometimes that made them think you already knew something that you didn't, so they admitted it. Was that what Inspector Dyson was intending? I decided I should be on my guard. But against what? I supposed it was working: I already felt nervous and guilty, even though I had nothing to feel guilty about.

Or had I? I hadn't been quite straight with the police. I'd omitted to tell them about Mrs Jameson's argument with Julia before we left for the theatre, or seeing her in the garden as I went down to the beach. Frankie's words returned to me. There's no reason to tell the police everything, is there?

I thought about Mrs Jameson, disappearing into the library with Inspector Dyson after lunch. What had she told him – and was that why I was here now?

#

I'd waited more than an hour when Sergeant Cox returned, looking apologetic, and brought me a fresh cup of tea. Inspector Dyson strutted into the room behind him, pulled out a chair opposite me and sat heavily. He glared at me in silence for a long moment.

I stared back, remembering Frankie's advice to say nothing. Let him explain what I was here for.

'You've had quite a career, haven't you?' he said eventually.

'Dancer in an illegal nightclub. Journalist on a trashy newspaper. Hanging around with gangsters and criminals, artists and perverts. How many murdered corpses have you seen in the past two years, Miss Swallow?'

I gaped at him, open mouthed. Then I realised he was serious, and waiting for an answer.

'I work as a secretary for a private detective agency,' I said. 'The nightclub, the newspaper, all the rest – that's part of my job. I am sometimes required to work undercover, in a variety of roles.'

'How many corpses?'

I counted up mentally. 'Nine,' I admitted. 'In the course of our investigations.' It did seem a lot.

'That must take a toll,' interjected Sergeant Cox. 'Especially for a nicely brought-up young lady like you.' He tutted sympathetically. 'You must have horrible nightmares, Miss.'

I didn't dream of murders, thankfully, but I smiled at him anyway.

'I suppose I've become accustomed to it,' I told him. 'Although it's never pleasant, of course.'

'Nine,' repeated Inspector Dyson. 'And how many of those nine corpses did you happen to discover yourself?'

I thought again, shivering as I revisited each murder scene in my mind, reliving the shock each time at the violent ways in which people could die.

'Three. Four, if you include Miss Donatello. But I only saw her from the terrace. Mr Ashcroft found the body.'

I didn't like the way he was looking at me, as if I was something unpleasant he'd got on his shoe. 'The King discovered one of them, at Chelsea,' I added, unnecessarily. Discovering a body could happen to anyone, even royalty.

'Four corpses, and you just happened to be first on the scene each time. Did you know the Kent police have a record of an outstanding accusation against you for assault, Miss Swallow? A gardener in Kingsmead says you tried to break his arm and pitched him into a heap of manure.'

Oh dear. I remembered the man well. It had happened last May, when Mrs Jameson and I were investigating a case of horticultural sabotage before the Chelsea Flower Show. I'd been forced to use my jiu-jitsu skills to escape an awkward situation in the gardens of Kingsmead Place.

'I didn't try to break it,' I said. 'I warned him that I could if he didn't let go of me. He wasn't actually injured.'

Sergeant Cox gave me a reproachful glance. 'Well, that's not a very ladylike way to behave, Miss. I suppose that's what comes of spending time with all those criminals.'

'I need to be able to defend myself,' I said. I tried to gather my thoughts. Why were they bringing up all these past cases? The true culprits for the murders had been discovered, and mostly brought to justice. Mrs Jameson and I had made sure of that.

'What does any of this have to do with Miss Donatello's death?' I asked.

'That's exactly what I've been asking myself, Miss Swallow.' Inspector Dyson leaned forward, jutting out his chin. His face was unpleasantly close to mine, and I could smell the fish paste sandwiches he'd had for lunch.

'What were you doing last night between twenty past ten, when you arrived back at the hotel, and five to eleven, when you joined the guests in the hotel bar?'

What had I been doing? I tried to remember.

'We'd just got back from the theatre,' I began. 'We'd been to

Margate, to see *The Scarlet Pimpernel*.'

'We know that,' growled Inspector Dyson.

'I asked Mrs Jameson if she wanted anything, but she said she didn't. She was going to have a walk on the terrace before going to bed.'

'Never mind about what she did,' he snapped. 'We've already spoken to her. Tell me what you did, Miss Swallow.'

I gulped. What had she told them? 'I looked in to the bar. I think… yes, James Lockwood asked if I wanted a drink. I said I'd have one later.'

I thought back, with a sinking feeling in the pit of my stomach, then continued, slowly. 'I wanted to see if Miss Donatello was still by the gate, where we'd seen her as we came in.' Oh, golly. I'd been an idiot.

'Go on.' The inspector's voice was grim.

'So I went down the driveway and had a look, but she'd gone. I couldn't see her on the road.'

The room seemed hotter than ever, suffocatingly hot. I knew now, or at least I thought I did, what was happening.

'What did you do then, Miss Swallow?'

'I strolled along the cliff top,' I admitted. 'It was a nice evening. I walked along to the top of the steps to the beach, and looked at the moon rising above the sea.'

I wasn't sure how long I'd stood there. I'd been lost in thought, remembering another sultry night on a different beach. A night of music and champagne and velvet darkness, when Hugh had kissed me. Until, of course, we'd been interrupted by a scream and the discovery of another corpse.

Sergeant Cox shook his head sorrowfully. 'You should have said so before,' he said. He was right; I should have done. In all my concern about Mrs Jameson and what she'd told the police, I'd forgotten that I hadn't told them the full extent of my own movements.

'I'm sorry,' I said. 'I don't think you asked before. I forgot. It was only for ten minutes or so, I think, and I didn't see anyone.'

'You went down to the beach,' said Inspector Dyson. 'Didn't you?'

'No.' I looked him firmly in the face. 'I stayed at the top of the steps. I wouldn't have gone down to the sand, in my new shoes. They would have got ruined.'

'So you took them off,' he said. 'You took off your shoes, went down to the beach and saw the woman who had been threatening you ever since you arrived. There was an argument, and she demanded money to keep quiet about your past. You used your martial arts training to subdue her, and then you put an end to her. After which, you calmly returned to the hotel for a drink. You're a pretty cool customer, Miss Swallow, aren't you?'

'What?' I stared at him in amazement. 'She wasn't threatening me. I'd never met her before Wednesday. I don't know anything about her.'

Sergeant Cox sighed regretfully. 'But that can't be right, Miss Swallow. She knew all about you, didn't she? She'd left a letter for you, in the post box at the hotel. We found it this morning.'

Inspector Dyson was holding an envelope, written in the same childish hand as the one addressed to Mrs Jameson that we'd seen earlier. It too had been slit open. But this one was addressed to me.

Chapter 22

'Show me!' I held out my hand.

Inspector Dyson took the letter from the envelope. 'It's very clear, Miss Swallow. Listen: "You should do what I tell you, or you'll wish you had never been born. I know all about you. I'm going to tell them everything. You help me, or I'll make sure everyone knows your secret." There.' He looked at me in triumph. 'Explain that, will you?'

I was at a loss for words. Julia Donatello had written that to me? But it didn't make sense. She knew nothing about me. Whatever did she mean? I frowned, scanning my memory for guilty secrets that would make me wish I'd never been born if they were brought to light. I came up short.

'May I see?' This time, the inspector passed me the sheet of pale blue paper, flimsy and cheap. Large scrawled writing with blotches and crossings-out, like a schoolgirl just learning to write. She'd signed it, a loopy signature which sloped downwards.

I read the words again, the vague threats and tone of petulance. She sounded like a child, making threats in the playground. I almost laughed.

'She's bluffing,' I said. 'Look. She doesn't actually know

anything about me. She doesn't even give the slightest hint of what she knows. She's guessing that I have a secret, because most people do. It's a standard blackmailing technique.'

Sergeant Cox looked interested. 'How do you mean, Miss?'

'I'm surprised you haven't come across it, Sergeant. She's on a fishing expedition, that's all. If I told you that I knew everything about you, and I'd tell Inspector Dyson here your guilty secret, what would you think? You'd assume I knew something that you'd prefer him not to know. Even if I knew nothing of the sort.'

Sergeant Cox cast an uneasy look at his superior. I wondered which minor misdemeanours or private troubles were going through his head.

'She wanted me to use my influence to persuade Mrs Jameson to investigate this case of hers,' I told Inspector Dyson. 'This is just a clumsy attempt to get me to do what she asked. I'd already told her I wouldn't get involved.'

Inspector Dyson took the paper back. 'What an ingenious explanation, Miss Swallow. I can see you are familiar with blackmail and the criminal mind.' That didn't sound like a compliment. 'And yet, you are the only person, to whom Miss Donatello was sending threatening letters, who was near or on the beach at the time she died. I'm afraid you'll have to do better than that.'

I shook my head in exasperation. 'Listen to me, Inspector. Julia Donatello sounds to me like a woman on the make. One of her ploys must have landed her in hot water.'

I had a sudden thought. Miss Fraser in the library, with a troubled look and an envelope by her elbow, addressed to her and Miss McDonald in scrawled handwriting. Asking about Mrs Jameson's detective agency. Had Julia Donatello targeted them, too?

Inspector Dyson raised his eyebrows, so I went on, trying to make him understand.

'She told Major Redfern some nonsense about running from the mafia, and got him to pay her bills. She had clandestine meetings with Mr Treadwell in Margate, and no doubt intended to get money out of him in one way or another. She was trying to use one of the waiters to get access to the hotel, and she even stole the wallet of a customer at the Captain Digby. I think… she may have written to other guests at the hotel. And then, she was trying to involve me in whatever business she had with Mrs Jameson.'

I stopped abruptly, a little out of breath.

'And what business was that, Miss?' asked Sergeant Cox.

'I don't know. Mrs Jameson didn't tell me,' I said, shortly. I wished I hadn't mentioned it.

'Dear, dear. And you her personal secretary,' said the sergeant. 'She can't have trusted you, can she? I wonder why that was.'

So did I. If only she'd taken me into her confidence, I would have understood. Or at least, I would have tried to understand. In my heart, I felt that Julia Donatello's business with Mrs Jameson would explain why she was dead. The only person who could help me with that was refusing to talk about it. I felt out of my depth without Mrs Jameson to guide me.

There was no clock in the stuffy room and, without windows, no way to tell how much time was passing. How long had I been here? I'd lost track. It was so frustrating not to know what was happening outside. Frankie must have told Mrs Jameson what had happened. So why wasn't she here? Or perhaps she was, and the police hadn't told me.

113

Was anyone going to come and help me? I supposed I should ask for a lawyer, especially if Dyson seriously suspected me. But I didn't know any lawyers, except for Mrs Jameson's man in London.

Inspector Dyson had folded the letter back into its envelope and was watching me closely.

'You're very ready to blacken the name of a dead woman, Miss Swallow,' he observed. 'Not very charitable, is it?'

'Well, it doesn't sound like she was being very charitable to me,' I snapped. I was losing my temper, rattled by the accusations and the letter.

He smiled, a patronising grin that made me long to slap him.

'Now, now. No need to be nasty.' He dropped his smile and shoved his face close to mine. 'Let's go back to last night. You arrived at the hotel bar at five to eleven. You accepted a drink from James Lockwood and joined the other guests. What happened next?'

Once more I ran through the events – the argument over the card game, the move out to the terrace, the ridiculous fight, which I hadn't mentioned before. From his expression, I could see he already knew about that.

'And then you just happened to notice a body on the beach,' he said. His voice sounded a fine note of incredulity. 'Again.'

I dragged my mind back. 'Actually,' I said, 'Mrs Treadwell saw it first. She was leaning on the wall smoking a cigarette. I went to ask her to intervene in the fight, to try to restrain her husband. She pointed out the body, although she didn't realise what it was. She asked what I thought it was, and I called to the others.'

'But you knew, didn't you, Miss Swallow?'

I took a deep breath. 'I thought I knew what it might be. As you have reminded me, I have seen corpses before.'

'You told the men to "get her out of the water". You knew it was a woman, because you knew it was Julia Donatello. And the question I'm asking myself is, how did you know that?'

I paused. Oh, goodness. This was turning into such a muddle. 'It was the white dress. She was all in white when we saw her at the hotel gate. I suppose that's why I connected the two things.'

Inspector Dyson snorted. 'Go on. What did you do next, Miss Swallow? Did you call the police, or go down with the others to confirm your suspicions?'

I hesitated. 'They were going down through the tunnel. I hate tunnels, especially in the dark, so I said I'd go around and down the steps from the road.'

'Hmm. That would be very convenient, if you wanted to have an excuse for why your footprints were on those steps, I suppose.'

I sighed. Then I remembered.

'But they wouldn't have been the same footsteps, Inspector. I changed out of my sandals before I went down.'

He raised his eyebrows. 'You'd discovered a dead body, and your first thought was for your shoes?'

'No!' I was exasperated. 'First I went to call Mrs Jameson,' I began. Then I stopped. Bother. I hadn't mentioned that before.

He leaned forward. 'You went to your employer's room?'

I nodded. 'But there wasn't an answer when I knocked on her door. So I thought I might as well change my shoes so I could walk properly on the sand. Then I ran through the garden and down the stairs from the road to the beach.'

There was a glint in Inspector Dyson's eye. 'And where was

Mrs Jameson, Miss Swallow, when you knocked on her door at eleven o'clock at night?'

I closed my eyes. There was no way around the question. And although my conscience might allow me to withhold information from the police, it didn't allow me to lie.

'She was at the hotel gate,' I said, reluctantly. 'I saw her when I went down to the beach.'

When I opened my eyes, I saw that Inspector Dyson was satisfied. Whatever he'd hoped to find out, I'd just told him. I shuddered, feeling like the worst sort of Judas. But I'd had no choice. I could not in all conscience have pretended I hadn't seen Mrs Jameson at the gate of the hotel.

'That must have been a relief. Did you tell her what had happened, and where you were going?' Sergeant Cox took up the baton, his voice encouraging.

I shook my head.

'Speak up,' snapped Inspector Dyson.

'No.' It was almost a whisper.

'But why not, Miss Swallow? You'd tried to tell her before.' Sergeant Cox sounded genuinely perplexed.

'She turned aside and walked away through the trees. I don't think she saw me. I waited until she was gone, then I went down to the beach.' I hadn't answered his question. I didn't suppose they would let me get away with that for long.

There was a knock on the door, and a constable put his head around. Inspector Dyson turned on him in fury.

'What?' he yelled. 'Can't you see I'm busy?'

'Sorry, sir. There's a gentleman here who says he's a solicitor come to represent Miss Swallow. He wants to know if you've cautioned her and arrested her, sir.' The constable looked apologetic, and rather scared.

Inspector Dyson got to his feet, pushing back the chair so hard it fell to the ground. 'Miss Swallow is here of her own volition. She hasn't asked for a lawyer. There's no need for this interruption.'

I began to feel very sick. I should have asked for a lawyer at the start. I shouldn't have let the police question me without one, especially once they began to make serious accusations. I wondered who the solicitor was. Had Mrs Jameson got her man in London to come down?

'Actually,' I said, getting to my feet, 'I do want a lawyer. And I don't want to be here any more.'

Inspector Dyson looked furious, but there wasn't much he could do. 'I would strongly advise you to continue to co-operate with us, Miss Swallow. If you've done nothing wrong, there's nothing to be afraid of. That's what I always say.'

'I'm leaving,' I said firmly. 'If you want to speak to me again, you'll need to ask my solicitor. Or put me under arrest.'

I felt as if I'd been far out at sea, getting further and further from shore, out of sight of any help. And now, finally, someone had thrown me a lifeline. I just hoped it hadn't come too late.

Chapter 23

I stumbled through to the police station waiting room. The first person I saw was Frankie, looking truculent, her shirt-sleeves rolled to the elbow and her cap pushed back on her head.

'About blooming time!' she cried. 'What's been going on, Marge? We've been waiting for ages.'

I looked around for the mysterious lawyer. The only other person in the waiting room was James Lockwood, holding his Panama hat in his hands and looking embarrassed. I remembered him telling me that he had trained as a solicitor before the War.

'I hope you don't mind,' he said. 'Miss O'Grady here was quite frantic. We agreed that you shouldn't talk to the police without legal representation, and I offered to help. I hope I haven't put you in an awkward situation.'

I laughed with relief. 'Not at all. Thank you so much for coming. It's very kind of you. I'm extremely pleased to see you both.'

Where was Mrs Jameson? Every time I'd found myself in trouble in the past, she'd been there to bail me out. Quite literally, on occasion.

'I've got the car outside,' said Frankie. 'Let's get you back to the hotel.'

'Can we walk for a bit first? I've been stuck in there for ages.' I glanced at James. 'If that's all right with you?' I remembered that his leg pained him if he walked too long. But I was in no rush to get back to the increasingly oppressive surroundings of Kingsgate Bay. And I wanted to find out from Frankie what Mrs Jameson had been doing.

He nodded, and grasped his stick. 'I could do with a walk myself,' he declared. 'Let's go down to the gardens.'

I blinked in the bright sun as we exited the police station, which was located out of town, away from the sea shore. The contrast with the dark interior was stark. Broadstairs was bustling with holiday-makers; mostly families and well-to-do older people, all out enjoying the sunshine and sea air. It was a little more sedate than Margate, but still lively. The clock tower showed the time as just after half past four, and I was surprised it was not later.

I breathed deeply, exchanging the stale atmosphere of the little room where I'd been questioned for the dancing marine breeze. We strolled through the town to the Victoria Gardens, where a brass band was playing on the bandstand and smartly dressed families promenaded past the rather faded flowerbeds.

'Look,' said Frankie. 'There's a bloke selling ice-cream.' The brightly painted cart had 'Morelli Finest Italian Ices' written on it in curly handwriting, and the man serving was dark-haired, with a moustache and a boater with a green and white ribbon. I wondered if he was the suspicious Italian that Major Redfern had warned us of. He looked genial and friendly, not at all my idea of a mafia assassin.

'I'll get us some, shall I?' James joined the queue, while

119

Frankie commandeered three deckchairs. It felt surreal to be here, behaving like ordinary holiday-makers, after the intensity of the interrogation at the police station. The band swung into a lively rendition of *It's a Long Way To Tipperary*, and a couple of children got up to march around on the grass, playing at being soldiers.

'Where's Mrs Jameson?' I asked, as soon as James was out of earshot.

Frankie looked troubled. 'She's at the hotel. I told her, of course, straight away. She said she was sure you'd be fine, but then went to the booth to make a telephone call. I heard her asking the operator to put her through to Mr Green's office.'

Mr Green was her solicitor in London. That was something, I supposed. 'What did she do then?'

'Went to her room. I haven't seen her since.' Frankie must have seen the dismay on my face. 'I'm sure she's working on it, Marge. She wouldn't just leave you. But anyway, I was worried and I got talking to Mr Lockwood. The police said they'd spoken to everyone and we were free to leave the grounds, although we should give an address if we planned to check out of the hotel altogether. Mr Lockwood rather decently offered to come down with me and find out what was happening. What was happening, anyway?'

I sighed. 'It was pretty grim,' I said. 'I thought they were going to charge me with murder at any minute. But then I think I might have told them something I shouldn't have done.'

James returned with three cornets of vanilla ice-cream. 'They shouldn't have questioned you without asking if you wanted a lawyer, Marjorie. If it came to it, a barrister could argue that whatever you said couldn't be used in court.'

'What did you say?' asked Frankie.

I applied myself to the ice-cream, enjoying its coolness as I tried to remember all that had happened.

'The trouble is, I don't have an alibi,' I said. 'The inspector made out that Julia Donatello was trying to blackmail me, so I murdered her on the beach after we got back from the theatre, and before I joined you in the bar, James.'

Frankie snorted in incredulity. 'That's rubbish!'

James gave me a reassuring smile. 'They were just trying to scare you into letting something slip, by the sound of it. Lack of an alibi doesn't mean anything, and they know it. Lots of people won't have had an alibi.'

'As if there was anything to blackmail you about.' Frankie grinned, teasing. She had made short work of her ice-cream, crunching down the wafer cornet in minutes. 'You're an open book, Marge. What made them come up with that nonsense?'

I explained about the letter. 'She was just fishing, though,' I said. 'You're right. I can't think of anything she could have been blackmailing me about.'

James laughed. 'Poor woman. She must have picked the only person at the hotel who wouldn't have immediately thought of a dozen secrets that they wanted kept quiet. If she'd threatened to blackmail me, I'm sure I'd have fallen for it.' I couldn't help but wonder what secrets he was thinking of. I noticed he was looking at me quite intently. His eyes were nice, a clear hazel colour with dark lashes.

He passed me his handkerchief, which was starched, ironed and had a monogram in the corner. 'You have a dab of ice-cream on your nose,' he observed, gravely. 'If you don't mind me pointing it out.'

I blushed, thanked him and wiped it off.

'I'm sure there's nothing to worry about,' he said. 'Unless

you accidentally confessed to murder, there's nothing they can use. And even if you did, you could say it was under duress and without legal advice, and the judge would throw it out.'

I nodded, but I was still troubled. 'The thing is,' I said, 'I told them about seeing Mrs Jameson, as I was running down to the beach. And I'm worried that was the information they were after all along. I don't think they really suspected me at all.'

Chapter 24

We finished our ices and walked back through the town in silence. The shops were closing, people heading back to hotels and guest houses, or to the railway station to take the train home to London.

Frankie was annoyed with me for having told the police anything, although as I pointed out, I couldn't very well have lied.

'You could have declined to comment,' said James. 'That's what a solicitor would have advised.' I gave myself another mental kick for not thinking of that, or at least asking for a lawyer.

'Oi, oi,' muttered Frankie. 'Look who's here.' She pointed.

We glanced across the street to a pawnbroker's shop, the three golden balls on the sign glowing in the sunshine. In the shade of its awning, a man in a blazer and rather battered-looking straw hat was peering into the window. It was Major Redfern.

We crossed the street.

He straightened, with a puzzled frown on his face. He looked to be about to go into the shop, when James hailed him.

'Afternoon, Major. What are you up to?' he asked.

The man jumped and reddened. 'Nothing, really,' he said. 'Just stretching my legs. I was fed up of being penned in at that blasted hotel.' He glanced at me, then his gaze slid away. 'They've finished with you, have they, Miss Swallow?' His voice was stiff.

I smiled. 'I hope so.' I waited for him to move on. I wanted to see whatever had caught his attention in the window display.

'We've got Mrs Jameson's Lagonda,' said Frankie. 'Do you want to come back with us?'

He gave another glance towards the pawn shop door. A man with a long green linen apron over his suit, spectacles perched on his bald head, was turning the sign around from open to closed.

'Thank you,' said Major Redfern. 'I'd prefer to walk. Might drop in at the Captain Digby later, Lockwood, if you're heading that way.'

He tipped his hat to us and strode off in the direction of the cliffs.

I looked in the window, where the shopkeeper was already removing the more expensive items: a pair of fashionable arrow-shaped diamond clips, a gold bracelet set with rubies, and a gentleman's pocket watch. But the centre of the display remained: a string of coral and jade beads. They looked identical to the distinctive necklace worn by Julia Donatello.

'Look,' I told Frankie. 'Those are the beads she was wearing in Margate, with Mr Treadwell. I'm sure it's the same set.' I grasped the handle of the shop door, but it was locked. Frankie banged on the door. The man, removing the beads from the window, glanced up in annoyance. He pointed towards the closed sign. Frankie knocked again.

After a moment, the door opened and the man looked out,

his face red and shiny with the heat. 'What? It's gone five. I'm doing no more business until Monday. You'll have to come back then.'

'Those beads,' I gabbled, before he could close the door. 'The jade and coral set. Where did you get them from?'

He sighed. 'I never divulge ownership,' he said.

'They may be of importance in a criminal trial,' said James, quickly. 'I'm Lockwood, a lawyer involved in the case. I can ask the police to come back tomorrow with a warrant, but…'

The man shook his head hastily. 'No need to make threats, sir. This is a lawful business. Nothing to hide, here.'

He held the door open and we filed inside.

#

The shop was hot and smelled pungently of mothballs. In the back I saw racks of fur coats, in hock until they were needed in the winter again. The front room was lined with glass cases in which gleamed dozens of treasures: old-fashioned jewellery, watches, carriage clocks and porcelain figurines.

The man laid a faded green velvet cloth on the glass counter and draped the beads over it. The jade beads were round and polished to a high sheen, the pale green of early garden peas. The lengths of coral were spiky and rough, fanning out across the velvet. They made a striking contrast.

'Have you seen any others like these?' I asked.

He lowered his spectacles to his nose and inspected them. 'I haven't. They're real, all right, none of your glass imitations. I'd say they came from overseas. I've not had any like them in here before, and I see most things.'

'From India, do you think?' asked Frankie.

The man shrugged. 'Could be. You do get jade from there.

125

But most of it comes from China, or Burma.'

James leaned across the desk. 'Will you tell us who brought them in? It could be important.'

The man scratched his head. 'The thing is, I need to protect my clients. Discretion is everything in this business. You wouldn't like it, sir, would you, if I told people that you'd pawned your watch?'

'Of course,' I said. 'I do understand. However, we think the woman who owned these beads is dead, so there's no confidence to betray. An Italian woman, young, with dark hair and a white dress. She was murdered.' By the start he gave, the shopkeeper recognised the description.

'She's been using two names,' James added. 'Julia Donatello is one. Bianca Colomba is another.'

The man shook his head and got out the ledger from under the counter. 'I don't know either of those names,' he said. 'But I do recognise your description of the lady who brought them in. Very young, quite pretty. I'm sorry to hear she's come to a bad end.' Although from his disapproving tone of voice, not surprised.

He turned back the pages until he came to the entry for the beads. 'Miss Fosci, it was. Miss Anna Fosci. I had it off her passport. I gave her three pounds for them. I don't suppose anyone will be back to redeem them, now. I hope I can make up the money when I sell them.'

James had his wallet out. 'I'll take them,' he said. 'If you let me copy down the details from your book.'

The man whisked away the pound notes James held up, and turned the ledger around to face us.

'Anna Fosci, date of birth 29 June 1903, place of birth Naples, Italy.' James pulled out a fountain pen and diary, and noted the words down. 'Currently residing at the Captain Digby Inn, Kingsgate, Broadstairs. Received on Friday July 10, 1924, one set of coral and jade beads, £3.'

Anna Fosci. If that was the name on her passport, I supposed that must be her real name. I took a moment to think of the quick gabble of her voice, the sharp eyes and small teeth. What had brought Anna Fosci all the way from Naples to this corner of England?

Chapter 25

Mr Ashcroft ushered me to the dining table alone. 'Mrs Jameson says she will take dinner in her rooms,' he explained. 'She wishes to eat privately this evening. She asked if you would go to see her after dinner, at nine o'clock.'

His eyes did not meet mine and his professional smile seemed directed somewhere over my right shoulder. 'Are you sure you wouldn't also prefer a tray in your room, Miss Swallow?'

'No, thank you,' I said, a little puzzled. My room was small and had no convenient table to eat from. As I took my seat, I noticed the chatter in the dining room die down, pause for a moment, then start up with a new intensity, albeit at a lower level. With an unpleasant shock, I realised the diners were talking about me.

Geoffrey Treadwell had his back to me, but Mrs Treadwell gazed coolly across the room from their usual table, her mouth pursed with disapproval. Mr and Mrs Goldsmith, usually so friendly, looked away with furrowed brows as I smiled towards them. Even Mrs Redfern, who was also dining alone, glanced quickly my way then returned to her perusal of the menu.

I tried not to mind. I supposed all the guests had heard that

I'd been called to the police station, and had drawn their own conclusions. I wished Sarah and Bertie were there, with their easy friendliness. They wouldn't suspect me, I was sure. But they would be at the theatre until after ten o'clock.

I tried to focus on the important event: my dinner. If I was to dine alone, I might as well order what I fancied. But it was too hot to be properly hungry.

'Ready to order, Miss?' It was Alfred, the waiter who caused such havoc in the heart of Etta the chambermaid. I took another look at him. He was really rather good-looking, with thick black hair slicked back from his handsome face and dark eyes.

I smiled. 'What would you recommend?'

'The Dover sole is nice,' he said. 'It comes with a cucumber mousse. Not too heavy on a warm evening.'

He was capable of being quite charming, I realised. Perhaps Etta was onto something. I placed my order and waited, fidgeting and trying to keep cheerful.

It was not pleasant to dine alone, surrounded by suspicious faces. I was rather hurt that Mrs Jameson had not come down from her room to see how I was, after my ordeal at the police station. I'd been eager to tell her about our discovery of the true identity of Anna Fosci. I was less keen to warn her about what I'd told the police, admittedly, but she did need to know. I tried to keep my chin up, to look self-possessed and confident, but I rather envied Frankie the freedom of meals in the servants' hall.

'Hello,' said James, appearing just as I was trying to decide whether it would be completely outrageous to order myself a glass of wine. 'Do you mind if I join you?'

I turned with a grateful smile. 'Please do. I'd be glad of your company.'

He sat, adjusted his leg and laid down his stick. He surveyed the hostile room with surprise. 'What's up with all of them?' he asked. 'They look like they've been drinking vinegar. Talking of which, shall we have a decent bottle of wine?'

James had been at the Captain Digby with Major Redfern, he explained. 'I showed him the jade beads. I hope you don't mind; it seemed like a good opportunity. I thought he might react better if it was just me.'

'Good idea.'

Alfred poured us each a glass of chilled Chablis, and I took a sip.

'What did he say? Had he bought them for her?'

James knocked back his glass, then started in on his salmon mousse. 'He says not, although I don't know whether I believe him. He might have felt a fool if he gave them to her and she promptly pawned them. But he did say he recognised them. She wore them the last time he saw her, on Thursday night.'

She didn't have them the first two times I'd seen her, and she struck me as the type of girl who liked to flaunt nice jewellery when she had it. I thought it through. Perhaps she'd been given them on Thursday, by Major Redfern or Geoffrey Treadwell. Or, of course, by an as yet unknown suitor. She'd pawned them on Friday afternoon, which was why I hadn't seen her wearing them when she spoke to Mrs Jameson at the gate of the hotel, shortly before we left for the theatre.

'Who do you think is behind this, Marjorie?' James asked, his hazel eyes serious. 'I mean, I'm assuming it wasn't actually you.'

I choked on my wine. 'I'm glad to hear it.'

'From a fictional perspective, you see, it won't wash. Not

now that Agatha Christie has done it,' he said, his eyes twinkling. 'You can't make the detective the murderer. Agatha just about got away with it, but if another author tried it, everyone would cry foul. You simply can't have it happening in real life. It would be far too unrealistic.'

I knew he was teasing me. I tried to smile, but to my dismay I felt tears rising to my eyes, and the corners of my mouth turned down. I looked away, blinking, hoping he wouldn't notice my distress.

'I'm so sorry,' he exclaimed, contrite. 'I'm being an oaf. It's been an upsetting day for you. It must be horrible to be suspected, and I shouldn't have joked about it.' For the second time that day, he produced a clean handkerchief for me.

'Sorry,' I gasped, quickly whisking away the treacherous tears. 'It wasn't that, honestly. I suppose it's just all been a bit of a strain.'

Chapter 26

I made an attempt to be an entertaining and rational dinner companion for the rest of the meal. However, I was quite glad to be able to run up to my small room and be alone for a few minutes, without having to put on a brave front.

I washed my face, combed my hair and tried to compose myself. Mrs Jameson had asked to see me at nine o'clock, alone in her sea-facing suite. I hadn't seen her since luncheon, when she'd snapped at my attempts to discuss the case, and warned me sharply not to test her patience.

A cold fear had been growing since I'd returned from the police station. Had Mrs Jameson decided I was too troublesome as an assistant? After all we'd been through together, was she going to dismiss me, send me back to Catford in disgrace? I wasn't sure I could bear that. I'd have to move home to my parents' flat, say goodbye to all my friends in Bedford Square. The thought of that was almost worse than the possibility that Mrs Jameson might be behind Julia Donatello's – no, Anna Fosci's – death.

I'd have to go back to the employment agency, try to find a new secretarial position. Would Mrs Jameson even give me a reference? I thought grimly of the sort of employers who would take on a young woman becoming notorious for involvement in illegal nightclubs, newspapers and assault claims. I remembered my previous attempts to find secretarial employment: the car salesman who chased me around the showroom, the gorgon at the government department who unnerved me with her superiority.

Perhaps I could set up on my own, advertising my services as a private detective. Take on all the cases of lost cats and divorce court evidence that Mrs Jameson's agency declined to touch. I might make a go of it, I supposed. I'd learned a lot about how to conduct an investigation. But the thought of a life reporting on errant spouses and missing felines was not encouraging.

The clock pinged, marking the hour. Swallowing down my fear, I rose and walked swiftly to Mrs Jameson's door. It wouldn't do to be late, on top of everything else.

I knocked firmly on the door, my heart playing a tattoo against my ribs.

'Come in.' Her voice was clear.

I entered and stopped in surprise. Mrs Jameson wasn't alone.

'Good evening, Miss Swallow.' Mr Green, Mrs Jameson's solicitor, half-rose from the sofa. He was a small, precise man, hair brilliantined down from a strict centre parting, his formal pin-striped suit as correct as if he'd been in his office in the City of London. 'Mrs Jameson has asked me to attend this meeting.'

So, it was a formal meeting, not a cosy chat. Not that Mrs Jameson really did cosy chats.

'There you are, Marjorie.' Mrs Jameson, sitting in an armchair beside him, gave me a tired smile. She hadn't changed for dinner and wore the plain green linen skirt and matching jacket she'd had on at lunch-time. Her usual turban was replaced by a green chiffon scarf tied around her greying hair. I noticed with alarm that her small overnight bag was packed and stood ready by her side. Papers were stacked neatly on the table.

'I hope your interview at the police station wasn't too arduous. I thought in the circumstances it would be prudent to ask Mr Green to hear what happened, and see whether there is anything he can do to prepare,' she said. No inquiry about how I was, I noticed with a pang. It felt as if she was distancing herself from me.

'Of course.' I hovered, wondering whether to sit. Mrs Jameson waved me impatiently to the sofa, beside the upright figure of Mr Green. He uncapped a fountain pen and opened a notebook. I was unnerved by this reversal: usually when Mrs Jameson conducted interviews, I was the one taking notes.

'Now,' she began, 'tell us what happened when you arrived at the police station. Frankie has explained about how the police asked you to accompany them, of course. And I know that she asked Mr Lockwood to go with her to collect you. Tell me everything that happened in between.'

Suppressing a sigh, I told her about the police accusations, the way Inspector Dyson and Sergeant Cox had used the experiences of my working life to make me sound suspicious, so it looked like I had something to hide. I explained about the letter from the woman I still thought of as Julia Donatello.

'It was a classic fishing expedition,' I said, childishly pleased to see a nod of approval. 'I wouldn't have fallen for it, if I'd received it. But the inspector pretended to believe – or perhaps did believe – that she really was threatening me, and that was my motive for murder. Of course, the difficulty is the time I spent out of the hotel, overlooking the beach, after we came back. Because I suppose that's when the murder must have happened.'

Mrs Jameson had been watching me through narrowed eyes, jumping in to ask questions if anything I said was unclear. I felt terribly tired, and not just from the two glasses of wine I'd had at dinner. Being interrogated for the second time that day was exhausting.

'I suppose it must have,' she mused. 'And you saw nobody, heard nothing? Did you not look down onto the beach at all?' She sounded incredulous, as if she didn't quite believe me.

'I was looking out to sea, mostly.' I could hear the defensiveness in my voice. I remembered the shimmering silver path laid by the full moon as it rose. It had looked as if you could trip along the path without getting your feet wet, all the way across the Channel. 'I looked up at the hotel a few times. I could hear the music from the gramophone in the bar.' Mellow jazz music, of the sort I'd danced to with Hugh in France.

I shook off the memory and tried hard to remember if I'd noticed anything on the sands, or anyone passing on the road. 'I'm almost certain nobody passed me. Certainly not close by, nobody walking. Perhaps a car or bicycle might have gone by on the road. But I didn't see the body on the sands, and I didn't hear any voices, arguments, screaming or anything like that.'

'Where exactly were you standing?'

'By the top of the steps.'

'Hmm.' Mrs Jameson looked at her solicitor, who was listening in silence. 'You might go down and take a look later, Mr Green. I don't believe you would be able to see the body from there. The cliffs are quite high, and as the body was further along to the north, where the cave is, it wouldn't be possible to see that part of the beach.'

Despite all her protestations that she didn't want to be involved, Mrs Jameson had taken in every detail of the investigation. Either that, or she knew exactly where the body was, and whether you could see it from the top of the stairs, because... but no. I refused to believe it, even now.

'And what happened at the police station after that?'

I'd been dreading this part of the conversation. 'They asked how the body was discovered. And I told them, and said that I called for you, but got no answer,' I admitted.

Mrs Jameson, who had been gazing towards the window as if making abstract calculations, snapped her eyes back to me.

'You didn't tell me that,' she said. Her tone was even, but cold.

'No. I'm sorry. You didn't seem to want to know anything about it,' I reminded her. 'At the time, I assumed you were asleep, so I went and changed my shoes and ran down to the beach.'

I saw something change in her eyes. A realisation that froze the air between us.

'Which way did you go to the beach?'

I swallowed. 'By the road. I hate tunnels.' Which she knew perfectly well, after I'd got stuck in one during our investigations on the Riviera.

'And what did you see, Marjorie?' Her voice was low, measured. She knew, I realised. She knew what I must have seen, if I'd gone through the gardens, and down to the beach by the road.

The silence grew between us; five excruciating seconds, then ten. She held my gaze, her sharp grey eyes pinning me like a butterfly on a board.

'I saw you,' I admitted. 'Standing by the gate. Then you walked off through the gardens.'

She nodded, slowly. 'Write that down, Mr Green. Marjorie, have you told the police this?'

I was torn between fear and shame. I broke her gaze and looked down at my hands, gripping each other tightly in my lap. I nodded. 'But not until this afternoon,' I said. 'Not until I had to.'

She gave a heavy sigh. 'I see.'

Chapter 27

We sat in silence for a few minutes. I wanted to defend myself, to remind her that I'd tried to talk to her about the death, the investigation, and had been rebuffed every time. She had chosen not to confide in me. She'd been secretive and touchy ever since Sister Agnese's visit. What was I supposed to think?

Mr Green cleared his throat. 'If I might make a suggestion, Mrs Jameson? Perhaps you might explain to Miss Swallow what Miss Donatello wanted. Or why you had gone to the gate.'

'I cannot see how that would help,' said Mrs Jameson, coldly. 'I went to the gate for the same reason as Marjorie. I wanted to see if Miss Donatello was still there.'

I sighed. Why on earth hadn't she said so, in that case? To me, or to the police, when they asked.

'Oh!' I exclaimed, remembering. 'We found out her real name. The pawn shop in Broadstairs took her details from her passport.'

It was a relief to have something to offer. I scrabbled in my handbag and found the scrap of paper that James Lockwood had torn out of his pocketbook for me. 'Anna Fosci,' I said, handing the paper to Mr Green. 'From Naples, in Italy.'

'Anna Fosci?' repeated Mr Green. He shot a glance at Mrs Jameson. She gave an almost imperceptible shake of the head.

'Tell me about the pawn shop,' she said, switching her gaze back to me with a slight softening. 'How did you get this information?'

I started in on the story about seeing Anna Fosci wearing the distinctive jade and coral beads in Margate, and how we'd spotted Major Redfern looking at them in the Broadstairs shop.

'So we went in, and Mr Lockwood said he was a lawyer involved in a murder case, and made the man show us the ledger. He bought the beads, too,' I added.

Mrs Jameson exhaled. 'That's good,' she said. 'Mr Green, please speak to Mr Lockwood in the morning. Well done.'

In any other circumstances, praise from Mrs Jameson made my day. But I was too confused by her earlier coldness for it to truly register. And why did she seem to be handing over the investigation to Mr Green? Surely, now that we were both involved, Mrs Jameson and I should work on it together. Unless, of course, Mrs Jameson had reason to keep me away from the investigation.

My answer came sooner than I had expected. There was a knock on the door, and Mr Ashcroft opened it without waiting to be told to enter.

'I apologise for this intrusion, Mrs Jameson.' His tone was cold, and he looked disapproving, rather than sorry.

Behind him, Inspector Dyson and Sergeant Cox crowded in through the narrow doorway. The big room seemed suddenly too full of people.

Mrs Jameson rose. 'Please pass me my shawl, Marjorie.' She folded it neatly over her arm, and picked up her overnight bag.

She turned to Inspector Dyson with raised eyebrows.

He was holding a pair of handcuffs. I gasped as he ran through the formal words of the police caution, before attaching one cuff to Mrs Jameson's wrist.

'My solicitor, Mr Green, will accompany me to the police station,' she told the inspector. 'Marjorie, please remain at the hotel with Frankie until Mr Green informs you otherwise.' She locked eyes with me, as I stood helplessly by. 'Do not put yourself in danger. Mr Green will handle this.'

'Come along, then,' Inspector Dyson said.

Distressed, I followed down the stairs with Mr Ashcroft as Mrs Jameson, head held high, was escorted firmly through the lobby and into the courtyard.

#

Everyone had stopped to stare. James came hobbling out of the bar with Major Redfern. The girl on reception was agog. Mildred Treadwell, on her way up the stairs, flattened herself against the wall with horror as the inspector and Mrs Jameson passed. Even Mrs Heath paused in haranguing one of the maids to watch.

'Oh, goodness.' I was almost in tears after the strain of the past hour. Mrs Jameson, I realised, had been prepared for this. I was not.

'This is really very awkward,' said Mr Ashcroft. 'It's bad enough having a body discovered at the bathing cove. I've already had cancellations for next week. No-one likes the idea of sunbathing at the site of a tragic death.'

The manager's usual smooth manner had deserted him. He wiped away beads of sweat from his forehead, then glanced around at the guests, his face contorted with anxiety.

His gaze locked onto me. 'The police taking you for questioning, and now your employer being arrested for murder – this really is too much. I'm sure you understand my position, Miss Swallow. I'm afraid I have no option but to ask you and your party to leave.'

'Oh, please don't!' I turned to him in dismay. 'I'm sure it will all be cleared up soon.' Although I had no idea whether it would be cleared up at all.

James Lockwood appeared at my side. 'That's a pretty poor show, Ashcroft,' he said. 'You'll have my room to fill too, if you turf out the Jameson party. And if you've already had cancellations, I don't suppose you'll find it easy to fill the vacancies.'

'Me too,' said Major Redfern. 'I prefer the Captain Digby, anyway. Much more relaxed. I suppose Mother will grouch, but I have no intention of staying here if you put Miss Swallow out on the streets.'

'Whatever's happening?' Sarah Post came through the door, clutching a bouquet of orchids. 'We saw Mrs Jameson being driven away in a police car.'

Frankie arrived from her room over the garages, her hair sticking up and a smudge of engine oil on her cheek. 'Marge, what's going on? Where are they taking her?'

It was all getting too much.

'Mr Ashcroft, please don't evict us,' I said. I couldn't stand the thought of having to find us another hotel, on top of everything else. I clasped my hands together and gave him my most appealing look. I knew our rooms were paid for, having made the arrangements myself. 'Everything will work out, I'm sure of it.'

'You can't evict Marjorie and Mrs Jameson,' said Sarah,

shocked. 'Mrs Jameson will have the whole thing solved in no time. Won't she, Bertie? And I won't stay another night here if you don't let Marjorie stay. We'll tell all our friends not to come, too.'

'Eh?' Bertie looked as bewildered as I felt. 'Whatever you say, darling. Shall we have a drink?'

Under sustained fire from so many of his guests, the manager caved in. I breathed a sigh of relief.

'Now, Mr Ashcroft,' said the housekeeper, rounding on the beleaguered man. 'There's still this matter of the laundry to sort out. Etta swears she changed all of the sheets on the second floor, but that doesn't explain why there's still one missing.'

We left him to it and retired to the lounge bar.

Chapter 28

'We'll have to solve it ourselves, then.' Frankie took a swig of beer. She refused to countenance any doubts about Mrs Jameson's innocence. 'Don't be daft, Marge. How long have we worked for her? There's something rum going on, but if she hasn't told us, she's got a good reason for it. And I don't believe for a moment that she's responsible for that woman's death.'

Her certainty was comforting. Sarah Post was also refusing to imagine that anyone she liked could be a murderer, which was slightly less helpful. Bertie kept his own counsel, as did James. I supposed they didn't know her as well as Frankie and I did. But then, did any of us really know Mrs Jameson?

I thought back over the cases we'd worked on together, and all I had learned about my employer's past. She had come to Europe from America as a young woman, travelling with her aunt, who had married an English lord. Mrs Jameson then met and married an artist, lived in Paris and then Rome. She'd been widowed twenty years ago and since then had led a peripatetic existence, before returning to England two years ago.

She had friends in surprisingly high places, including the English aristocracy, politics, universities, and the Metropolitan Police. One of her greatest friends, Inspector Peter Chadwick, had worked with her during the War on mysterious intelligence jobs that both of them refused to tell me about.

In the first case we'd worked on, a woman had threatened Mrs Jameson with blackmail, and then died. The killer, of course, had not been my employer, who had indeed solved the case. But Mrs Jameson had received a letter, warning her that 'we know what happened in Rome'.

In our second adventure, the case of the American ambassador's niece, I learned that the ambassador had done Mrs Jameson a great favour when he was a consul in Rome, twenty years earlier. Mrs Jameson had told me he had bent the rules for her, in the interests of natural justice. Then, while working undercover at a newspaper, I'd discovered that the same ambassador had acted as her protector after her husband's accidental death in Rome.

That husband, I knew, was the once-famous English symbolist artist Julian Jameson. After we'd seen one of the paintings she'd modelled for, during our stay on the Riviera, she had admitted that he had treated her with great cruelty. And during our first case, she had told me that nobody knew what they were capable of, until they were put in an impossible situation. Including murder.

I had slowly become accustomed to the idea that my employer and mentor might have murdered her husband. It gave me a shock, to realise that I'd accepted that and it did not horrify me as it should.

But did that mean she was also capable of murdering a young woman who seemed to know about her past? I really hoped not.

'We should call Inspector Chadwick,' I said.

'Who?' asked James.

'He's an old friend of Mrs Jameson,' I explained. 'He's known her since the War. He's a detective with the Metropolitan Police, at Scotland Yard.' If anyone knew what Mrs Jameson was capable of, it would be upright, fearless Detective Chief Inspector Chadwick. And if he believed her innocent, I decided, so would I.

'Not a bad idea,' said Frankie, unexpectedly. She was usually against involving the police, if it could be avoided. But even she respected Inspector Chadwick.

I checked the clock. It was half past ten, so unlikely he would be at his office. I didn't have his home telephone number, although I supposed Mr Green might know it. But would he give it to me? Mrs Jameson had been very clear that I should leave everything to the lawyer. I was sure, however, that Inspector Chadwick would want to know.

'I'll ring Scotland Yard and leave a message for him,' I said. 'He'll tell the Kent police to let her out, I bet. And probably come and take charge of the investigation himself. Now, what else can we do?'

We reviewed the evidence. James wrote it all down, and drew up a timeline with Frankie. Bertie mainly yawned, while Sarah made improbable but enthusiastic suggestions about who might have been the murderer, based on who she liked or disliked among the guests.

'Major Redfern is very suspicious,' she said. 'Always sloping off to the Captain Digby on the sly. And I don't like the way Mildred Treadwell looks at me when I come down for lunch. Her husband's pretty gruesome, too. He was watching me sunbathe on the terrace yesterday, although he was pretending to read his newspaper. I bet it was him.'

'Don't be daft,' said Frankie. 'Look at the timeline. We saw Anna Fosci at the gate, when we got back from the theatre. The Redferns and the Treadwells were in the lounge, until Mrs Treadwell saw the body.'

'Oh.' Sarah looked despondent. 'Well, it must have been the Goldsmiths, after they went to bed. Maybe they acted together. No! One of those Scottish women who are always striding around with golf clubs, looking healthy. Maybe they knocked her over the head with a five iron.'

Bertie yawned again. 'Do put a sock in it, darling. The woman was strangled. Come on. Let's go to bed. Leave it to the proper detectives, and get some sleep.'

They went up to their room.

'I should go up too. Work to do tomorrow,' said James. He finished his whisky and set the glass down, looking contemplative. 'You know, if it wasn't for his alibi, my money would be on that Treadwell fellow,' he said quietly. 'The major's all right. But Treadwell's a cad. Don't like the way he talks about women. And I'm sure I saw him with that Italian girl earlier in the day.'

Frankie and I exchanged glances.

'What time?' I asked.

He rubbed his chin. 'Not sure. Early evening, I suppose. I was strolling along the cliffs before dinner. Of course, it might not have been him. Hard to tell, from a distance. But there was a very stony silence between him and that wife of his in the restaurant. They barely said a word all evening, and she refused to play bridge. That's why I ended up being dealt in.'

When he'd gone, I told Frankie about Helen Fraser's unexpected question in the library the day before the murder, and the letter that had been on the desk.

'I wonder if they were being blackmailed,' I said. 'I mean... I know there's nothing wrong about it, but some people might be suspicious of a school teacher if rumours went around about her and her friend. They share a house together in Edinburgh, James said. His sister knows Helen Fraser.'

Frankie gave me a quick look and laughed. 'Not those two,' she said firmly. 'Trust me. Miss McDonald isn't on that bus.'

'Hmm.' I didn't bother asking Frankie how exactly she knew. 'But Anna Fosci wouldn't know that. She might have been fishing, the same as the letter to me. And Miss Fraser seems very protective of her friend.'

Frankie nodded thoughtfully. 'Fair point.' She grinned, teasingly. 'But according to the maids, they both sleep in their own beds.'

We didn't sit up much longer. We agreed to meet again in the morning after breakfast. I placed my telephone call to Scotland Yard from the booth in the reception hall, then yawned up the stairs to bed.

I lay awake for a while, all the same. The events of the day had been too overwhelming to dissolve easily into sleep. I went over what had happened after we'd returned from the theatre, again and again. The glimpse of Anna Fosci at the gate. The card-players in the lounge. My stroll to the cliffs, and however long I'd spent gazing over the sea. Why had I not seen or heard anything? If Anna Fosci had struggled, if there had been a scuffle and an attempt to run away, surely she would have screamed?

Unless, I supposed, the murder had happened after I returned to the hotel bar. In that case, she could not have been dead for more than half an hour when I went down to the beach.

I puzzled it over. I was sure that when I'd felt for a pulse, her body had been cold. Even allowing for the fact that she'd been soaked from the sea, that seemed too quick. I wished I could have asked the police what time the doctor had given for Anna Fosci's death.

Chapter 29

I was still mulling it over when I went down to breakfast the next morning. Mr Green was sitting at our usual table. I stopped halfway across the room when I saw him, neat and tidy as ever in his city suit. I felt scruffy by comparison in my cotton frock and tennis shoes, but it was too hot for formality. He looked up and beckoned me over.

'Sit down, Miss Swallow. I'm staying in Mrs Jameson's suite, at her request. I fear that I had a more comfortable night than she did.'

'Haven't they bailed her?' I asked, sitting down and arranging my napkin on my lap. I remembered my night in a police cell in France the previous year, and how scared I'd been. I hated to think of Mrs Jameson in the same position.

'Regretfully not,' the lawyer said. 'I will be pressing for that, of course. It was really quite outrageous, to take her into custody late at night. I shall be protesting to the superintendent this morning.'

He paused to take a small bite out of his toast. He ate as precisely as he did everything else, marmalade spread thinly over the butter.

'Mrs Jameson has a message for you. To be exact, she wishes

me to remind you of her last words to you before she left. Please do not attempt to investigate this matter yourself, Miss Swallow. Mrs Jameson says you are apt to take unwarranted risks. She asks that you leave the affair entirely to me, and to the police. I assure you, I do not intend to leave her in custody for long.'

That was awkward. 'Frankie and I want to help,' I said. 'I thought we could put together a timeline, from everything we have learned so far. That might help, don't you think?'

He hesitated. 'I suppose there's nothing to be lost by you and Miss O'Grady writing down the facts,' he said. 'I can take it in to Mrs Jameson this morning. If it isn't too much trouble.'

'No trouble at all,' I assured him, slathering strawberry jam on my toast.

#

I checked again at the reception desk, but there had been no message from Inspector Chadwick. I went around the back of the hotel to find Frankie. She was drinking a cup of tea, sitting on a wall in the sun. Etta was next to her, smoking one of Frankie's Woodbines.

'G'morning, Miss.'

I smiled and sat next to her.

'Etta's fed up,' said Frankie, conspiratorially. 'That Mrs Heath's been having a go at her. So we're having a cuppa and a tab.'

'It weren't my fault,' said the young woman, indignantly. 'I told her. I did all the beds like usual on Saturday morning. And when I counted them up for the laundry list, I was one short. What does she think I'd want with an old sheet, anyway?'

'Ah, the missing sheet.' I remembered Mrs Heath haranguing

Mr Ashcroft about it. 'The mystery is still unsolved, I take it?'

She tapped ash from the end of her cigarette. 'One of the guests must've taken it,' she said. 'That's what I told them.'

'What would a guest want with a sheet, though?' I asked the question idly, kicking against the wall. I hoped she'd go soon, so I could talk to Frankie properly.

'Oh, you'd be surprised,' said Etta. 'We see all sorts.' She giggled. 'Sometimes they have fancy dress parties, you see. And people drape them round themselves, like in that film with Rudolph Valentino.'

My mind went blank.

'The Sheik,' said Frankie, with a laugh. 'Desert robes, Marge.'

'Of course. Or draped over themselves for ghosts, I suppose. But they'd put them back afterwards, wouldn't they?'

Etta shrugged. 'Unless they'd made a mess of them. Ripped them, or spilled stuff on them. Mostly, they just leave them for us to clear up. But sometimes they're too embarrassed and try to get rid of them without us seeing. Mrs Heath's had us looking all over, but we haven't found it yet.'

'Don't you know which room it was taken from, though?' I asked. 'I mean, if you'd been changing the beds and one had a sheet missing.'

For a second she froze, then threw me a quick, guilty glance. 'We have to work fast,' she said. 'You don't always realise.' She stubbed out her cigarette. 'I suppose I'd better get back to it. Before Mrs Heath accuses me of slacking off again.'

She almost ran back inside.

'She does know,' I said. 'Don't you think?'

'Fancy dress,' said Frankie, thoughtfully. 'There weren't any fancy dress parties on Friday night, were there?'

'Just boring old card games.' The only guests who would

enjoy a fancy dress party were Sarah and Bertie, and they had all their fabulous theatre costumes to choose from. They wouldn't need to resort to a bedsheet.

A missing bedsheet, after the night when a woman was killed. It hadn't seemed important when the housekeeper had mentioned it. But now I wondered. Where had that sheet gone?

Chapter 30

Frankie got to her feet and stretched. 'Come on, Marge. Let's finish that timeline we started last night.'

'Shouldn't we wait for James? He wanted to help,' I said.

She gave me a long look. 'Dunno, Marge. The thing is, I know it wasn't you, and you know it wasn't me. And we both know it wasn't Mrs J. But everyone else here's a suspect, I reckon. Don't get too pally with them.'

I took a breath to protest, then stopped. What, really, did I know about James Lockwood? That he was a writer, that he'd helped get me out of the police station by pretending to be my lawyer, that he'd pulled the same trick to get the owner of the pawn shop to let us in and look at the beads.

'He was in the hotel when we got back on Friday,' I objected. 'With the others. So he's got an alibi too.'

Frankie sighed. 'I know. Too many blooming alibis. But even so, let's keep it just to us, shall we? Until Inspector Chadwick gets here.'

We went into the library, now mercifully empty of police officers, and I set out the sheet of paper on which we'd begun to construct the timeline.

'Ten twenty (approx). Last sighting of Anna Fosci alive,' I

153

read aloud. I wished we had a more precise time. 'Mrs J to terrace, Frankie to garage, parked then went to bed, M to lounge bar. Present in lounge: James Lockwood, Major and Mrs Redfern, Mr Treadwell, all playing cards.

'Ten thirty-five (approx). M through garden to gate. AF not there. M walks along road to top of beach steps.

'Five to eleven, M returns to lounge bar. Present: James, Major and Mrs R, Mr and Mrs Treadwell, bar tender.'

Frankie rubbed her face. 'You were gone for quite a while, Marge. Are you absolutely sure you didn't see or hear anything?'

I shook my head. 'Not a dicky-bird. I've been trying to remember. And that's the odd thing. If she wasn't murdered then, if it was after I'd gone back in at eleven, then she could only have been dead for half an hour when we found her. And yet she was cold, colder than you'd expect on a warm night, even if she had been in the sea.'

There was a rap on the library door. I looked up in excitement, hoping to see Inspector Chadwick, but it was Mr Green.

He stood by the desk and looked over the timeline. 'Very helpful,' he remarked. 'Are you going to finish it?'

I took the pen and added the next times.

'Eleven twenty (approx). Argument between Mr Treadwell and Major Redfern. Mrs T goes outside to terrace. Mr T and Major R follow, with Mr Ashcroft. Sarah and Bertie Post return from theatre. M goes to terrace with the Posts.

'Eleven twenty-five (approx). Fight between Mr T and Major R. Mrs T sees body on beach. Mr T, Major R and Mr Ashcroft go down to beach by tunnel.

'Eleven thirty (approx). M goes to Mrs J's door, but no

answer. M changes shoes and runs through hotel to gate.'
I glanced up at Mr Green.

'Please make the timeline as comprehensive as possible, Miss
Swallow.' He didn't look at all perturbed.

'Eleven thirty-five (approx). M sees Mrs Jameson at the hotel
gate. Mrs J turns aside and walks back through garden. M
continues down road to beach steps and down to beach.'

I glanced again at Mr Green. 'That's when we discovered
the body.'

He nodded. 'Thank you. If you don't object, perhaps we
could follow in your footsteps and go down to the beach now. I
should like to have a full understanding of the situation before
I return to the police station.'

#

We walked down together. We must have looked a strange
party: Frankie in shirtsleeves, breeches and boots, me in tennis
shoes and a gingham frock, Mr Green in his formal business
suit and shiny black shoes.

We paused at the top of the steps. Mrs Jameson had been
right; we couldn't see the spot where the body was found.
The tide was quite high, although the shallow waves had not
reached the tide mark of seaweed on the sand.

'Down that way.' Frankie pointed along the beach.

We walked down the steps, half-covered in soft dry sand. It
was the first time we'd been allowed back on the beach, now
that the police searches had been completed. The place was
deserted, although I could see a few people looking down at
the bay from the garden of the Captain Digby. Ghoulish sight-
seers, I supposed, come to look at the beach where the Italian
girl had been murdered.

We walked in silence.

'About here,' I said, finally. 'See, if you look up to the hotel at the end of the bay, you can see the terrace. But you can't see the top of the stairs where we were standing a minute ago. It's blocked by the curve of the cliff.'

Mr Green stood and looked to his right and left, then made a note in his pocketbook. 'You can't see the Captain Digby, either,' he observed. 'Which may be why no-one spotted the body from there.'

'And we found her shoes just outside the cave,' said Frankie. She led us back to the cliffs, where the soft chalk wall had eroded into a high arch, just above the line of seaweed. 'From inside here, you can't see anything. Not the hotel or the pub.'

I walked inside, and the temperature dropped. I rubbed the goosebumps on my bare arms. The ceiling was high, but the cave was not deep. Green slime marked the walls, and the smell of seaweed caught in my throat. I turned. All I could see was the sea, empty to the blue horizon.

'Do you think she was killed in here?' Frankie's voice was low.

I shivered again. 'Maybe.' Too late to look for footprints, of course. The marks that our search party hadn't destroyed on Friday night would have been obliterated by the team of policemen. But I glanced around all the same.

I tried to imagine what might have happened. Had she been expecting to meet someone here, in this secluded spot where no-one could see? After we'd seen her at the gate, had she come down here, maybe waited for someone to join her? Or perhaps someone was here already. Perhaps she'd made threats, or they had. An argument, anger, fear. A struggle, shoes kicked off in an attempt to run. But she'd been caught and overpowered.

The body left on the beach for anyone to see.

'That's odd,' I said.

'What is?' asked Mr Green. He'd been staring thoughtfully around the cave.

'If she was killed in here, or just outside, why would the killer have left her body on the beach? Surely they would have wanted to keep it hidden,' I said. 'Would it not have made more sense to pull her body back into the cave?'

He stared at me with quizzical dark eyes. 'Good point,' he admitted.

'Or the murderer could have dragged her to the next cave along,' said Frankie. 'It goes back a long way into the cliff. There's a tunnel that's supposed to go all the way up to the Captain Digby, which they used to smuggle brandy and stuff. She wouldn't have been found for ages, if they'd put her in there. No need to have left her out in the open for anyone to see.'

'The killer might have panicked,' I said, thinking it over. 'Perhaps they didn't mean her to die. Maybe they ran off, thinking they would get help. And then they saw us all down on the beach, so they disappeared.'

'That's one possibility,' said Mr Green, cautiously.

There was another, I knew. The body had been left in the open because the killer wanted it to be found.

Chapter 31

We walked out into the sun. 'Thank you for your assistance, ladies,' said Mr Green. 'I think I have enough to go on now.'

I remembered something else that had been puzzling me. 'Mr Green, will the police tell you what the doctor gave for time of death?' I asked. 'Because when I got to her, the body was cold. But if she'd been killed after I went back to the hotel, she could only have been dead for half an hour, and that sounds a bit quick. It might be useful to know.'

Mr Green made another note. I thought I saw renewed respect in his demeanour. 'Thank you, Miss Swallow. You have been very helpful. I can see why Mrs Jameson prizes your assistance. Now, don't do anything silly. I'm going to see if I can bail her out.' He replaced his notebook and pen into his inside jacket pocket and walked back along the beach.

'Here, Marge. Take a look at this.'

Frankie had disappeared into the second cave, a few feet along the cliff. As she'd said, it went back much further. The opening was smaller and the roof of the cave much lower than the one we'd just left.

I ducked my head to see the back of the cave, but it continued into a tunnel beyond a sort of lintel. The tunnel looked to be man-made, hewn out of the rock.

'We ought to go through,' said Frankie. 'See if it really does go all the way up to the pub.'

'Not me,' I said, firmly. 'The police will have searched it, I'm sure. And you know I hate tunnels. Come on. Let's go back up to the hotel.'

Too late. Frankie was already scrambling through on her hands and knees. I groaned, crouched down and steadied myself on the rocks as I watched her.

'Careful,' I warned. I glanced back towards the sea. 'The tide is coming in. It's further up the beach than it was.'

'I can see something,' said Frankie. 'Looks like steps. Wait there, if you like. I won't be a minute. There's something up there.'

I walked to the mouth of the cave, feeling anxious. Outside, the sun blazed high in the sky, fierce and strong. I stepped out for a moment, and it felt like walking into an oven in contrast to the coolness of the cave. The waves lapped the shore, the sea looked tranquil and flat. The tideline was higher on this side of the beach, with seaweed inside the cave mouth. I could hear the water hissing as it rose and fell on the wet sand. In the distance, church bells clanged. It was Sunday, I remembered. I hadn't been to church for years now.

'Come on,' I called. 'What are you doing in there?'

'I think I've found something. It looks like… it looks like a sheet, bundled up at the top of a pile of rocks.' I heard her laugh. 'Marge, I reckon it's the blooming missing sheet from the hotel. But it's been cut into pieces. Hang on. It's stuck on something. I'm just going to…'

I heard a thump, and a loud curse.

'What's happened? Are you all right?' I ran to the back of

the cave and knelt on the sand, tried to peer through into the darkness. 'Frankie! Answer me.'

There was an agonising pause. 'Bother,' she said, or something like it. 'I fell. I've done something to my knee, Marge. Hurts like hell. I think it's bleeding.'

'Oh, no. Come out here, so I can see.' I glanced again at the waves. 'We should get back.'

More curses. 'Sorry. Can't move it. There's something wrong with it.' I heard panic in her voice. 'It's really bleeding, Marge. I can't see how to stop it.' She gave a sob.

Frankie, usually so unflappable, was crying. Frankie, who never cried, never backed down and wasn't afraid of anything. I was seized with fear. What on earth had she done?

I took one last look at the sea. 'All right. I'm coming through. Don't worry.'

Squashing down my fear of tunnels, I crawled through the gap under the lintel on my hands and knees. The rock brushed against my back, making me panicky. There wasn't much light. At the back of the cave the ceiling rose again, where a pile of rocks marked the beginnings of ruined steps. Frankie sat with her back to the pile, clutching her knee. I tried to stand and cracked my head, then scrambled to her side.

'Show me.'

But I could already see. Blood coated her hands, ran in rivulets down her bare shin. Quickly I pulled my handkerchief from my pocket and prised her hands away. A gush of blood through a rip in her breeches above the kneecap.

'Oh, Christ.' Frankie turned big, frightened eyes on me.

'It's all right.' I felt quickly for the wound. Frankie hissed in pain as I probed it, my fingers slippery.

'Sorry. I'm going to put a pad over it, and you're going to

help me hold it in place.' I folded the handkerchief and covered the wound. Immediately, blood began to bloom through the cotton. I pressed hard with the heel of my hand. I needed something to make a tourniquet.

'Hold that there. Press down hard, even though it hurts,' I instructed her. I unbuckled the thin belt from my waist, and looped it around Frankie's thigh. The fabric of her breeches was in the way.

'Do you have a knife?'

'Back pocket.'

I reached around and found her horn-handled penknife. I unfolded the blade, slit the bottom of her breeches and cut them away to mid-thigh. I could see better now. There was a jagged wound, bigger than my handkerchief could cover, and the blood still flowed. I needed to stop it, quickly. I pulled my belt tight, and Frankie grunted. At first the blood came faster, gushing over her fingers with the inadequate pad of cotton. She began to whimper.

I felt cold, remembering the nights on the ward during the War when I helped the nurses and surgeons strip away filthy dressings, exposing suppurating wounds that would need amputation. And the awful time an amputation went wrong; the patient bleeding to death on the table as the doctor struggled frantically to stop the waves of crimson.

'Do you have a clean handkerchief?' I asked Frankie. If not, I supposed I could tear a panel out of my skirt. 'I need something bigger to cover the wound.'

She looked at me, her eyes steady despite the fear. 'No. But there's the remains of that sheet up there,' she said, jerking her thumb towards the pile of chalk and flint rocks she was resting against. 'That's what I was climbing up to get. But I slipped.'

I glanced behind her. A bundle of fabric, white cotton.

'Hold this. I promise, the blood will slow soon,' I said, putting her spare hand on the knot of the belt. 'I'll see if I can get it.'

I scrambled up the rocks, careful not to slip. The chalk was damp with algae and treacherous. Jagged edges of flint glinted between the chalk boulders, sharp as an axe. That must have been how Frankie cut herself.

I reached out and grabbed. A piece of the missing sheet came from where it was lodged. I tore two strips from it with the knife, then crawled carefully back to Frankie.

'Here.' I made one strip into a folded pad, then used the rest as a bandage to hold it firmly in place. I pressed down on it. Frankie watched, her jaw set. She'd wiped away her tears with bloodstained hands, and the streaks on her face looked ghastly. I watched, biting my lip, knowing how much pain she must be in. A little blood bloomed on the cotton, then slowed. The patch, the size of a poppy, stopped growing.

'Oh, thank you, God,' I breathed. 'It's working.'

Frankie gave a strangled laugh that was more of a sob. She clutched my hand, both of our fingers sticky with blood. 'Thought I was a goner. You know what you're doing, though, don't you?'

I wasn't sure that I did, but I did know that Frankie needed proper medical help quickly. A tourniquet stopped acute blood loss, but keep the blood away from the tissues of the lower leg too long and it could lead to nerve damage.

'We'd better get you out of here,' I said.

She nodded. 'I don't think I can crawl, though.'

Oh, goodness. How would we get her out of the cave? I glanced back to the entrance where I'd squeezed under the lintel. Water was seeping through, leaving little traces of foam on the sand.

Chapter 32

I didn't know how high the water would come up. It was already past the mouth of the cave. I searched around in my head for useful information. Spring tide, perhaps? Didn't the tide get higher than usual around the time of a full moon? As a confirmed land-lubber, I had no real idea.

'Let me sit you up on these rocks a bit higher,' I said. 'I'd better get someone to help you.'

I wouldn't tell her about the tide. She had enough to worry about. 'Keep pressing down on that dressing. You can loosen off the tourniquet in a few minutes, but if the blood comes back then tighten it up. I'll be as quick as I can.'

I hauled her up a bit further on the rocks. She was staring at the line of water coming through the mouth of the cave, and I saw that she understood the situation immediately.

'You're going to get your feet wet,' she said. 'Better make a run for it. I'll be all right, Marge. You get going.'

I squeezed her hand a last time. 'I'll be quick,' I promised again.

I tucked up my skirt and knelt on the wet sand, the ripples of water narrowing the gap below the lintel. Focusing my eyes on the bright strip of sunlight beyond, I crawled forward, the wavelets breaking over my hands, lapping around my knees. My head bumped painfully on the roof. I looked down, taking calming breaths, at the trickles of clear salt water. Keep moving forward.

It felt like it took an hour. I drove myself on, into the light, trying not to think about the tons of chalk and earth above me, the unstable crumbling cliffs. The wet sand shifted beneath my knees, the waves trickled over my hands and shins. I wanted to scream, but bit down on my fear. I had to be strong; I could not let Frankie down. Finally, I emerged into the wide cave mouth.

I turned back to where the ripples ebbed and flowed in the passageway. 'I'm out! I won't be long. Are you all right?'

'Don't worry,' she called back. No-one was better at putting on a brave face than Frankie. 'I'll be fine.'

I ran across the beach, the sand gleaming wet and smooth. I was half-blinded by the sun after the gloom of the cave. I ran towards the hotel, waving my arms and shouting for help, although I couldn't see if there was anyone on the terrace. The beach was empty; Mr Ashcroft's prediction that nobody would want to bathe where a body had been found proving correct.

Finally, I heard a shout and spun around. Someone was waving from the road, up by the Captain Digby. I shaded my eyes, but in the dazzle I couldn't see who it was.

'I need help down here,' I called. Without waiting for a reply, I turned and stumbled on through the wet sand. I reached the foot of the steps, chest heaving and sweat streaming down my face. I'd lost my hat in the cave, and my hair was plastered to my damp forehead.

As I started to scramble up, I heard the roar of a motorcycle.

It came to a stop in a squeal of brakes, then a tall, broad-shouldered figure began to run down the steps two at a time, wearing a leather helmet and waxed jacket. I was almost floored by a wave of relief.

'Inspector Chadwick! Oh, thank goodness you're here.'

'Marjorie, what on earth has happened? I rode down as soon as I got your message,' he said, unbuckling the chin strap and removing his helmet. 'Where's Iris? What's she been up to now?'

'Never mind that. Frankie's badly hurt, and she's stuck in a cave,' I gabbled. I saw him take in my wet, bloodstained frock.

'Good God. Let's get this sorted out.'

I explained, and he took in the salient points. 'We need the coastguard. They have the equipment to carry out a rescue. Do you know where the nearest station is?'

'There's one in Broadstairs,' I volunteered. I'd noticed it while I strolled on the promenade with Frankie and James. 'Down by the harbour. About two miles away.'

He thought quickly. 'You go and fetch them. I'll go down to the cave and stay with Frankie. Take my Triumph. You know how to ride a motorbike, don't you?'

I did, although it had been years since I had done so. I remembered telling Frankie I'd like to ride one again. Not in these circumstances, though.

He handed me the leather helmet and began to unlace his boots. 'Take these.'

I buckled on the helmet, which was much too big but better than nothing, and stepped into the boots. I would look ridiculous, but that didn't matter.

'Tell the coastguard exactly what you told me. They've plenty of experience at cave rescues.' His stern face softened into a smile. 'Don't look so worried. Ride carefully, and I'll look after Frankie. Tell them I'm here.'

He launched himself down the steps. I ran up to the road, where Inspector Chadwick's Model H Triumph ticked gently in the sun. Thankfully, it was similar to the models that I'd ridden during the War. I stepped astride the motorbike, careful to avoid the hot exhaust pipe, settled myself on the leather seat and kicked down hard on the kick-starter. The engine was already hot, and it started on the second go. Slowly I eased off the brake and launched myself, a little wobbly, onto the road.

Chapter 33

I tried to keep my speed sensible on the way to Broadstairs, although I felt desperate at the thought of Frankie lying helpless in the cave. At least she would have Inspector Chadwick at her side. The motorbike flew along, fields to my right and the sea on my left, past the lighthouse and the golf links and the Kingsgate Castle hotel. I took the coast road, whizzing past families with buckets and spades, gulls whirling overhead. Plenty of heads turned as I passed, my skirt dancing around my knees in the wind. No matter. Again, I was reminded of my wartime experiences; the thrill of being sent on urgent business, the clarity that came with life and death situations.

I pulled up on Harbour Street in front of the white clapboard building by the sea. I ran inside, ignoring the looks of surprise from the fishermen and others loitering around the boats.

A bearded man in a short-sleeved white shirt with naval epaulettes greeted me, his steady demeanour no doubt the result of facing down many emergencies.

'Calm down, Miss,' he said, as I tried to tell him everything at once. 'Take it slowly.'

I took a deep breath and tried again. 'There's a badly injured woman stuck in a cave on Kingsgate Bay,' I said. 'The tide's coming in, and she needs urgent medical treatment. Please help. There's a police officer with her now, but I don't know how far up the water will go.'

He reached for a telephone on his desk. 'There's a coastguard cottage at Kingsgate,' he said. 'You should have gone there.'

He spoke rapidly to the operator, pausing to ask me exactly which cave, then relayed the information to the other coast-guard station. He replaced the receiver and looked at me more kindly.

'But you weren't to know, and they'll need my help anyway. I'll get my kit and see if I can get a taxi-cab over there now.'

'I have a motorbike,' I said, trying to regain some dignity. 'You could ride on the back. That would be quicker.'

He grinned and I saw a twinkle in his eye. 'Right you are, Miss. This'll be a first.'

#

By the time we wobbled into Kingsgate Bay, the coastguard with a duffle bag slung over his shoulder, there was plenty of activity on the beach. A line of three men was at the cave mouth, carrying rope and a stretcher. They were knee-deep in water.

'Oh, no,' I cried. 'Please don't say we're too late.' I'd never forgive myself for not knowing about the coastguard at the bay, if anything happened to Frankie and Inspector Chadwick. It had taken fifteen minutes to ride to Broadstairs. What if those minutes had made the difference?

We ran down. The coastguard, his face set, unearthed a first aid kit from his duffle bag. I'd explained Frankie's wound and how I'd applied a pad and tourniquet.

'You wait here, Miss. I'll see what's happening.' He gave me a comforting pat on the shoulder and waded into the cave with his colleagues.

'What's going on?' Major Redfern strode over from the cave entrance. 'The blighters won't tell me a thing. Have they found another body?'

I shuddered. 'Don't say that. Oh, don't say that, Major.'

The circle of onlookers grew as the minutes ticked past and people came down from the hotel, curious to see what was happening. James Lockwood arrived and stood by my side. The midday sun pounded onto our heads, scorching; the waves seemed to pause at the height of the tide. Everything was very still. The air above the beach shimmered, shifting in the heat, unreal. Gulls cried as they bobbed on the waves. There was the occasional shout from inside the cave, an instruction or a warning.

We stood in silence: Major Redfern, James, the Goldsmiths, Constable Perks, the police doctor. Several chambermaids came down, Etta among them, wringing her hands. Alfred and another waiter watched with us for a moment, then headed back to the hotel. Word had spread quickly about Frankie's predicament.

The doctor went to the mouth of the cave, where he spoke to one of the coastguards, then returned to stand a little away from the rest of us, his face sombre. I didn't ask what he'd been told. I felt as if I was in suspended animation, and as long as I did not know what was happening, nothing could change.

It took half an hour, but finally the stretcher reappeared. Inspector Chadwick walked beside it, soaked from head to toe, his expression grim. The men carried it up the beach and laid it down. The doctor scurried over and knelt beside it.

I clutched at Major Redfern. My head began to buzz, as if

suddenly full of flies. My knees started to give way.

'Woah, there.' He took one arm, and James the other. 'Let's sit you down, Miss Swallow.'

I let them lower me to the sand, never once taking my eyes off the inert figure on the stretcher. My breath was coming in tiny, shallow gasps. The men were talking to me, but I couldn't hear what they were saying. It didn't matter. Nothing mattered – nothing except the figure on the stretcher.

'Miss Swallow. Marjorie.' Inspector Chadwick crouched before me, taking my hands in his. 'Frankie lost consciousness. She'd lost a lot of blood, and she was in pain. She was being very brave, but it was probably best.'

I stared at him, desperate. What did he mean, it was probably best?

'We couldn't have got her out if she'd been conscious, I don't think. The water was almost to the top of the lintel. We had to swim through holding our breath. That's why it took so long.'

I didn't understand what he meant. I imagined that narrow passage between the front and the back of the cave, full of water. I wasn't sure I could have forced myself to swim through. How could they bring an unconscious woman out through that?

A faint smile twitched one side of his moustache, and I looked into his hazel eyes, wondering.

'Eventually they got her onto the stretcher, and I held her mouth and nose closed while they pulled her through the water. She's made it. She's alive, Marjorie. Thanks to you, she's alive.'

I gave a great sob of relief and collapsed into his arms.

Chapter 34

I held Frankie's hand as the coastguards carried the stretcher over the sands. She looked terrible, her usually merry face pale and drawn with pain. Her eyes flicked open, then scrunched closed against the sun. Mrs Goldsmith gave me her parasol to shield Frankie from the glare.

'You'll be fine now.' I avoided looking at her leg, the breeches soaked in blood, the coastguard's field dressing over the cotton pad. Her eyelids flickered again, and she gave a slight squeeze of my hand. 'They're taking you to the hospital in Margate. I'll visit as soon as they let me.'

I hoped the wound was clean enough to avoid the dangers of infection. It had bled freely, and the salt water might have helped. The nurses would clean it at the hospital; a gruesome task I'd assisted with myself. I prayed fervently that they would give her morphine before they started.

The coastguard men loaded her into the back of an ambulance that was parked at the top of the steps. I wanted to go with her, but the doctor said there wasn't enough room. I watched as it drove slowly away.

'Come,' said Inspector Chadwick. 'Let's get you sorted out in the hotel. And then perhaps I could have my boots back.'

I looked down at the ridiculous figure I made. Enormous

leather boots, laced to the knee. A bloodstained dress, stiff with dried saltwater, hanging loose with no belt. Hatless in the full glare of the sun, my hair no doubt all over the place.

'I suppose I'd better wash and get changed,' I said. I was suddenly aware that I was quite hungry. 'Maybe we could have some lunch.'

'You go up and change, Marjorie,' said James Lockwood. He glared suspiciously at Inspector Chadwick. 'I'll get us a table for lunch.'

'That's kind, but I should talk to the inspector,' I said. 'He's come down from London to help with this business about Mrs Jameson. We've worked together in the past.' I felt guilty that I had barely given my employer a thought since Frankie's accident.

James immediately looked less prickly and held out his hand. 'Marjorie was talking about you last night, inspector. I'm Lockwood. You look like you need to dry off. Can I offer you the use of my room?'

The two men shook hands. 'Chadwick. Inspector Chadwick, Scotland Yard. That's decent of you, Lockwood.'

We walked up to the hotel together.

While the men conferred with Mr Ashcroft at the reception desk, I went up to my room. Thankfully the bathroom was free. I ran a tepid bath, unlaced the boots and threw off my ruined dress. I plunged into the water, rinsing off the salt and sweat, the dust and sand and blood. If only I could wash away the horrors of the past week as easily. Frankie, badly wounded. Mrs Jameson, charged with murder. And me, getting everyone into trouble. If I'd not said anything about seeing her at the gate... or if I'd spoken to her about it earlier... if we hadn't been down on the beach with Mr Green to show him the cave...

Wallowing in self-recrimination was pointless, I knew. I pulled myself out of the bath, dried briskly and changed into my red and white linen frock. I'd have to make do with my old straw cloche, having lost my favourite wide-brimmed summer hat in the cave.

#

When I arrived in the restaurant for lunch, not two but three men were sitting around the table waiting for me.

James flashed me a quick smile and rose to pull out my chair. Inspector Chadwick, looking respectable again in a lightweight suit, was listening intently to Mr Green, the solicitor.

'What's the news?' I asked.

'Nothing yet from the hospital,' said Inspector Chadwick. 'I've asked them to call as soon as they have anything to tell us.'

I reached for a glass of water. The morning had left my mouth dry as sand. I gulped it down thirstily and eyed the bread rolls.

'The police are still holding Mrs Jameson,' said Mr Green. 'I've advised her to say nothing. Everything they have is circumstantial. The police need to come up with solid evidence, if they are to charge her with murder. And I don't believe they have it yet.'

He took a sip of water and gave me a disapproving look. 'I believe, Miss Swallow, I advised you not to do anything silly, when I left you on the beach this morning. Mrs Jameson will be very distressed to hear about Miss O'Grady's accident.'

'It wasn't Marjorie's fault,' said James.

Inspector Chadwick shook his head impatiently. 'The whole thing is ludicrous,' he said. 'I called the chief inspector of the

Kent force before I left. I mean, I have no objection to them making fools of themselves if they must, but this goes too far. As if Iris, of all people, would do such a brutal thing to a young woman...' he tailed off.

Except, I thought, that she always said you didn't know what you were capable of doing until you were in that situation. I badly wanted to speak to the inspector on his own. He knew her better than any of us. I wanted to ask what he knew about Rome, and how Anna Fosci fitted in with that story.

Alfred approached the table to take our orders. He leaned over my chair. 'Is Frankie all right?' he asked quietly. 'Everyone's worried about her.'

I smiled at him, touched by his concern. 'They've taken her to the hospital. I'll tell you more when we hear.'

James Lockwood took the jade and coral beads from his jacket pocket and laid them on the white tablecloth. 'Perhaps the police should start by finding out where these came from,' he said. 'The Fosci woman was wearing them the day before she died. She pawned them on Friday afternoon. Marjorie spotted them in the pawn shop on Saturday, and I bought them. I'd like to know who gave them to her.'

Inspector Chadwick picked them up and ran them through his fingers. 'Indeed. They're rather unusual. Look foreign to me. If you're amenable, Lockwood, I'll have them photographed and circulate the description to my contacts in Hatton Garden. Ten to one, someone will know where they came from.'

'Mrs Jameson says the timeline is key,' stated Mr Green. 'She says I should concentrate on that. Miss Swallow and Miss O'Grady have been most helpful in writing down their timings.

'But I've spoken to the police doctor. He admits the time of death puzzles him. He would have put it at much earlier – three or more hours before she was found. Of course, that would have been while Mrs Jameson and her party were at the theatre in Margate. But Anna Fosci was seen alive at twenty past ten, and her body was discovered at half past eleven.'

Inspector Chadwick pounced on his words. 'Seen alive by whom? Are the witnesses reliable?'

The men seemed to have forgotten I was there. 'By me,' I said. 'And Frankie, and Mrs Jameson. She was at the gate of the hotel when we came back from the theatre.'

'Oh. And you're completely sure, Miss Swallow?' The inspector leaned across the table, crumbling a bread roll in his fingers.

'Of course,' I said. 'We all saw her.' I reached for a roll and buttered it thickly. 'She was in her white dress and hat. She looked like a ghost.'

I bit into the roll hungrily. Then I stopped chewing.

'We have to go back to the cave,' I spluttered, through a mouthful of bread.

Chapter 35

'What? I didn't get any of that,' said the inspector. Mr Green brushed away the crumbs that I'd sprayed across the table, his nostrils pinched. James patted me on the back as I choked on my mouthful of bread. I poured another glass of water and drank it down.

'Sorry. We have to go back to the cave, as soon as the tide is low enough. I'd forgotten about the missing sheet,' I said.

'The missing sheet?' The inspector raised an eyebrow. 'Sounds like a detective story. Go on, Marjorie.'

'That's what Frankie was doing when she slipped. She'd found a bundled-up cotton sheet, pushed up on the rocks at the back of the cave. I had to tear a piece off it to bandage her leg.'

'I'm not following,' said James. 'What was so interesting about this sheet? Was it bloodstained or something? Or torn into strips and tied up to make a rope?'

'It was cut into pieces. And it's been missing since Saturday morning. Mrs Heath scolded Etta about it. We need to talk to Etta.'

'Who is Etta?' asked Mr Green. He'd pulled out his fountain pen and was taking notes.

'The chambermaid. Frankie and I talked to her this morning. She said she'd done all the beds on Saturday morning, but there was a sheet missing and they hadn't found it since. It caused trouble with the laundry, and the housekeeper was insisting they had to find it. She said she didn't know which room it was from, but I think she must have done, really.'

'I'm sure Mrs Heath will be very relieved,' said James. 'But I still don't get it. Why would someone steal a sheet, cut it into pieces and then hide it at the back of a cave?'

I was thinking hard, my eyes screwed up to remember the night we had returned from the theatre. It had been dark as we'd driven around the curve of the road. The entrance to the hotel grounds was guarded by tall chestnut trees, casting shadows from the lamp that illuminated the gateway. Frankie had slowed the car, and we'd seen the tall, slim figure in white, standing by the gatepost under the shadow of the trees. White dress, white hat half-obscuring her face. We'd all immediately thought it was Julia Donatello, standing where we'd seen her stand before.

But she had not attempted to speak to us. She hadn't waved or stepped out into the light. She'd just stood there, and when I'd run back to check a few minutes later, she'd gone.

I opened my eyes. 'Etta said the guests sometimes use the sheets for fancy dress parties. Roman togas, and so on,' I said, slowly. 'Arab sheiks. Ghosts. But if you cut up a white bedsheet, you could make it into a white dress. And stand by the gatepost at the entrance to the hotel, under the trees. A real life ghost. A white lady.'

'Good God,' said Inspector Chadwick.

'You mean...?' asked James.

'Someone could have pretended to be Anna Fosci, so that

everyone would believe she was still alive at twenty past ten,' said Mr Green. 'To cover up the fact that she'd been dead for hours. Which is why the doctor was so confused.'

A tremendous wave of relief washed over me. 'Which means...'

Inspector Chadwick was on his feet. 'Which means Iris is innocent. And someone...' He paused and looked around the restaurant, where the guests had all been covertly watching our table. 'Someone else is guilty. And all the alibis that people carefully presented from ten twenty onwards are worthless. I'm off to find that wretched Inspector Dyson, and get a few constables down to the cave to retrieve that sheet.'

Chapter 36

I gazed around the luncheon tables. Everyone had been eavesdropping on our conversation. Mr and Mrs Goldsmith were so excited they'd stopped quarrelling and sat, hands clasped across the table, gazing eagerly towards us.

In the middle of the room Jean McDonald and Helen Fraser sat with Mildred and Geoffrey Treadwell. They looked studiously away, and began a stilted conversation about the pros and cons of different makes of golf club. Miss Fraser caught my eye for a second, and her cheeks reddened.

Major Redfern, who had been sitting at the table nearest to us with his mother, got up and walked over.

'Found something out, have you? Come on, Lockwood. That London policeman knows about the Italian mafia, I'll bet. They're all over Soho, from what I hear.'

'Cedric, dear. Do sit down and finish your luncheon.' Mrs Redfern had a pack of cards beside her plate, I noticed, and was absent-mindedly shuffling them one-handed, in a rather expert way.

'Do excuse us, Major. We're just about to eat,' said James.

Alfred was hovering by our table with plates balanced up his arm. Even with all the excitement, I was hungry. 'Major

Redfern, we'll let you know if we find out anything about the mafia. I promise.'

'Inspector Chadwick will tell us as soon as he knows anything,' said Mr Green. 'There's nothing more to say for now.'

Defeated, the Major slunk away.

'If the time of death can be shown to have been while you were still at Margate, I shall insist they let Mrs Jameson out. If only you'd thought of it before. It would have saved a lot of trouble,' said Mr Green.

If Mrs Jameson had allowed me to discuss the case with her, I wanted to say, everything would have been different. We might have both questioned our sighting of Julia Donatello earlier. We could have told the police that we weren't sure it was her, at least. And then the police doctor would have given an earlier time of death, and both of us would have been in the clear.

For once, I paid little attention to my food. Despite the heatwave, the restaurant produced the usual Sunday fare of roast lamb with all the traditional accompaniments. I ate automatically, glancing from table to table. Who had benefited from the police thinking the murder took place after twenty past ten? Everyone with an alibi for that time, I supposed. Which meant everyone who had been together in the lounge bar from ten twenty until the body was spotted on the beach. And yet one person must have been absent for long enough to impersonate Anna Fosci.

'Mr Green, do you have that timeline?' He took it from his pocket, and I scanned our notes. When I'd first entered the lounge, who had been there? The bridge players: James Lockwood and Geoffrey Treadwell, Major and Mrs Redfern.

The bar tender, of course. Had Mr Ashcroft been there, or did he arrive later?

And where was everyone else? Jean McDonald had said that she and Helen had gone to bed early. And the Goldsmiths rarely stayed up past ten o'clock. I supposed that meant none of them would have had a strong alibi for the false time of death.

The question was, where had everyone been two hours earlier? And, of course, who had been standing at the gate in a white dress, waiting for us to come back from the theatre?

I glanced around the room. The woman we'd taken for Julia Donatello had been tall and slim. Jean McDonald was not much above five foot in height. Mrs Redfern was slight but stooped. Plump Mrs Goldsmith was as short as her husband. That left Helen Fraser, tall and athletic, and Mildred Treadwell, slim and elegantly lofty. I glanced back at the timeline. Neither of them had been in the lounge when we arrived back from the theatre.

There would be a record of who had been in for dinner, I supposed. Dinner was served in two sittings, six o'clock for those who wished to eat early, and eight. That meant we could place where people had been during their evening meal.

Major Redfern, I remembered, had planned to meet the woman he believed to be Bianca Colomba, at Neptune's Tower after dinner. What time had he said – eight o'clock? Half past? And he'd waited, planning to propose marriage, but she never arrived.

Or perhaps she had arrived. Perhaps she'd arrived without the beads he had given her, having pawned them in town. Perhaps he'd heard the rumours about her other entanglements or seen her with another man. And perhaps that had been too much for his short temper.

But then, why tell us that he'd planned to meet her at all? Surely it would have been better to say nothing. Unless... my head began to ache. Unless he knew he might have been seen and decided to have a story ready.

'You're very quiet, Marjorie. Penny for your thoughts.' James broke into my musings.

I smiled and set my knife and fork down. 'I'm sorry. It's just... this turns the case upside down, you see. I'm having to rethink everything I thought I knew.'

He chuckled. 'This is why I write romances. Nice, easy plots, no red herrings or double bluffs. Why don't you talk it through with us? Sometimes just saying it out loud helps, when I'm working on a plot.'

'Maybe.' I wanted, more than anything, to talk it through with Mrs Jameson. She had a way of taking in all the details and instantly picking out the most important of them. I felt at sea without her, awash in a rising tide of facts that refused to arrange themselves in order.

'I think Miss Swallow has done quite enough for one day,' said Mr Green, laying down his cutlery. 'She needs to rest.'

'That's true,' said James. 'Maybe you should have an after-lunch nap. Then I'm supposed to be playing bridge with the Major and Mrs Redfern this afternoon. Perhaps you could make up a four with us.'

I couldn't think of anything I'd want to do less. Then I paused, watching Mrs Redfern shuffling through her pack of cards. She looked so frail and innocent that one tended to overlook her. But appearances could be deceptive. How tall would she be if she stood up straight? And she gave the impression that she would do anything to protect her son.

'I don't know how to play, I'm afraid. But maybe I could learn. You can teach me the rules, James.'

You can discover a lot about people from the way they play games, Mrs Jameson had told me. Were the Redferns really cheating at cards, as Geoffrey Treadwell had suggested?

Chapter 37

To my surprise, I fell asleep as soon as I stretched out on my bed after lunch, a blissfully dreamless sleep that my tired mind tumbled into headlong. Mrs Jameson was innocent. I hadn't realised until Mr Green told us about the doctor's evidence quite how heavily the possibility of her guilt had weighed on me.

A rap on the door woke me. The room was stifling, despite the open window. I felt headachy and heavy with sleep.

'One moment,' I called. I checked the clock: I'd been asleep for barely an hour.

It was Inspector Chadwick. 'Sorry to disturb you, Miss Swallow. They've found the pieces of sheet in the cave,' he said. 'Can you come and take a look?'

I splashed my face with cold water, then dressed quickly.

The sections of damp cotton were laid out on the library table, on top of a layer of newspapers. One large rectangular section was doubled over, tacked together at the sides, with a slit to make a neck-hole. A big section from the bottom had been hacked away roughly, and bloodstained handprints showed around the tear.

'That was where I tore a piece off to dress Frankie's wound,'

I confirmed. 'I used her penknife.' I tried to keep my voice steady. 'That'll be her blood.'

I picked up the piece and held it in front of me. It would drape from my shoulders almost to my ankles.

'But ignore that missing section, and this would make a dress, if you didn't look too closely. It'd fall to about mid-calf length, if you were tall, with another strip to tie around for a belt.'

'There are a couple more pieces here,' said Constable Perks.

I examined them. 'That would make a belt,' I said, indicating a long strip of fabric. The other section was round, like a dinner plate. I stared at it for a moment. 'A hat,' I pronounced. 'She was wearing a white cotton sun-hat. If you pinned that over a simple straw hat, it would look just like it.'

The remainder of the pieces looked like off-cuts. For a moment I was back in my mother's sewing room where she made up dresses for customers, her mouth full of pins as she wielded the shears, unused fabric falling to the floor, then gathered up carefully for making into handkerchiefs or fabric trimmings.

I looked again at the bigger piece. The stitches were large and wonky, and had started to unravel from the end of one seam. The work had been done hastily, and not by anyone skilled at sewing. White cotton thread, tied in a big knot. The needle holes showed, suggesting they'd used a darning needle, not the small quicksilver needles my mother used for light fabric.

'Whoever made this didn't know how to sew properly. Or else they were in too much of a hurry to make a good job,' I said. I couldn't imagine Mildred Treadwell or Helen Fraser making their own clothes.

'Well?' said Inspector Chadwick.

Inspector Dyson, who had been leaning against the table, his expression sulky, gave a shrug.

'Speculation,' he said. 'We don't know how long that sheet's been there, or if it was used in the way you suggest. Or even if it comes from the hotel.'

'Don't talk nonsense, man!' Inspector Chadwick exploded with annoyance. 'At the very least, you must admit that this calls your timeline into question. And your own medic swears your corpse was dead three hours before she was found.'

'The sheet was missed on Saturday morning,' I reminded him. 'So, it can't have been there longer than that.'

Constable Perks shifted uneasily. 'There's a woven label attached to the seam on this piece, sir. It gives the hotel's name. I think it probably is from here.'

Inspector Dyson rounded on him. 'If you'd done your job properly when you searched the beach, you'd have found it yesterday,' he said, furious.

'Indeed. And you would not have taken an innocent woman into custody,' said Inspector Chadwick.

The two men faced each other, animosity bristling from every pore.

'If your lady friend had been honest with us from the start, we wouldn't have suspected her, would we?' Inspector Dyson sneered.

For a moment, I thought Inspector Chadwick might punch him. Instead, he shook his head and turned away.

'Have it your way. I'll make a call to Scotland Yard and suggest that the Kent Constabulary are relieved of their jurisdiction over this murder, as they are clearly not competent to investigate,' he said. 'Scotland Yard knows Iris Jameson well. Commissioner Groves is a particular friend of hers. If he knew she was in custody, he'd be here himself, and your career wouldn't be worth tuppence, Dyson.'

Inspector Dyson swallowed, his Adam's apple shifting. He didn't seem to have shaved since Friday night. His mouth worked, as if he was rehearsing what he would say, if only he could get the words past his fury.

'I'll speak to her solicitor,' he said eventually. 'We may be able to arrange bail.'

Inspector Chadwick relaxed his grip on the chair, colour returning to his knuckles. 'You do that,' he said.

Chapter 38

The policemen went off in search of Mr Green. I still felt guilty that it had been my testimony which had put Mrs Jameson in a cell. What else could I do to help clear her name?

I stared for a moment at the sheet. Whose room was it from? If we knew that, we'd know the murderer – or at least, we'd know who had helped them construct an alibi. I jumped up in excitement.

One person knew, all right, even if she'd pretended not to. Etta the chambermaid would be cleaning rooms somewhere in the hotel. Perhaps I could find out before Mrs Jameson was back from Broadstairs.

Etta wasn't working on my floor, or the one below. I trotted down to the reception desk, where the disapproving Mr Ashcroft made me wait five minutes while he finished a conversation with a supplier.

'I was looking for Mrs Heath,' I said. 'Do you know where I can find her?' The housekeeper would be more likely to know the whereabouts of the chambermaids than he would, I supposed.

'Is anything wrong with your room, Miss Swallow?'

'No, I just wanted to ask her about something.'

He raised his eyebrows. 'She's very busy. Please don't keep her longer than is necessary.' His deference towards guests no longer extended to me, I'd noticed. Not since he'd asked me to leave, and the other guests had intervened to stop him. 'We're one chambermaid down. Mrs Heath is having to do her work herself. I expect she's in the east wing.'

'Which maid?' I asked, alarmed.

He sighed. 'I don't see that it's any of your business. But Etta Morrison hasn't come back after lunch.'

This was bad news. 'Do you know where she's gone?'

'I do not. Now, if you will excuse me, I too have a busy afternoon.' He picked up the telephone again.

I ran over to the east wing and tracked down Mrs Heath. She was stripping a room with a briskness that made me fear for the furnishings. Yes, she confirmed, Etta had been at table for the servants' lunch. However, she'd not been seen since. Mrs Heath had only realised she was missing when one of the guests had complained that their room had not been made up yet.

'Not a word, the little minx. Off with some boyfriend, I suppose. I've a mind to give her notice.' She swept a duster vigorously over a chest of drawers, dislodging a china vase with a posy of wilting flowers.

Boyfriend. Perhaps Alfred would know where she was. But I had an anxious feeling in my stomach. I'd mentioned her by name, when I'd talked at lunch about the missing sheet. In a room full of potential suspects, I'd named the woman who might have been able to tell us who had taken the sheet. Once more, my indiscretion had put someone in danger.

'I'm sure she'll have a good reason,' I said. 'Mrs Heath, you didn't find out which room that missing sheet had come from, did you?'

She straightened and gave me a suspicious look. 'Why, what do you know about that? Did Etta tell you? Because she hasn't told me.'

I ran down the stairs and out into the courtyard. As I crossed it, on my way to the kitchens, I bumped into James. 'Ready for your lesson, Marjorie? We're meeting the Redferns at four. I could show you the basics before they arrive.'

'My lesson… Oh!' I'd forgotten about the game of bridge. 'I just have to find someone. I shan't be long.'

He grinned. 'Off sleuthing again? What are you up to this time?'

'Tell you later.'

James lowered his voice. 'I saw that solicitor fellow going off with your friend from Scotland Yard. He said they've found that sheet you were talking about, and they're going to the station to get them to free Mrs Jameson.'

'Have they both gone?' I wanted to tell Inspector Chadwick about Etta.

'They have. By the way, I telephoned the hospital. They said Miss O'Grady is doing well. The doctor's sewn up the cut and she's being made comfortable.'

'Oh, thank you.' Two pieces of good news. I felt that we were turning the corner. With Mrs Jameson and Inspector Chadwick working together, I had no doubt that we would find the guilty party soon.

But would it be soon enough for Etta Morrison?

'I'll join you in a minute,' I promised. 'Shan't be long.'

When I arrived at the kitchen door, the staff stopped working and crowded around to ask about Frankie. Alfred was among them, his dark eyes seeking me out.

191

'She's doing well,' I assured them. 'The hospital says she's been treated and is recovering. Thank you all so much for asking about her.' I looked around. 'Where's Etta? I saw her on the beach this morning when they were getting Frankie out of the cave. I'd like to tell her how she is.'

The cook shook her head and looked uneasy. One of the waiters, a tall thin boy with pimples on his chin, nudged Alfred, who turned to him with a scowl. Two of the kitchen maids looked at him, then quickly looked away.

'What is it?' I asked.

'Haven't seen her, Miss,' said the second waiter. 'Not since this morning, anyways. Down on the beach, when Miss Frankie was being got out of the cave. Like you said.'

'She ate her lunch at midday,' volunteered the cook. 'But I've not seen her since.'

I sought out Alfred. 'Do you have any idea where Etta may have gone?' I asked him.

He shrugged, but he didn't meet my eyes. 'Not me. No special reason why I should.'

One of the kitchen maids giggled, then clasped her hands over her mouth after the other gave her a shove.

'Come on, back to work,' said the cook. 'Enough standing around gossiping. Thank you for coming to tell us about Miss Frankie, Miss.' She chivvied the maids back inside. Alfred followed.

His fellow waiter hesitated. Then: 'Alfie and Etta fell out, Miss, over that Italian girl. Etta gave him a hard time about it; pretended she was interested in one of the guests. That's why Alfie's a bit funny about her, see. Maybe he thinks she's gone off with someone else. He's awful jealous. He threatened to thump me once, just for walking to the village with Etta.

Thick as thieves, those two.'

Chapter 39

I didn't like it, but I couldn't interrogate Alfred against his will. I'd tell Inspector Chadwick about the missing maid as soon as he got back – with Mrs Jameson, I hoped.

I traipsed back to the lounge, where the long windows to the terrace stood open in the vain hope of catching a breeze. The air was still and heavy. The atmosphere was ominous, a held breath before a roar.

Mrs Redfern, bright eyed, was deftly dealing cards. Major Redfern gazed glumly at his hand, his mind seemingly elsewhere. James passed me my cards and fanned them out.

'Now, as you're learning, I'll look at your cards and play both our hands. But usually, partners can't see each other's cards. See?'

I nodded. Mrs Redfern gave me a quick smile. 'You'll soon pick it up, dear. We'll make allowances for you. Now, Cedric, you lead.'

I can't pretend that I did pick it up. My head was too full of questions to follow what was happening. James and I lost the first trick, which I could see annoyed him, even though he pretended not to mind.

Mrs Redfern and her son bid quickly and without hesitation,

glancing one to the other with complete understanding. I began to think that Mr Treadwell was right. Either they had simply partnered together so long that they could guess the other's cards from their play, or they had agreed some kind of communication system.

After we'd lost two tricks, the Treadwells came in, dressed in tennis whites and swinging their rackets. Geoffrey Treadwell collapsed into an armchair, red-faced and sweating, but his wife looked cool and elegant as she strolled through to the sunlit terrace. She leaned against the wall, in the shadow of a palm.

A prickle ran down my back, a flash of memory. The woman we'd thought to be Julia Donatello, standing beneath a tree. A tall, slim woman in white.

'I said, your turn, Marjorie.' James leaned over, pointing to the card I should play. His voice was a little testy.

'Sorry.' I set it down without even looking at it.

'There we are, then.' Mrs Redfern's voice, satisfied, as she set down her card. 'Our game.'

James frowned. 'You're not concentrating, Marjorie. You need to pay more attention.' But I had other things on my mind.

Where had Mildred Treadwell been on Friday night, when we'd come back from the theatre? Her husband had been playing cards with James and the Redferns, as we were now. I'd walked into the room and James had asked if I wanted a drink. Had she been there?

'You won't beat those two, Lockwood,' said Geoffrey Treadwell, with a harsh laugh. 'No matter how good you are. I need a drink. Mildred, do you want a G and T?'

That was it. Mildred Treadwell had walked into the lounge

with a gin and tonic, and criticised her husband's playing. But how long had she been in the vicinity? Would she have had time to stand by the gate, let the car go by, change out of the white dress and then rejoin us, within a few minutes?

Geoffrey Treadwell had taken Anna Fosci to tea, and I'd seen him pawing her in the Dreamland gardens. Had Mrs Treadwell found out and taken her revenge on the woman? She was tall, athletic, with a powerful forehand at tennis. But would she really have murdered a woman for flirting with her husband?

Major Redfern had set down his cards. 'Now, Cedric,' warned his mother. I looked up, alerted by her anxious tone.

'That's the second time you've accused me of cheating, Treadwell,' he growled. 'We were interrupted, before. Maybe there's unfinished business.' He got to his feet.

'Oh, don't start all that again!' I exclaimed. 'Please, Major. You're just very good players, that's all Mr Treadwell meant. Can't we leave it at that?'

The whole scene was suddenly, powerfully redolent of Friday night. Mrs Treadwell leaning on the wall, the cards on the table, Major Redfern squaring up to Geoffrey Treadwell. I shuddered, remembering how the next moment we had discovered a young woman's body, rolling in the surf. And now another young woman was missing.

'I say, look down there,' said Mildred Treadwell, casually leaning over the terrace wall.

I rushed to her side, and let out a gasp of relief. Walking across the sands, deep in conversation, were Inspector Chadwick, Mr Green, and Mrs Jameson.

'They seem to have let her out,' drawled Mrs Treadwell. 'Does that mean she's not the killer after all? How tiresome. I suppose that dreadful Inspector Dyson will be questioning us all again.'

She seemed merely annoyed by the idea, not frightened. However, that was no guarantee of innocence. Some of the killers Mrs Jameson and I had met were so convinced of their own cleverness, they couldn't imagine being caught.

'Of course she's not the killer,' I snapped. My own guilt at suspecting Mrs Jameson made me irritable.

'Well, one never knows about Americans. They're so unpredictable,' she said. She turned back to the lounge and raised her voice. 'Geoffrey, come out here. If you get into another fight with that man, I swear I'll divorce you.'

She didn't sound like someone who would murder a rival to keep her husband.

Mr Treadwell followed her instructions. 'I've no intention of getting into a fight,' he muttered. 'But it's damned fishy the way they always win, all the same.'

I returned to the lounge. 'Mrs Jameson is here, with Mr Green and Inspector Chadwick,' I said, happily. 'I'm going to go down and join them.'

'That's good news,' said James. 'Major, did I tell you I gave those jade beads to the man from Scotland Yard? The ones from the pawn shop. He's going to get them traced. We'll soon find out who gave them to the Italian woman.'

Major Redfern, who had been staring belligerently after Geoffrey Treadwell, turned sharply to James. 'What? What do you mean?'

His face was a picture of guilt.

'If you gave them to her, Major,' I said gently, 'I think you'd better tell the Inspector.'

He flushed a deep magenta and turned away.

197

'What beads?' asked Mrs Redfern, puzzled. 'You can't mean the ones I'm missing, Cedric?' She turned to me. 'I had a lovely coral and jade set, that my late husband gave me in India. I haven't been able to find them. But you say you saw them in a pawn shop?' Her nose wrinkled in distaste.

'No idea what you're talking about,' shouted Major Redfern. 'I'm going out.' He stomped from the room.

I ran after him.

'Leave me alone,' he said. 'I'm taking your advice, all right? I'm going to tell the police.' He turned a furious face on me. 'Mother will be very upset. I thought they would stay in the family, see? Once we were married. Mother never wore them anymore. I don't believe Bianca pawned them herself. Whoever did this thing must have taken them from her. I shall tell the police. They must find out who took them into that pawn shop.'

He marched down the steps to the basement.

I trotted through the grounds and out onto the road. I paused at the top of the steps and looked down onto the shimmering sands, the tide now far out, exposing slippery chalk rocks fringed with seaweed. Mrs Jameson walked alone by the water's edge. Inspector Chadwick and Mr Green stood together, and the Major strode across the sands towards them.

Chapter 40

I walked down the steps, more slowly now. My first rush of relief was replaced by apprehension. What would Mrs Jameson have to say to me? I wondered if we would ever be able to repair the trust that had once been so firm between us.

She turned at my approach, and I was relieved to see her smile. But her eyes were sad, as if she too knew something had been lost.

'Ah, Marjorie. There you are.'

I smiled at the familiar greeting. 'Here I am, Mrs Jameson.' I was taken by surprise by a sudden tightness in my throat.

We both looked down at the smooth wet sand. She traced a figure of eight pattern on it with the tip of her parasol.

'I'm sorry,' I said.

'So am I.' She sighed. Neither of us needed to ask what the other was sorry for.

'However, here we both are.' She looked up. I wondered if I was imagining the shine of tears in her eyes. 'And although it pains me to admit it, you were right. We do need to discover who murdered Anna Fosci.'

'Who was she, Mrs Jameson? Did you know her in Italy?' I asked.

She shook her head. 'I had not met her before that morning on the beach. But Peter Chadwick has wired the Italian police. They have a record of an Anna Fosci, a petty criminal arrested several times in Naples, Rome and Florence. Theft, extortion and obtaining money under false pretences. She left Italy ten days ago.'

'A confidence trickster,' I said. 'And a blackmailer. Why did she follow you here?'

Mrs Jameson sighed again. 'She believed she had learned something that would allow her to extort money from me.'

There was a pause. I waited to see if she would tell me more.

She gave me a severe look. 'Are you attempting to use my lengthy pause technique?' she asked.

I laughed guiltily. 'Well, maybe. A bit.'

This time her smile was mischievous. 'I thought so. For the record, it doesn't usually work on me. However, I believe I do owe you something of an explanation.'

We walked across the sand, back towards the steps to the hotel.

'Miss Fosci had not chosen the name Julia at random,' Mrs Jameson began. 'She claimed to believe that she was the daughter of my late husband, Julian Jameson.'

'Oh!' My mind flew to what I had overheard of their conversation. Father, mother, convent, hospital. Perhaps Anna's mother had given birth there, in a nursing home for unwed mothers run by the nuns. And her daughter had learned of her true parentage when her mother died, spoken to the nuns, and then followed the trail to England. Perhaps Sister Agnese had come to warn Mrs Jameson of her arrival.

'Miss Fosci had presumably learned of my husband's un-savoury reputation.' Mrs Jameson stopped walking and gazed out to sea, as if a focus on the distant horizon enabled her to share these deeply personal, no doubt distasteful revelations. 'It must have seemed perfectly possible that he would have an illegitimate child. She seemed to think that I would be taken in by this story, hand over a suitable inheritance in return for her silence.'

She paused and gave a grim smile. 'She was wrong. About being able to blackmail me, and about what she believed she had learned. I am certain she was not Julian's child.'

I frowned. 'But why would she come all the way from Italy to blackmail you, if she didn't have proof?'

Mrs Jameson shook her head and put up her parasol, shading her face from my gaze. 'Unfortunately, that's something we will not be able to ask her,' she said. 'It's an unpleasant topic, Marjorie. I don't wish to talk about it any more.'

'Of course.' And yet, for all her promise of an explanation, I felt Mrs Jameson had held something back. There must be plenty of rich men with unsavoury reputations who could have twenty-one-year-old daughters. Why had Anna Fosci fixed on one who was no longer alive, and why would she expect his widow to pay up?

'I take it that it was your idea to involve Peter?' Mrs Jameson strode on, leaving me with my questions unanswered. 'I had hoped not to trouble him, but I admit he has been useful. He has been telling me about your discovery in the cave, and the implications for the timeline.'

'Frankie's discovery,' I said.

'Indeed.' She shook her head. 'I have come to expect recklessness from you, Marjorie. But I shall be having a sharp word with Frankie, as soon as she is recovered.' Her voice was severe. However, Mrs Jameson adored Frankie and was most unlikely to do any such thing. 'I simply cannot spare either of you. I hear you were very brave and resourceful. You saved her life.'

The look of pride she gave me then went straight to my heart. I beamed.

'Now, let's get down to business,' she said, turning back to the hotel. 'We can work from the library, assuming that ridiculous Inspector Dyson has finished with it. Order afternoon tea, and we can review the timeline and put all the pieces together.'

'Oh!' I exclaimed. 'I haven't told the inspector yet. There's a girl missing, a chambermaid, and I think she might be important. She could probably tell us which room the sheet came from.'

Mrs Jameson whirled around. 'Run and tell Peter. We cannot let whoever has done this take another young woman's life.'

Chapter 41

'I don't know, and I'm not saying anything,' said Alfred.

'Come on, lad. You're not in trouble, but it's important we find Etta,' said Sergeant Cox. He laid a fatherly hand on the waiter's shoulder. 'She might be in danger, Alfie. You wouldn't want that, would you?'

Alfred shook his head, stubbornly. 'I told her.' He jerked his head towards where I sat with Inspector Chadwick, behind the desk in the library. 'Haven't seen Etta since this morning. She was down on the beach, when we heard that Frankie – Miss O'Grady – was hurt. I had to go back to the hotel because I was serving at lunch. I ain't seen her since.'

The police had already searched the hotel and its grounds, and constables had called to see if Etta Morrison had returned to her parents' cottage in Minster, a village fifteen miles inland. So far, there was no trace of the missing maid.

Inspector Chadwick rose. 'Let him go for now, sergeant,' he said.

Before the waiter disappeared out the door, Sergeant Cox tapped him on the lapel. 'Listen to me, Alfred Featherstone. If any harm comes to that young woman as a result of you keeping your mouth shut, you'll have me to deal with. Do you understand?'

Alfred ducked his head and hurried out of the room.

'You should have let him stew for a bit, Inspector Chadwick,' said Sergeant Cox, reproachfully. 'He knows something. Not that I think he'd hurt her, mind. Leastways, I hope not.'

I shivered. 'The other waiter told me he's jealous where Etta's concerned,' I said. 'That he threatened to punch him because of her.'

Sergeant Cox sighed. 'Well, he's got a temper on him. I've known him and the family since he was a baby. He was always a bit quick with his fists as a little lad, but I hoped he'd grown out of it. I'll call on his mum this afternoon. She wasn't keen on Etta, I do know that. She said Alfie could do better.'

A possibility was growing in my mind. What if Anna Fosci had tried to make trouble for Alfred, as she'd seemed to make trouble for everyone? Perhaps she'd threatened to tell Etta something about him. His alibi for Friday night no longer held. He'd served at dinner, I supposed. But what if he'd met her on the beach before dinner?

'Keep a close eye on him,' said the inspector. 'Haven't you got a constable who can shadow him, undercover? He'll lead us to her, if he knows where she is.'

Sergeant Cox looked dubious. 'There aren't that many of us, sir. He'll recognise most of the constables. They were all at school together. But I'll see what I can do.'

He followed the waiter out.

Chapter 42

As soon as Sergeant Cox had closed the door behind him, Mrs Jameson and I returned to the revised timeline, spread out on the desk.

'The police doctor estimates the time of death at between half past seven and half past nine,' she said. 'We were in Margate, of course, although I spoke to her at about half past five, before we left. Do we have any confirmed sightings of her after that? And who was at which sitting for dinner?'

'I'll see what I can get out of the Kent police,' said Inspector Chadwick. 'She stayed at the Captain Digby tavern, didn't she? I'll go over later and check when they last saw her.'

He picked up the booking list that Mr Ashcroft had been induced to supply. 'Mr and Mrs Goldsmith, Miss McDonald and Miss Fraser, Major and Mrs Redfern all went to the six o'clock sitting,' he read. 'Which means they would have been finished by eight. Mr and Mrs Treadwell and Mr Lockwood were booked for the eight o'clock sitting, which means they would have been finished by ten. Maybe earlier.'

He stared at the list, glumly. 'Doesn't help much. Anyone from the early sitting would have been able to bump her off afterwards, and anyone from the late sitting could have squeezed in a quick murder first, or even afterwards if they didn't mind getting indigestion. But my money's on the early crew, if it was a guest.'

I chewed my nail, thinking. 'But if it had been before eight o'clock, the body would have been on the beach for three hours. It was right out in the open, and it's light until almost ten. Surely someone would have seen her?'

'Good point,' said the inspector. 'Assuming it was on the beach all that time.'

I remembered my previous suspicion that the body had been moved, perhaps from inside the cave to outside on the beach, where the killer wanted it to be found. But not, I supposed, until after 10.20pm.

'Perhaps it wasn't,' I said. 'What if the murderer moved the body? Frankie and I thought she would most probably have been killed in the cave, where nobody could see her. But whoever did it wanted us to find the body while they had an alibi. After we'd seen – or thought we'd seen – Anna Fosci at the gate.

Mrs Jameson smiled. 'Good. That should help us to pin it down. Let's take them one at a time. We need someone free at the time of the murder, someone impersonating Anna Fosci at the gate at twenty past ten, and someone able to move the body to a position where it would be found later.' She nodded with satisfaction. 'It's always the cover-up, Marjorie. That's how we'll find them.'

'And we need a motive,' I said. 'It sounds as if she'd been trying to get money out of lots of people.' Including Mrs Jameson.

'Let's start with the men,' said Inspector Chadwick. 'Strangling is a man's crime. That army fellow, the one who charged up and informed me he'd given the dead woman a set of beads belonging to his mother. What do we know of his movements?'

'Major Redfern. He said he went to meet her after dinner,' I said. 'He planned to ask her to marry him, but she didn't arrive.'

I scribbled down the times. 'He was playing cards in the lounge when we got back from the theatre, with his mother, James Lockwood and Mr Treadwell.'

Mrs Jameson narrowed her eyes. 'He has a potential motive, especially if Anna Fosci had pawned his mother's jewellery and been flirting with other men.

'However, that doesn't explain who was at the gate. It cannot have been his mother, if she was in the lounge when we returned. Marjorie, can you find out how long they'd been playing?'

I made a note.

Mrs Jameson stared at the timeline, thoughtfully. 'Of course, if Major Redfern is innocent, it's possible that Anna Fosci was dead by the time of their appointment, since she failed to keep it. That would point to a time of death in the first hour of the doctor's estimate, between half past seven and half past eight.'

'Your Mr Green got the Met to look up Redfern's army record, Iris,' said Inspector Chadwick. He checked the notes that the solicitor had left for him. 'Nothing wrong there – he was mentioned in dispatches after Gallipoli. He went back to India, but he had to retire on health grounds. Malaria and what-not. Shell shock, I suppose, although they don't spell it out. Incidentally, Green says Redfern and his mother have a reputation for sharp practice with card-playing. They came back to Blighty four years ago and live in a villa in Dulwich off his army pension and what they can make at cards.'

He gave a shrug. 'Unmarried at his age, living with his mother – call me prejudiced, but that suggests a suspicious character to me.'

Mrs Jameson laughed. 'Peter, he can't be older than you. You're not married, either.'

He flushed and gave her a look full of meaning. 'Police work doesn't mix well with family life,' he muttered. 'Anyway, this is beside the point. I was speaking in general terms.'

He looked rather wretched at her teasing. I decided to come to his rescue.

'Then there's Geoffrey Treadwell,' I said. 'Frankie and I saw him having tea with Anna Fosci in Margate on Thursday afternoon. They were... well, they looked very cosy. When I told him later that we'd seen him, he said he'd told the police, but asked me not to tell his wife.'

Inspector Chadwick produced Mr Green's notes again. 'Treadwell works in the City, in a stock-broking firm. Married for ten years, lives in a great barn of a place outside Guildford. Two boys, both at boarding school. Apparently some of my colleagues in the Fraud Squad know his name. Rumours of insider trading, but although he sailed close to the wind, nothing was proven.'

He glanced at me. 'A bit of a ladies' man, as they say. According to one of the men who tailed him during the fraud investigation, he would look out for young women in financial distress and take advantage of them.'

'Like Anna Fosci,' I pointed out.

'And where was this charming character on Friday evening?' asked Mrs Jameson.

'Dinner at eight,' I said, writing it down. 'Oh! And James said he saw him and Anna Fosci together on the beach before that, earlier in the evening. That must be the last confirmed sighting. And if she died between half past seven and eight...'

I looked up in excitement. 'It could have been him, Mrs Jameson. Then there's Mrs Treadwell. I saw her in her tennis dress this afternoon, standing under a palm on the terrace. It gave me quite a turn. It could have been her we saw by the gate. Also, could she be the murderer herself? I've watched her playing tennis. She's very strong. What if she'd found out about Mr Treadwell and Anna Fosci?'

Mrs Jameson gazed into space, tapping her index finger on her chin. 'Interesting. If she'd come across them on the beach that evening... but then they would have had to agree to cover up the crime, whichever of them committed it. Not impossible, I suppose.'

'Right, then.' Inspector Chadwick looked over my shoulder. 'Three suspects. Who else knew the victim?'

'Alfred, the waiter,' I interjected. 'She flirted with him on Wednesday, and he and Etta had a row about it. What if Anna Fosci met him on the beach and threatened to make trouble for him? And he killed her in the cave, then came back after dinner to move the body.

'And what if it was Etta pretending to be Anna Fosci at the gate? Maybe she was protecting Alfred. Maybe he'd told her what had happened, and she agreed to help him make up an alibi.'

Mrs Jameson scanned the timeline. 'It would be tight,' she said. 'With the dinner service.'

Inspector Chadwick lit his pipe. 'Well, we're keeping tabs on young Alfred. He's a possibility, Marjorie. But so is everyone else.'

'Then there's Helen Fraser,' I said. I realised I hadn't told them about her appeal for Mrs Jameson's help before the murder, or the envelope she'd had, with Anna Fosci's writing on it. Quickly, I explained.

Mrs Jameson sighed. 'I wish I'd known.'

I opened my mouth to protest.

'I know, Marjorie. I'd been behaving abominably. You thought you were doing the right thing by telling her I wasn't taking cases. Well, we can't rule her out. She's tall enough to have been the one in the white dress by the gate. And her grip on a golf club is pretty merciless. Perhaps I should have a word with her this afternoon.'

The inspector sighed. 'You do that, Iris. Now, what about the people at the Captain Digby tavern where Miss Fosci was staying? I'd better find out what inquiries the Kent police have made at the pub. There may be a loose end or two that hasn't been tied up.'

Mrs Jameson didn't answer. She was staring at the timeline with narrowed eyes.

'What?' asked the inspector. 'Iris, you've seen something.'

'Leave her alone for a bit,' I advised. 'She'll tell us when she's worked it out.'

Chapter 43

For want of anything better to do, I accompanied Inspector Chadwick to the Captain Digby. Before we left, he telephoned the hospital in Margate for news about Frankie.

'Comfortable,' he relayed. 'That's good, isn't it?'

I grimaced. 'It's what the nurses always say if someone isn't actually dying.'

We walked out along the road beside the bay in silence. I wondered if I dared to ask Inspector Chadwick about Rome, and what he knew about Mrs Jameson's husband. It was worth a try, I supposed.

'Do you know…'

'Has she told you…'

We both spoke at the same time, and stopped. Inspector Chadwick smiled. 'Please, after you.'

I took a deep breath. 'Mrs Jameson says Anna Fosci followed us to Broadstairs in the hope of extorting money. But her explanation doesn't really make sense. Do you know what happened in Rome?'

He stopped walking, and stared out to sea with his broad shoulders hunched. He stood in silence for a moment, as if unsure where to begin, then gave a great sigh.

'When I first met Iris, in Paris before the War, she was in a bad way. Frightened, if you can believe that, Miss Swallow. Constantly looking over her shoulder, haunted by what she'd been through in Rome.'

'With Mr Jameson?' I asked.

His eyes hardened. 'With that brute. Anyway, everything changed, once she had work to do. I can't tell you exactly what either of us was doing, but I was there for Special Branch, and Iris began working in a similar capacity for the Americans. We rather hit it off,' he said. 'Ended up spending a good deal of time together.' His neck had flushed brick red, and he stared determinedly at the horizon, his jaw set.

I gazed at him, realising for the first time the nature of his feelings for my employer. I'd assumed they were merely former colleagues, that the ten year age difference between them ruled out anything more than friendship. I began to see that I was wrong.

'She has the finest brain of anyone I've ever worked with. Brave, resourceful, brilliant at languages. And she could charm anyone. She was tremendously attractive – well, she still is, of course. You can imagine what an asset she was. Saved hundreds of lives through her discoveries, including mine. It was the making of her.'

His eyes shone and I surprised myself with a little pang of jealousy. I knew she was formidable, but I'd never before considered how attractive Mrs Jameson must have been in her youth.

'She told me a little of her former life in Rome. There are some things she doesn't talk about, for good reason. The death of her child, for one.' He leaned on the wall and stroked his moustache. 'That almost broke her, I think.'

'And the death of her husband?'

The question hung in the air between us for a moment.

'That, too.' He turned to face me, his eyes troubled. 'I don't know exactly what Anna Fosci thought she had discovered. But you are right that it concerned Julian Jameson. I'm sure Iris will tell you the full story one day. But I don't advise you to press her on the subject. Believe me, Miss Swallow, you would understand her actions if you knew.'

I longed to question him further, but knew he would not tell me anything Mrs Jameson wished to keep secret. Perhaps she would tell me herself, one day. I would have to be content with that, for now.

#

The Captain Digby was dim inside, the evening sun filtering in through small windows facing inland and illuminating dusty dark wooden beams and tables.

The manager was behind the bar when we arrived, but as soon as Inspector Chadwick presented his warrant card, he came out to sit with us in a quiet window nook overlooking the sea. He introduced himself as Mr Badgett and was voluble, happy to gossip.

'Not to be funny, but she was trouble,' he said, wiping his face. The low ceilings trapped the heat and the whole pub was stifling. I wished we could sit outside. 'Right from the word go. I shouldn't have let her stay, really, but one of my regular barmaids was off sick and we were busy. I said she could board in one of the box rooms, if she tended bar. She did quite well the first night. Pretty face, you see. The men like it.'

'And when did she arrive?' asked Inspector Chadwick.

'Let me show you.' Mr Badgett heaved himself up and fetched the ledger where the inn's bookings were recorded.

'Monday. She was calling herself Bianca Colomba then, but I understand from your colleagues that wasn't her real name. Then on the Tuesday morning, there was this business about the wallet. One of our regular summer visitors was staying here with his family. He'd been out for a walk with Bianca, along the cliffs. So he said.'

The man gave the inspector a sideways look. 'And he couldn't find his wallet when he got back. That was when Major Redfern intervened. There was a bit of a row, and afterwards the major offered to pay her board, so she didn't work behind the bar again.

'Then the man said he'd made a mistake, and he'd found his wallet, but the family left early. The same day, back to Streatham with the kids in tow. I reckon his wife was suspicious.'

'Hum.' Inspector Chadwick stroked his moustache, thinking. 'I'm sure you've been asked this before, but when did you last see Miss Colomba?'

'Would have been about seven on the Friday evening, I reckon. She was out a lot.' He shook his head. 'With one man or another. Trouble, like I said.'

'With Major Redfern?' I asked.

'Amongst others.' He smiled a little sadly. 'Nice chap, the major, for all he's got a nasty temper when he's had too many. I felt like I ought to warn him. I could see he was going silly over her. But you can't tell a man, can you? Not when he's falling for a girl.'

Mr Badgett turned to the back of the ledger and pulled out an envelope. 'Glad you came by, Inspector. I've been wondering what I should do with this. I thought I'd ask Sergeant Cox, but he's been that busy, I haven't seen him.'

He laid it on the table. Hotel stationery, with the crest of Kingsgate Castle in the corner, addressed to Miss Julia Donatello, c/o The Captain Digby Tavern, in a neat, educated hand. The postmark showed it had been posted on Friday.

'Arrived Saturday morning, but nobody got around to looking at the post until today,' he said. 'What with all the excitement. I didn't like to open it.'

Inspector Chadwick's eyes glittered. 'Pass me a knife,' he said. He pulled on a pair of cotton gloves, similar to the evidence gloves I'd been taught to carry in my handbag.

He slit the envelope open and carefully extracted the contents. A ten pound note, folded neatly. A letter, in the same hand as the envelope, also on hotel stationery. 'Please leave us alone, now. Your understanding of the situation is entirely wrong. Take this and be done with it.'

No signature, and none needed. I felt quite sure I knew who had sent the money.

'Foolish,' remarked Inspector Chadwick. He replaced the letter and the money in the envelope. 'Thank you, Mr Badgett. Thank you very much.'

'Something important?' asked Mr Badgett, who'd been trying to read the note upside-down.

'Possibly,' said the inspector. 'I suppose I'd better get back to the hotel. Before I go, though, think back to Friday night, if you would. Did anyone from the hotel come in during the evening?'

The man nodded. 'Major Redfern, poor chap. He came in on his own, looking very crestfallen. He had a whisky and soda, asked if I knew where Miss Colomba was. I didn't, of

215

course. Gadding about with one of the others, I supposed.

'I thought he'd be in here for the night, and told the girl behind the bar to keep a count and let me know when he'd had four whiskies. You get to know when a man reaches the danger point, and that was his. Anyway, his friend came in and said they were supposed to be playing cards at the hotel. They'd gone by ten, when I called last orders.'

'His friend?' I asked.

'Writer chap. Got a wooden leg.'

I nodded. 'James Lockwood. The man who had lunch with us, Inspector Chadwick. He must have come over after dinner.'

The inspector made a note. 'And he was one of the bridge players? So that would fit with what the major told us.'

We thanked the manager and were making our way out, when we bumped into James in the doorway, looking flustered.

'I say, what's all this about one of the chambermaids going missing? I hope we haven't got another murder on our hands.'

Chapter 44

'The police are making every attempt to find Miss Morrison,' said Inspector Chadwick, reassuringly.

'Yes. Well, they haven't made much of a job of finding the killer of that young woman, have they?' James leant his stick against the table. 'Apologies to your profession, Inspector. But I'd say this is urgent. I'd like to help.'

'Etta Morrison?' asked the pub manager. 'I didn't know she was missing. When did that happen?'

I checked the clock: it was almost half past six. I was also getting anxious about the amount of time that had passed since Etta was last seen alive.

'She's not been seen since lunchtime,' I said. 'But it's true, James. The police have been searching everywhere. All over the hotel, in the town and around the bay.'

He stared out of the door and across the road. 'What about the golf course?'

I frowned. 'What do you mean?'

He rubbed his chin. 'Well, perhaps I shouldn't say. But that Treadwell fellow, I don't like the way he is around the women who work at the hotel. Some of the things he says.'

Inspector Chadwick pushed the door open. 'I'm sure the golf

course is being searched, Mr Lockwood. I'll talk to Sergeant Cox. We're going back to the hotel now. But go on. What does Mr Treadwell say about the female staff?'

We walked through the garden to the footpath beside the road. The white glare of the sun had faded, leaving a sullen, heavy feel to the air. Over the sea, the sky had a bruised, purpling look.

James glanced at me, his face reddening. 'He makes remarks about their personal appearance. The maids, and… and the other guests. Young women, I mean.' He looked away. 'I'm sorry, Marjorie. It's very distasteful. He talks about what he'd like to do if he got them alone in his room. That sort of thing. I'm sure you don't need me to spell it out.'

If James Lockwood thought I was too naïve to know how some men treated women they believed to be their social inferiors, he was wrong.

'When was this?' I demanded. 'Has he said anything specifically about Etta?'

James bit his lip. After a moment, he said: 'Something happened yesterday morning. My room is on the same corridor as the Treadwells, you know. I was writing, and I heard a noise – sort of a shriek. I put my head out, and saw her coming out of their room. She looked upset; her face was red, and her cap had come off.

'She said it was nothing, and told me not to say anything about it, in case Mrs Heath got the wrong idea. But once I heard she was missing, I thought I should let you know.'

'How horrible!' I exclaimed. 'Poor Etta.'

Inspector Chadwick nodded slowly. 'Thank you, Mr Lockwood. You were right to tell me. What time would you say this happened?'

'Around half past ten. I like to write straight after breakfast, and I'd been going for a couple of hours, I suppose. I usually ring down for coffee at about that time.'

I wondered if Alfred knew about Geoffrey Treadwell's assault on his girl, or indeed if any of the other chambermaids had suffered the same insult. I remembered Treadwell in the tea garden, his arm creeping around Anna Fosci's shoulders, his hand on her knee. I shuddered.

We arrived back at the hotel gates. 'Tell me what I can do, Inspector,' said James. 'I know I'm a bit of a poor specimen now, but I'd like to help find the girl. Do you have any leads I can follow up?'

'Leave it to us, Mr Lockwood,' said the inspector. 'Thank you for your help.'

He strode off, presumably to find Sergeant Cox.

'Pompous ass. What do you say, Marjorie?' asked James. 'Shall we do a bit of sleuthing of our own?'

I didn't like to hurt his feelings. And perhaps he could help, anyway.

'We've been keeping an eye on one of the waiters,' I said. 'Alfred, the dark-haired chap. Etta's his girl, you see. Why don't you see if he's serving at dinner? And whether the Treadwells are eating early.' We'd missed the first sitting. 'I'll see if I can find Mrs Jameson. I don't know if she's eaten yet.'

He nodded, briskly. 'I'll do that. Rendezvous back in the lounge bar at eight, shall we? We could have a drink, then all have dinner together.'

\#

My employer was no longer in the library. I checked the terrace, then tapped on the door to her suite.

'Come in.'

Mrs Jameson sat at the table in her lounge, a trolley stacked with plates and silver domes beside her.

'There you are. I've ordered dinner for us, and for the inspector. I thought we could eat while we talk. What have you done with Peter?'

'He was going to look for Sergeant Cox,' I said. I'd have to remember to let James know we wouldn't be dining together after all. 'We found out something interesting. It sounds like Mr Treadwell did something to upset Etta in his room yesterday morning. And we found a note at the Captain Digby, with ten pounds, which I bet you anything came from Helen Fraser.'

There was a firm rap on the door.

'Oh, splendid.' Inspector Chadwick surveyed the feast with pleasure. 'I haven't eaten properly since breakfast.'

We sat around the table and Mrs Jameson served up poached salmon and potato salad, while we brought her up to date on our findings and Inspector Chadwick showed her the letter that Mr Badgett had given us.

'We need to talk to Treadwell about Etta Morrison,' said Inspector Chadwick. 'He was also seen with Anna Fosci the evening she died. And I don't think anyone saw her after that, until her body was found. That Sergeant Cox seems a sensible fellow. I'll see if he can round him up.'

'And his wife,' I added. I couldn't shake the image of Mildred Treadwell, tall and slim in her white tennis dress. 'And Miss Fraser.'

'Mm.' Mrs Jameson chewed thoughtfully. 'I had an interesting conversation with Helen Fraser this afternoon. She says that Miss McDonald hopes to set up her own academy for girls. She feels very strongly about the need for girls to have a good education that will equip them to make an independent living. Miss Fraser intimated that she planned to invest in the scheme. However, she says it is important that Miss McDonald's reputation is spotless, if the cream of Scottish society is to entrust her with their daughters.'

She read again the note that had accompanied the money. 'Miss Fraser told me they had received an unpleasant letter, which she has now burned. But she claimed not to know who it was from, and she certainly didn't tell me she'd sent cash. One should never pay a blackmailer. It only encourages them.'

'What do you suppose the blackmail was about?' asked Inspector Chadwick. 'The usual thing?'

'Frankie says there's nothing like that about Miss McDonald and Miss Fraser,' I interjected. 'But that wouldn't stop a blackmailer, especially if they knew their victims were keen to avoid any hint of scandal.'

Mrs Jameson sighed. 'Indeed not. Miss Fraser says that Miss McDonald lost her fiancé in the War. She was, of course, bereft. He was a writer, I understand; wrote some very fine poetry about his wartime experiences.'

Which would explain, perhaps, why Miss McDonald was so scathing about James Lockwood's romances.

'Miss McDonald was left with nothing, and that's why she is so keen to ensure that women are given the chance for an independent life. Miss Fraser has money, so sees it as her duty to help. But as you say, that wouldn't stop a blackmailer.'

She shook her head, looking fierce. 'Really, if the Fosci woman wasn't already dead, I would shake her until her teeth rattled. It's one thing to flutter your eyelashes at men until they give you presents; quite another to threaten to ruin a woman's life.'

She pushed away her empty plate. 'Marjorie, have you spoken to the other servants about this business with the chambermaid and Mr Treadwell? She may not have reported it to the management, but I bet she'd have told the other maids, if only to warn them.'

I shook my head, my mouth full of salmon.

'Do it after dinner,' said Mrs Jameson. 'By the way, Peter, what's happened to that Inspector Dyson, who was so impolite to me in Broadstairs police station?' she asked. 'I thought he was leading the investigation.'

Inspector Chadwick grinned. 'Not any more, he isn't. I had a quiet word with the commissioner, who had a not-so-quiet word with the chief of the Kent constabulary. Inspector Dyson has been encouraged to take a few days off. I'm the officer in charge.'

Chapter 45

One of the pot boys let me through to the servants' private quarters, where the three chambermaids were sipping cups of Horlicks before bed. They ate early, went to bed early and rose at dawn to get all the public rooms ready before the guests came down.

A snub-nosed girl of about fifteen jumped up from the scrubbed wooden table. I recognised her from the beach. She'd been one of the maids who came down to watch while the coastguards rescued Frankie from the cave.

'Is there any news about Etta, Miss?'

'I'm afraid not. I came to ask you about something that happened to her yesterday morning with one of the guests.'

They exchanged looks, uneasy. One of them collected up their empty cups and took them to the sink.

'We all like Etta,' volunteered the girl who had spoken first. 'We don't want to get her into trouble.'

The third girl rose, pleating her apron together in her fingers. 'And she'd kill us if she found out we'd told on her. I saw you with that policeman earlier.'

'I'm just trying to help her,' I said. 'I'm not in the police. No-one's going to get into trouble for talking to me, honest.

But I'm worried about Etta. I think something bad might have happened, and she might be in danger. I need to know if she told you anything about it.'

'All right.' The first girl sat back down and stuck her elbows on the table. 'I'm Jane. Try me.'

'Listen, Jane.' I pulled out a rickety chair and sat down opposite her. 'I know what it's like. I've worked with men who couldn't keep their hands to themselves. It's horrible. But you're stuck, aren't you? You can't say anything to your boss about it, because ten to one you get the blame. But you can't always keep out of their way, either.'

Jane shrugged. 'Way of the world, ain't it, Miss? Nothing to be done about it.' I felt sad that such a young girl already knew what to expect from certain men.

I pressed on. 'I heard that one of the guests on the second floor tried it on with Etta yesterday. And that she was upset, but didn't want Mrs Heath to hear about it. Did she say anything to you? Warn you about him, or anything like that?'

They swapped glances again. This time they looked more puzzled than worried.

'Not exactly,' Jane said. She hesitated. 'Second floor?'

I nodded.

'She'd got friendly with him,' said Jane. 'That I do know, because Alfie was getting mardy about it. But Etta said it served Alfie right for making eyes at that Bianca. The Italian woman.'

'They made it up, though,' said one of the other maids. 'Etta and Alfie. After that woman got herself killed.'

I frowned. 'You're sure about that? Etta was friendly with the man – he didn't push himself on her or anything?' Although, I supposed, if he had been friendly with her earlier in the week, that might have made him more likely to try to force her attentions if she later decided she'd had enough of him.

Jane gave a decisive nod. 'I don't think there was anything like that about it. She said she didn't mind helping him out, but he'd told her not to say anything about it. And then she got scared, after the woman got herself killed and Mrs Heath kept going on about that blooming sheet.'

'So Etta did know who took the sheet?' I asked. 'Are you sure? Did she help him with it?'

The maids exchanged looks again.

'It wasn't her fault, mind,' said Jane. 'She wouldn't have done it if she'd known what was going to happen. I mean, you wouldn't, would you, Miss?'

Chapter 46

I ran back to the library, which had once more been requisitioned by the police. By the time I got there, Geoffrey Treadwell had arrived, and was slumped in a low armchair in front of the desk.

Inspector Chadwick sat at the desk in a straight-backed chair, Sergeant Cox standing behind him. Mrs Jameson was in one of the comfortable club chairs, off to one side. She indicated a chair next to her. I slipped into it and scribbled a note. She glanced at it and raised her eyebrows.

Geoffrey Treadwell looked rather seedy. His face was florid, and he sweated freely in the stuffy room. He was fidgeting, turning his cigarette case over and over in his hands. He turned to look at me and Mrs Jameson.

'What are they doing here?' he demanded.

Inspector Chadwick raised his eyebrows. 'Mrs Jameson and Miss Swallow are here to assist me, Mr Treadwell. I hope you don't object.' His tone suggested it would make little difference if he did. 'I want to know about your relationship with Anna Fosci, and also with the servants at this hotel.'

'I want my lawyer present,' stated Treadwell.

'Of course.' Inspector Chadwick got to his feet. 'In that case,

I shall arrange for our conversation to take place at Scotland Yard. Sergeant Cox, will you inform Mrs Treadwell that her husband is accompanying me to London this evening?'

'Wait,' Treadwell called, springing out of his chair. 'You can't do that.'

Inspector Chadwick smiled. 'I rather think I can, Mr Treadwell. Please give me the telephone number of your solicitor, and I will call him immediately. He can meet us there.'

'Oh, dash it all, Inspector.' Geoffrey Treadwell collapsed into the chair. 'Just ask your questions and get it over with. No need to make a song and dance about it.'

Inspector Chadwick sat back down.

'You met Anna Fosci on Friday evening,' he stated. 'You were seen walking with her on the beach. Tell me what happened, Mr Treadwell.'

He licked his lips and glanced from me to Mrs Jameson.

'Who saw me?'

'That isn't the question.'

Treadwell swallowed and ran a finger around his collar. 'I just happened to run into her. We'd had tea, the day before, in Margate. I was having a stroll on the beach before dinner, and when I saw her, I naturally said hello.'

Inspector Chadwick glanced at me. 'Miss Swallow, please tell us what you saw when you observed Mr Treadwell taking tea with Anna Fosci in Margate.'

'He had one arm around her, and his hand on her knee,' I reported. 'He told me afterwards that he had just happened to run into her there, too.'

Geoffrey Treadwell seemed to sag a little.

'Not against the law, is it?' he muttered.

227

'Indeed not,' said Inspector Chadwick. 'And what did you talk about with Miss Fosci on the beach on Friday evening?'

He rubbed his face. 'Dash it. We walked along the sand for a bit. I don't know, the weather or something.'

'And did you put your arm around her again, Mr Treadwell?'

The man looked up sharply, as if he suspected Inspector Chadwick of mocking him. Which he probably was.

'No, I didn't. My wife might have seen from the hotel terrace.' He glared at the inspector, as if daring him to make something of that.

'Not if you'd stepped inside the little cave,' said Mrs Jameson, her voice silky. 'No-one can see you once you're in there, unless they are out at sea. Although someone might have seen you leading the young woman towards the cave, of course, if they had been on the clifftop at the time.'

He reddened, and I saw at once that Mrs Jameson had made a lucky guess.

'I wanted to show her the rock formations,' he said, improbably.

'Indeed?' The inspector leaned forward. 'What are they, would you say? I understand the chalk deposits were formed by calcareous algae, resulting in some impressive fossils laid down sixty odd million years ago. Did you find any fossils in the cave?'

Next to me, Mrs Jameson pressed her handkerchief to her lips, eyes cast down. I realised she was having trouble suppressing her laughter.

'Oh, leave off this rot.' Treadwell slammed his fist into his hand. 'She was a little minx, Inspector. Playing me for a fool. She would barely let me near her; said she'd had a better offer, and I'd have to come up with more than a cream tea.'

Mrs Jameson's mouth twitched, and her eyes were dancing with merriment.

'And did you?' she murmured. 'Come up with a better offer, I mean.'

He rounded on her. 'I don't like what you're implying, Mrs Jameson.'

'Too bad,' she drawled. 'What happened, when Anna Fosci refused your advances and told you that her price had gone up? Did you get angry, Mr Treadwell? Did you try to force yourself on her? Did she struggle?'

He'd half risen from his seat, before Sergeant Cox's hand on his arm restrained him.

'No.' His voice was low and vehement. 'No, I did not. She was a silly little girl, and I know plenty like her. I had no doubt she'd come to a bad end. But I wasn't going to lose my head over her. I told her to take her better offer, and be damned.'

He sat back and stared at Inspector Chadwick defiantly. 'I went back to the hotel and had my dinner. Then I sat in the lounge bar all evening, played a few rubbers of bridge, and knew nothing more of the affair until my wife saw her body on the beach at almost midnight. You're not going to tell me nobody spotted her in all that time?'

'You do seem to be the last person who saw her alive,' said Mrs Jameson.

'But I wasn't, was I? What about the chap she was going to meet after me? Major Redfern, the silly fool. He's got a nasty temper. You've seen it yourself, Miss Swallow.' He turned to glare at me.

'Let's leave that aside for now, Mr Treadwell,' said the inspector. 'What was Etta Morrison doing in your room yesterday morning, at half past ten?'

'Eh? I have no idea who you're talking about.'

'Miss Morrison is a chambermaid at the hotel,' said Mrs Jameson. 'Perhaps you didn't know her name.'

'Why the devil should I? If she was in my room, I expect she was cleaning it. That's what she's here for.'

'That is her job,' Inspector Chadwick agreed. 'But that would not explain why she left your room in tears.'

Treadwell stared at us, and his bewilderment seemed genuine. 'I have no idea. Why don't you ask my wife? She was there all morning. Said she had a headache. Perhaps she shouted at the girl for waking her up. Wouldn't put it past her. Now, are we done here? Because I've had about enough of all this rot.'

Chapter 47

Sergeant Cox ushered Mr Treadwell away.

'Really, Peter,' said Mrs Jameson, laughing. 'Calcareous algae? Where did you get that from?'

Inspector Chadwick grinned. 'There are some very improving volumes in this library. I had a browse while I was waiting.' He turned over the leather-bound volume on the desk. '*The Geology of the Coastal Region of Dover, Ramsgate and Thanet,*' said the gold-embossed cover. 'What did you make of the fellow?'

'An unpleasant character,' observed Mrs Jameson. 'But he seemed quite convincing when he said he had no idea why Etta was in his room.'

I was bursting to tell them what I'd discovered from the servants. Quickly, I ran through what Jane had said.

'Indeed,' said Inspector Chadwick, pulling at his moustaches. 'That puts a bit of a different light on it. What do you think, Iris?'

Mrs Jameson tapped her fingers on her chin, eyes abstracted. 'It does,' she said after a few moments. 'But it might simplify things considerably. Give me a minute to think about it.'

The door to the library opened again. 'Got rid of that useless

Inspector Dyson, eh? Good show. Sergeant Cox said you wanted to talk to me. Is it about the mafia?'

Major Redfern sat heavily in the chair recently vacated by Mr Treadwell. His eyes were slightly unfocused, and the smell of whisky hung around him.

'Major Redfern, please confirm the last time you saw the woman we now know was called Anna Fosci, and your arrangements to meet her on Friday night.' Inspector Chadwick was brisk. However, the question seemed to flummox the major.

'Last see her. Hmm.' He clutched his jaw, lost in thought. His eyes misted over. 'Poor child.'

'Did you see Miss Fosci on the day she died?' asked the inspector, his voice betraying impatience.

'Oh. No, I didn't.' His eyes filled with tears. 'Thursday night, after dinner. That was the last time. All rather lovely. We sat outside the Captain Digby, in that little garden. Watched the moon rise over the sea. That's when I decided I'd ask her to marry me the next night, in the Neptune Fort, under the moon.'

He cast his face down. 'Fool that I was. I should have asked her there and then. She was shivering. It was still warm, but she felt the cold. Not used to our climate. I put my jacket around her. She always needed protection.'

I was quite moved by his description. Then I remembered that Frankie and I had seen Anna Fosci in Margate just a few hours previously, having a cuddle with Geoffrey Treadwell.

'Tell me about the arrangements for Friday,' said the inspector. 'You agreed this on Thursday night, did you?'

Major Redfern nodded. 'I told her I had something special to ask her. I went into Broadstairs the next day to look for a ring.' He pulled a little red box from his jacket pocket. 'Found this. I don't think I showed it to you before, Miss Swallow.'

He opened it. A square-cut amethyst sparkled from a filigree silver setting. 'I thought it was pretty. Hoped she'd like it.'

'It's very pretty,' I said gently. It was lovely, the filigree giving it a delicate touch. 'Where did you find it?'

I remembered him on Saturday afternoon, standing by the pawn shop in the High Street, staring at the coral and jade beads. Was that the first time he'd seen his mother's beads in the window, or had they been there when he was hunting for an engagement ring on Friday?

'Little shop by the harbour,' he said. He put the box away and wiped his eyes. 'I suppose they might take it back. Think I'll keep it, though.'

Inspector Chadwick intervened. 'And the plan was to meet Miss Fosci on Friday at 8.30pm?'

He nodded. 'After dinner. I knew Mother would make a fuss about it. Plan was to bring the girl back to the hotel with me, introduce her once it was a fait accompli. D'you see?'

'But she didn't come,' Mrs Jameson said.

He stared at her, his jaw jutting. 'No. Waited an hour. Then I went to the pub. Planned to stay there all night, but Lockwood came to get me. You know the rest.'

'Or did she?' Mrs Jameson's voice was soft.

He frowned. 'What d'you mean?'

'Did she come and meet you, then turn you down? Or perhaps you saw her on the sands, and went down to the beach. Had you seen her with someone else, Major Redfern? Geoffrey Treadwell, perhaps?'

He lurched to his feet. 'What's he been saying? The fellow's a cad. Don't trust him an inch.'

233

'Mr Treadwell walked on the sands with Miss Fosci earlier in the evening, Major,' said Inspector Chadwick. 'Did you see them together?'

'No!' He sat down again, as if winded. 'She didn't like the fellow. Told me as much – she said he wasn't respectful of women.' He frowned. 'I didn't think it was him, though.'

'Who, Major?'

'The figure on the sands. I saw someone walking over the beach while I was waiting in the Fort. Too tall to be her, or I would have gone down. It was half past nine, and I was just about to give up. Getting dark, I suppose. I couldn't see all that well. But you say it was Treadwell, hey?'

Mrs Jameson narrowed her eyes. 'Not necessarily, Major Redfern. Not necessarily.'

Chapter 48

A few minutes later, Sergeant Cox came in and encouraged the major away. He shambled out of the room, no doubt back to the bar.

'Well, that seems to put a lid on it,' said Mrs Jameson. 'Don't you think, Peter?'

He strode to the library window and looked out. The light was fading, and the wind had got up, billowing in the trees.

'We don't have enough for a court of law,' he said, frustrated. 'It's all circumstantial.'

'Perhaps... perhaps we could arrange something,' I said. 'Let the killer think they have a chance.' Mrs Jameson had set up traps for murderers before, although they were rather a risky tactic.

I told them what I had in mind.

Mrs Jameson narrowed her eyes. 'Let me see... yes. Yes, that might work.' She walked to Inspector Chadwick's side and looked out into the night. 'There are thunderstorms forecast. It's time to bring this business to an end.'

She stood silently for a moment, thinking. Then she turned and her eyes were bright and penetrating.

'Marjorie, go with Sergeant Cox to the dining room and get

Alfred to come here immediately. Tell Mr Ashcroft it's very urgent and he'll have to manage without him. We can't risk Etta's safety any longer. The killer will be forced to make a move, and she's the obvious target. Then wait in the lounge bar until we send you the signal to follow.'

I peeped around the door of the dining room from the courtyard. Alfred was standing by the Treadwells' table while Mildred Treadwell pointed at something on her plate, making a moue of dissatisfaction. Mr Treadwell snapped a few words at him, and he picked up the plate and took it away.

James Lockwood was dining alone, his back to us. As he'd promised, he was watching Alfred closely, tracking his progress across the dining room with the rejected dish.

'Quickly,' I whispered to Sergeant Cox. 'Round to the kitchen.'

The kitchens were buzzing with activity. The maids dashed around with trays of blancmange and spooned ice-cream into bowls. The pot boys were elbow-deep in dirty dishes, while the waiting staff darted in and out.

'She says the strawberry blancmange tastes too much of strawberry,' announced Alfred, rolling his eyes as he carried Mildred Treadwell's dessert plate over to the chef. 'Have we got any of the chocolate ice-cream left?'

'All right, young man,' said Sergeant Cox. 'I need to ask you to come with me. Right now, if you don't mind.'

Alfred began to protest. 'I'm in the middle of service, Mr Cox. I can't just drop everything.'

'Sorry, Alfred, but it's for Etta,' I said. 'It's really important.'

'Come on, lad. Don't make me arrest you. Come with me.'

Sergeant Cox escorted the protesting figure away, to the dismay of the remaining staff.

'What's going on?' Mr Ashcroft came in from the dining room. 'The Treadwell party say they've been waiting five minutes for a replacement pudding. What are you doing here, Miss Swallow?'

'I'm awfully sorry,' I said. 'Inspector Chadwick needs to talk to Alfred. I know it's inconvenient, but it's terribly urgent.'

I slipped away to the lounge, while Mr Ashcroft grabbed a bowl of ice-cream and tied a waiter's apron around his waist.

#

I waited for about fifteen minutes, dodging questions from Mr and Mrs Goldsmith about Mrs Jameson's arrest and sub-sequent release. Jean McDonald was sitting alone, pretending to read a doorstep of a Russian novel, but I could see she was listening hard. She seemed nervous, and looked up quickly every time the door opened, or someone passed on the terrace.

Finally, Sergeant Cox opened the door and beckoned to me.

'It's all set. Alfie's left the hotel,' he whispered. 'Time to get going.'

I put on my jacket and followed Sergeant Cox outside into the courtyard. Heavy clouds had rolled in from the sea and the sultry air was restless. The moon was invisible, the night dark.

I sniffed the air. 'It's going to rain.' I should have put on my mackintosh, but it was too late to fetch it now. Lamplight shone in the library window, where a figure watched me go, then pulled the curtain.

Sergeant Cox pointed down the driveway. 'He went that way. You'll need to be quick. Mr Lockwood's following him.'

I hurried through the portcullis gate. I could see a figure ahead of me, wrapped in a raincoat with his hat pulled down.

He turned right out of the gate, taking the road down to the bay.

I ran to catch him up. 'Wait for me, James!'

He spun around. 'Marjorie! I've been looking for you all over the place. I was worried when you didn't meet me in the lounge before dinner. But you shouldn't be out here. I think there's a storm coming.'

I laughed. 'Detectives don't get put off by a drop of rain. I am sorry about dinner. Mrs Jameson wanted me. Where are you going?'

He paused. 'I've been keeping an eye on that waiter, Alfred. I think you're right. He does know something. He was talking to Treadwell, then he disappeared into the kitchens and didn't come back.

'After ten minutes or so, I abandoned my pud and went to see if I could find him. I caught sight of him just now leaving the library and heading down the drive, so I followed.'

'Come on, then,' I said. 'We'd better hurry. Was he on his bicycle? We won't catch up with him if he's cycling.'

I strained to see in the eerie twilight. A finger of lightning streaked over the sea, reaching down to touch the horizon. A second later came a low rumbling, as if rocks were shifting in water.

'He's on foot.' James hesitated. 'Look, I'm not sure this is a good idea. Why don't you go back to the hotel and wait for me? I don't want to put you in any danger.'

'I'll be all right,' I said. 'Look, isn't that Alfred? Down by the far side of the bay, almost at the tavern. We should hurry.'

'I'm going as fast as I can,' said James, his voice grim. We were heading uphill again, around the curve of the road. James hobbled along surprisingly fast, his jaw clenched against the pain.

I glanced behind us. Lightning danced again over the sea, and the thunder grumbled. The wind was getting up, and I could hear the waves crashing on the beach.

'He's going down the path across the golf course,' said James. 'We're not far behind him now.'

The first fat drops of rain began to fall as we reached the Captain Digby pub. The door was flung open, and a tall figure emerged, wrapped in a practical rain cape. I caught a glimpse of her face, distraught beneath her hat. She saw me, then turned and hurried away from us along the golf course path.

'Miss Fraser,' I called in alarm. 'Helen, wait!'

Chapter 49

The path made its way between tall gorse bushes, their sweet coconut scent mingling with the metallic smell of the rain as it swept in from the sea. The tall figure ahead of us kept going, head down.

'You're going to get drenched. Why don't you shelter at the Captain Digby?' James pushed aside the overgrown bushes. 'Damn. These things are prickly.' He sucked his finger.

A sheet of lightning lit up the sea, illuminating a mass of seething waves. When the thunder came, it cracked loud as mortar fire. I saw James flinch, throwing an arm up over his face as if sheltering in the trenches. But he kept on, almost running along the path that led around the golf course, heading straight towards the sea. Helen Fraser strode quickly ahead of us. The desperation I'd glimpsed in her face alarmed me.

The rain was pelting down hard now, plastering my hair to my face. My linen dress clung to my legs. Lightning flickered again, splitting the indigo sky and lighting up the ruined towers of the Neptune Fort.

'That's where he has gone,' James muttered. 'Got him.'

Helen Fraser, however, walked straight past, heading into the seething storm. I hesitated as James pushed aside hanging fronds of ivy, shiny with lashing rain, and disappeared through the archway into the fort. Should I go with him, or follow her? This hadn't been in the plan.

'Please, Helen,' I called to her back. 'Be careful!' She raised a hand but did not turn her head.

I ducked into the fort and followed James.

Standing at the far side, huddled together under an umbrella, were Etta and Alfie. She clutched his arm, shivering in a belted tan mackintosh. Tall, slim. Put her in a white sun hat, cover her tawny hair, and you'd easily mistake her for Anna Fosci.

Alfie stared back at us, his jaw set in defiance.

'Thank goodness.' James advanced towards them. 'It's all right, Etta. You're safe now. That man can't do anything to you. Come on, let's get you back to the hotel.'

She shook her head. 'I ain't coming.'

'I know you're scared,' he said. 'But there's nothing to be frightened of. Is there, Miss Swallow? Come back with me, and we'll get everything sorted out. All right?'

She looked uncertain. 'Everything?' She turned her gaze on me. 'I don't want to get into trouble.'

James smiled. 'Nothing to worry about. The police already know. You've got nothing to be afraid of.'

'She's not going anywhere with you,' said Alfred. He pulled Etta closer to him. 'You stay with me, Etta.'

'Let go of her,' said James. He clutched his stick in one hand. 'I may be an old crock, but I swear I won't let you hurt that girl.'

'Nobody's going to hurt anyone,' I said, anxiously. 'Etta, why don't you tell me what happened on Friday night?'

James turned on me. 'Later,' he snapped. 'We're all getting soaked standing around. We need to get you both back, and away from that man. Plenty of time for talking later.'

'I didn't mean any harm by it,' said Etta. Her voice cracked. 'I thought it was just a bit of a joke. Dressing up to look like a ghost, to give everyone a scare. That's what you said, Mr Lockwood. A white lady, like in the stories.'

'Shut up!' he roared. James flung down his stick, his face furious, and limped over to her. 'Shut up, you stupid girl.'

He grabbed her shoulder. Alfred shoved him backwards, balling his fists with a look of fury.

'Don't you touch her,' he yelled.

Etta shrieked as James pulled a gun from the pocket of his trench coat and pointed it to her head.

'Nobody move,' he gasped.

I staggered to a halt, halfway across the fort. How stupid of us! Why did we not consider that he might have a service revolver? I swallowed, remembering the last time I'd stared down the barrel of a gun. But that had been a cold-blooded killer, and James was an angry, damaged man. No less dangerous for that.

'James, please put that down,' I said, as calmly as I could manage. 'Nobody here is going to hurt you.'

He glanced my way, but kept the revolver trained on Etta. She looked terrified, as well she might.

'This is your fault, Marjorie,' he said. 'You should have left Etta alone. She'd have kept her mouth shut.'

'I will, I promise,' said poor Etta.

'Too bloody late,' said James.

He didn't know what to do, I realised. We'd backed him into a corner like a trapped animal. If Etta was to escape unharmed, I had to show him a way out.

'James, lower the gun. We'll let you go, won't we, Alfred?

Alfred was staring at the gun in dumb horror. He hadn't let go of Etta's hand. 'All right. Don't hurt her,' he said, although I could see it cost him.

'James. You can drive to Ramsgate in half an hour; get the night boat to Ostend. But don't hurt anyone,' I begged. 'I'll tell the police you went to London.'

'Like hell you will,' sneered James. 'You've set me up, haven't you? How many people are waiting outside?'

'Nobody,' I lied. 'James, this is your chance. But put the gun down now.'

The ivy stirred and Helen Fraser pushed through into the fort. 'What on earth's going on?' she asked.

James whipped around to face her. I dived for his gun, at the same time that Alfred grabbed his arm. There was a loud crack, and I saw James's face contort in pain. Etta screamed again.

For a moment I had no idea what was happening. I saw the gun on the ground and snatched it up, as James slumped to the floor.

'Etta!' shouted Alfred. 'Are you all right?'

She flung herself into his arms.

Inspector Chadwick, Mrs Jameson and Sergeant Cox pushed their way through the curtain of ivy into the fort.

'That's enough,' said Inspector Chadwick. 'James Lockwood, I'm arresting you for the murder of Anna Fosci and the attempted murder of Etta Morrison. Cox, will you do the honours?'

'He's hurt,' I said. I thrust the gun at the inspector and knelt beside James. He was clutching his thigh, and I could see blood oozing slowly between his fingers. 'Where's the wound, James? Show me.'

'You bitch,' he gasped. 'Treacherous, filthy little...' I decided not to listen to the rest of the sentence. I'd been called worse, but not much.

'I suppose that's what you said to Anna Fosci,' I said. 'When you met her on the beach on Friday night, after you'd seen Geoffrey Treadwell kissing her in the cave. She turned you down, did she?'

He looked up at me, his face splashed with mud and his hair soaked. His expression was not anger, as I'd expected, but anguish.

'You don't bloody get it, do you?' he said. 'None of you bloody get it. You expect us to come back from all... all that... and just get on with it? Like nothing had happened.'

'Lots of men had a hard time in the War,' I said, stoutly. Good men, who were thankful to be alive, back in civilisation and out of the hell of the trenches. 'And most of them do just get on with it.'

He shook his head. 'Well, bully for them. And the rest of us can go hang. Half-men. And you say you feel sorry for us, but we can see it. Disgust. Even that Italian tart. Horror at the thought of actually touching us.'

'I am sorry,' I said. 'Truly.' I couldn't think of anything else to say.

Sergeant Cox stepped forward with handcuffs. 'Come along, sir. Let me take a look at your leg. The police car is waiting on the road.'

Chapter 50

I watched them disappear down the path, the prisoner supported between the two policemen.

Mrs Jameson held an umbrella over my head, although in truth there was little point. I couldn't have got much wetter.

'Well done, Marjorie. You saved the day. Etta and Alfred, you were very brave. Now, let's get you to the Captain Digby to dry off. The police can come back to take your statements later.'

Miss Fraser walked with us, her expression grave. However, the desperation I'd seen on her face earlier was gone.

'What were you doing out on the cliffs?' I asked. 'I was worried about you.'

She gave me a quick glance. 'I'd rather foolishly sent some money to... to a person who had tried to get money from me.'

'Anna Fosci,' I said, understanding. 'You sent it to the pub.'

She nodded. 'I thought I had better retrieve it. In the circumstances.' She sighed. 'It was stupid of me, I know. The manager told me that he'd given the envelope to the police. I was worried that they would think I had something to do with... But it's all over.'

She took a deep breath. 'I wasn't sure where I was going

after I came out of the tavern. Just walking, thinking it over. But then I heard shouting from the fort, so I came back to see if you were all right.'

I smiled. 'That was kind of you, Miss Fraser.'

'I am sorry I was unable to advise you earlier, Miss Fraser,' said my employer. 'And that I let you walk into such a dangerous situation. We weren't close enough to stop you without alerting Mr Lockwood. Perhaps… if you would like, I could advise you on the best way to handle blackmail. Should the situation arise again.'

Miss Fraser gave her a long look. 'Miss McDonald and I have nothing to hide, Mrs Jameson. Let's hope that it doesn't.'

#

Inside the Captain Digby tavern, we sat wrapped in blankets, while lightning sliced across the sky and thunder roared around the bay. Rain lashed down against the thick flint walls.

Mr Badgett lit a fire and Etta and I huddled close to it, drying off.

'I'm worried about what to say to the police, Miss,' she told me. 'Am I in trouble?'

I tried to reassure her. 'You weren't to know.' Although if she had come forward and spoken to the police after Anna Fosci's death, she would have saved everyone a lot of trouble.

'Like I said, I just felt sorry for him, because of his leg. And he seemed really nice. When I cleaned his room in the mornings, he used to stop writing and have a cup of coffee, and we'd chat. He made me laugh, reading out bits that he was writing. And I told him I wanted to be an actress one day, like that Sarah Post. He said he'd tell her about me, see if she could help.'

Sarah would be furious to have missed all the excitement, I

reflected. I'd ask her to talk to Etta and give her some advice on the business.

'Then on Friday night, he came round to the staff kitchen, just before I went to bed. He asked if I could help him. He said he wanted to play a joke on his friends, because they'd gone to the theatre without him.'

'That was us,' I said.

'I'm sorry, Miss. I didn't know. I was supposed to be a ghost and give them a scare by standing by the gatepost. But then I was to run away quickly afterwards, so they wouldn't know if I'd been real or not.'

She took a breath. 'I suggested just draping the sheet over my head like a ghost in the movies, but he said no, it had to look like a frock, or it wouldn't work. He said there was a legend about it, a white lady who haunted the castle. I cut it up and sewed it together as best I could. I've never been much cop at sewing.

'He said he'd get rid of the sheet and Mrs Heath would never know. But she's a right tartar. She spotted we were one sheet down right away, and I didn't know what to say. I had to pretend to look for it, even though I knew full well what had happened to it.'

Mrs Jameson brought us coffee. 'Did you not realise the connexion to the murder of Anna Fosci?' she asked.

'Not for a while.' Etta took the cup gratefully. 'Thank you, that's lovely.'

I folded my hands around my cup. My dress steamed gently by the fire and my hair was going frizzy as it dried.

'It was only after the police had interviewed us all, and they asked if anyone had seen her after twenty past ten. I said I hadn't – which was true – but then I realised that was the time

I was standing by the gate. I didn't want to get in trouble for taking the sheet, so I said I'd gone to bed at the normal time.

'I asked Mr Lockwood about it, yesterday morning. I said I thought that I should perhaps tell the police, in case it had caused a muddle. He got quite cross and told me not to be silly.'

She cast her eyes down. 'He shouted at me. He said the police would arrest me for hiding evidence. I was a bit upset, so I ran out and almost bumped into Alfie, who was bringing up Mr Lockwood's coffee. I think Alfie thought… he thought there was something wrong. That Mr Lockwood had tried it on. So afterwards, I told him all about it.'

Alfred was standing by the window, watching the storm. He turned and gave Etta a smile that warmed my heart.

'He was that worried,' she whispered. 'He tried to get me to tell the police, but I was too scared. Then at lunch, he heard you all talking about the sheet. He said Mr Lockwood was pretending not to know anything about it. That's when we agreed I should go and stay at his mum's house and keep out of everyone's way, until the killer was caught.'

'Alfred was right to be worried for your safety,' said Mrs Jameson. 'Mr Lockwood wanted you out of the way. I'm just sorry we didn't think of him having a gun. I would never have suggested you meet Alfred at the fort if I had.'

'He really might have shot me,' Etta said, a tremor in her voice. 'And before, I thought he was nice. I trusted him, but now I feel like such an idiot.'

I squeezed her hand. 'So did I,' I said. 'But you don't always know who you can trust. Not until you know them well, anyway.'

I looked up to see Mrs Jameson giving me a quizzical look.

'Indeed,' she said. She sat beside us and held her hands out to the fire. 'Trust has to be earned. And it goes both ways, Etta. That young man of yours has shown himself trustworthy, I'd say.'

She turned to look at me. 'It's not easy to rebuild trust, when it's breached. But sometimes, it's worth a try.'

Epilogue

We stood before a tall arched doorway, the stone darkened with centuries of smoke and dirt. The granite setts of the narrow Via Giulia were still in shadow between the tall houses. Even so, the clear blue sky high above shimmered with heat.

'Palazzo del Gonfolone,' said Mrs Jameson. The stone archway framed double doors, heavy dark wood with bronze rings set into them. The stucco walls were a patchy ochre, discoloured with grime and streaked with green. 'I lived in this building for seven years.'

Frankie and I craned upwards at the rows of shuttered windows, painted a dull brown. It wasn't like my idea of a palace. I thought of the crisp white frontage of Buckingham Palace, with its orderly railings and scarlet-uniformed guards. Palaces in Rome were different, it seemed.

Mrs Jameson noticed my expression. 'It's nicer on the inside,' she conceded. 'There's a courtyard with a fountain, and the rooms are well-proportioned. Our apartment was on the top floor, and the light streamed in during the mornings. You could see the river from our breakfast room.'

She reached out her gloved hand to the bronze ring, and for

a moment I thought she was going to knock. But she simply rested her fingers there, her head bowed.

She turned and smiled at us, her eyes sad. 'Thank you for indulging my nostalgia, girls. Now, it's too hot to walk uphill. Frankie, dear, see if you can find some kind of conveyance.'

We had arrived in Rome late the previous night and were staying in the comfortable Hotel de Russie. We had taken a pony and trap from the railway station, after a four day journey in which we had crossed the English Channel by steamer then taken endless trains through France and Italy. Mrs Jameson had promised us a week to see the sights of Rome. Today, she said, was business.

We walked through the streets to the road beside the wide Tiber river, where tall plane trees provided some welcome shade. Black-gowned priests walked past, smoking cigarettes and chatting. Frankie put her fingers in her mouth and let out a piercing whistle.

A thin-faced fellow trotted up in a smartly painted carriage, drawn by two glossy chestnut horses. Although there were plenty of motor cars on the streets of Rome, most of the hire trade still seemed to be horse-drawn.

'Convento Ospedaliero di Santa Francesca Romana,' announced Mrs Jameson. 'Trastevere.'

The man touched his cap, and we trotted off across the bridge over the river, the carriage jolting on the stones. We plunged into a maze of narrow streets crammed with picturesque red-tiled houses, turning this way and that past shady pavement cafes and markets selling glossy vegetables. Bright-eyed rats scampered among the market refuse at the side of the road.

Then we were winding up into the hills, through steep

streets shaded with tall, billowing pine trees. The driver took the hairpin bends in his stride and the horses appeared used to the steepness of the incline.

We finally drew up in a scruffy little square, at the base of a set of wide steps. A couple of men lounged against the wall, both dressed in black shirts cinched into tight-waisted trousers. They wore tin helmets pushed back on their heads, and were smoking. Their uniform was familiar from the newsreels of the March on Rome, two years ago.

'Look at those ugly so-and-so's,' muttered Frankie, balling her hands into fists.

The driver gave them a wary look. 'Be careful,' he muttered. 'Fascisti. Dangerous.'

Mrs Jameson paid the fare, giving him the usual generous tip and asking something I didn't understand.

'He'll wait,' she said. 'Quickly, up the steps. Frankie, keep quiet and take my arm.' Frankie, out of her usual chauffeur uniform and wearing a sober dark jacket and trousers with a cloth cap, did as she said, although I could see she was itching to make a rude remark. She'd made a complete recovery from her injury in the cave, although it had left a nasty scar.

The men watched us go, but said nothing.

#

The steps led to a paved plateau, beside which was a shaded colonnade. The floors above had barred windows. Faded frescos of saints decorated each archway, behind big terracotta pots containing silver-leaved olive trees.

'This is pretty,' I said, stopping to catch my breath from the climb up the steps. The bustle of the city, the noise of lorries and street pedlars, fell away.

At the end of the colonnade, a studded oak door swung open.

'Signora Jameson,' exclaimed a lilting voice. 'Iris. And your friends. You are very welcome.'

It was Sister Agnese. She beckoned us inside, taking a cautious look down the steps. We walked into a dimly lit chapel, its simple geometry leading to a mass of candles before the richly decorated altar.

'The soldiers are still there,' said Mrs Jameson, after they had embraced and exchanged greetings.

'I supposed they would be. So far, they have left us in peace,' said Sister Agnese. 'The man who calls himself Il Duce, their leader Mussolini, professes himself a good Catholic. But we shall see.'

She held out her hands to me and Frankie, with her warm smile. 'I am so happy to see you both again. Now, come through to the refectory, where we can talk in privacy.'

We sat in a white-painted room with a long wooden table, where a young nun fetched us thimble-sized cups of sweetened, tarry dark coffee. She glanced in confusion at Frankie.

'È bene, è una ragazza,' said Sister Agnese. Frankie gave the young woman a broad smile, and hitched up her breeches.

'I wanted to tell you in person. As you were so good as to come and warn me,' said Mrs Jameson. 'And I would like my friends to know the full story.'

Sister Agnese nodded. 'That is good. Letters… one does not know who is reading them these days. Even letters to a convent,' she said.

Mrs Jameson looked down into her coffee cup for a moment. 'She found me,' she said. 'Anna Fosci, to give her real name.'

'Not Julia?' asked Sister Agnese.

'Not Julia. And not, as she told you, the daughter of Julian Jameson.'

Sister Agnese sighed. 'I am sorry. I did wonder if that was true. But stranger things have happened.'

Mrs Jameson continued. 'Anna Fosci was a thief and a chancer. But unfortunately, it was not only with me that she tried to play games. She's dead, Sister Agnese. Killed by a man who was too angry to lose.'

Sister Agnese's eyes widened, and she pressed her hands across her mouth. 'Mio Dio. Che orrore.' She crossed herself.

Mrs Jameson's face was sombre. 'Horrific, yes.' She sighed. 'She told me she was entitled to money. To half of Julian Jameson's estate. She threatened me with exposure, if I did not pay her.'

Mrs Jameson gave a grim smile. 'Poor child. From what I have learned of her since, she was born in the poorest part of Naples. Her mother worked in a brothel, and she left as soon as she could, to avoid the same fate. Instead, she became a thief and a trickster. I wish I had taken the time to speak with her. I might have been able to help. But as you know, I don't take kindly to being threatened.'

I held my breath. What exactly had Anna Fosci threatened to tell people? Did I dare to ask?

'Threatened with what?' asked Frankie, bluntly.

Mrs Jameson gave a half smile, although her face was twisted with complicated emotion. 'I will show you.'

She rose, and Sister Agnese led us through a small courtyard where a cluster of cypresses dappled the gravel with shade. Above the doorway was a statue of St Francis of Assisi, and a plaque announcing, 'Ospedale per Incurabili'.

We walked through a peaceful, sun-filled room, where men

and women lay in beds beneath windows open to catch the light breeze. A corridor opened onto small private rooms. Nuns in brown habits with white aprons and veils flitted among their charges.

Sister Agnese opened a door.

'Buongiorno, Signor, come stai oggi?' she asked in a cheerful voice. She walked in and beckoned to us. 'You have some visitors.'

Mrs Jameson walked through, head held high. She did not look at us. Frankie and I exchanged glances and followed.

A grey-haired man sat before a table, his back to us. He had a purple wax crayon in his hand and was scribbling intently on a sheet of paper. After a moment, he looked around. His face – the handsome face I'd seen in newspaper photographs, with its hint of sensual cruelty – was amiable but vacant. He looked incuriously from one to the other of us.

I bit back an exclamation of surprise. Julian Jameson, supposedly dead for more than twenty years, was alive.

'Iris,' he stated, pointing at Mrs Jameson. His gaze passed over me and Frankie as if we were not there. He smiled at Sister Agnese, the open mouthed smile of an infant. 'She shot me,' he said. His voice was not angry, or accusatory. Merely surprised.

'Hello, Julian,' said Mrs Jameson. 'I'm glad to see you're working again.'

He looked down at the paper and smiled with pride. It was covered in purple scribbles, the sort a child might do before learning how to draw properly. I could discern no design, no order to the loops and whorls.

'She shot me,' he said again, conversationally. Then he applied himself once more to his drawing.

Mrs Jameson sighed. 'Nothing has changed,' she said.

Sister Agnese shook her head. 'Nothing has changed for twenty years, Iris. That is the way, sometimes, with brain injury. But he is not unhappy. He is contented here with us to look after him. You have done everything you can.'

Mrs Jameson walked to the window and gazed out. 'I wanted to see him again. And to tell you what had happened to Anna Fosci. She had visited him, I understand. I wonder how she came to know about him.'

Sister Agnese shook her head. 'The police, the American embassy… many people were involved in the decision to tell the world that Mr Jameson had met an accidental death.'

'Too many,' agreed Mrs Jameson. 'It's always the cover-up that gets you. Secrets have a habit of leaking out.'

'Not from this place,' said Sister Agnese, firmly. 'We put our confidence in God, Iris. We need no other judge or jury here.'

#

Somewhat to my surprise, the horses and carriage were still waiting in the dusty square at the foot of the steps. One of the black-shirted soldiers peeled himself away from the wall and strolled over to us. He held out his hand.

'Documenti?'

Mrs Jameson took her passport from her handbag and handed it to him.

He gestured to me and Frankie. 'Sono Americani?'

She nodded. 'My son and my daughter,' she said. 'We have been visiting the sick and saying prayers.' Frankie and I stood very still, our eyes on the ground.

'Bene.' The man stood aside, and we climbed into the carriage. The driver clicked his tongue, and the horses carried us quickly away.

'Cimetero Inglese,' called Mrs Jameson from the window. The man raised his whip in acknowledgement.

My head was still whirling with all we had learned. I gazed at Mrs Jameson's profile. Her jaw was firm, her nose aquiline, her fine grey eyes fixed on the streets outside. She had always believed, she told me, in natural justice. Which was not necessarily the same as human justice, administered by human courts. I knew Julian Jameson had treated her with cruelty. Even so, was what we had just seen natural justice?

She turned from her observation of the streets outside the carriage. 'One more stop,' she said. 'And then you can ask me any questions you like.'

'All right,' said Frankie. 'It's a deal.'

This would be Frankie's last trip with us, she'd told me. She'd found premises for the motor mechanic shop she had long wanted to set up for herself. She'd been carefully saving up her wages ever since we met, and a gift from a grateful client of Mrs Jameson had given her the capital she'd needed. I would miss her horribly, even though she would be only a few streets away from the house in Bedford Square.

The carriage finally drew up on a tree-lined street. 'Cimetero Inglese,' called the driver.

The English Cemetery. We walked along the gravel paths shaded by cypress trees. It was a tranquil, verdant place, interspersed with white marble gravestones. A few people lingered by the stone raised to the memory of the poet John Keats.

'Through here,' said Mrs Jameson, leading us past a bush covered in bright pink flowers. She stood before a simple headstone with only a name and two dates: William Jameson, born 1900, died 1904. She did not bow her head but rested her hand on the stone.

'Your son,' I said. My heart contracted.

'Our son,' she said. 'Who died of a fever, which might not have killed him if his father had done as I begged and arranged for a doctor to visit.' Her voice was controlled, any anger long dissipated. Only sorrow remained.

'Julian was working on a portrait of me. I was not allowed to leave the studio all day, although I was worried about William, who had felt too hot and became feverish overnight. He was left with the servants, who were too frightened to go against Julian's wishes. When I was finally released to go to him, it was too late.'

I found my throat too tight to speak.

'No blooming wonder you shot him,' said Frankie. 'I'd have done the same.'

Mrs Jameson gave a small laugh, which might have been a sob. 'I didn't shoot him then. William was the only reason I had for staying in Rome. After the funeral, I bought a train ticket to Switzerland. I hadn't decided where to go after that. Julian came back unexpectedly while I was packing. He could not bear the thought of being left, you see. It offended his sense of pride. He barged into my room with his gun.'

She swallowed. 'I thought he was going to kill me. I grabbed the gun, and turned it back on him. I suppose it might have gone either way. But as he says, I shot him. He's been saying it ever since. I still don't think he quite believes it.'

She shook her head. 'Perhaps it would have been better to be honest about it at the time. But the Italian judiciary were not known for leniency, and I was very frightened. I called on the American consul, whom I had met while trying to arrange my departure. He helped. It was expensive, but I had plenty of money. The servants testified the agreed story to the police, the police talked to the British embassy about the death of one of their citizens, the consul had a quiet word with the nuns of the Convent of Santa Francesca Romana. The announcement went out: Julian Jameson had died of an accidentally self-inflicted gunshot wound. I left for Geneva as soon as the arrangements were made.'

She looked at the ground. 'Well, now you know the truth. If you wish, Marjorie, you are free to leave my employment with three months' wages and an excellent reference. And I won't hold you to any vows of silence.' She looked me straight in the eye. 'I put my trust in you to do what you think is right.'

I wiped my eyes. 'Natural justice,' I said. 'I don't want to leave your employment, Mrs Jameson. I've never had a better job in my life.'

I held out my hand, and we shook on it.

'Now,' said Mrs Jameson, 'we have the whole of Rome to explore. Where shall we go next?'

* * *

Author's note

This is the sixth Marjorie Swallow book, and the last one in this series. However, Marjorie and friends may return for another series in future.

I hope you've enjoyed the Marjorie Swallow mysteries. If you would like to keep in touch and find out what I write next, sign up to my newsletter at my website, annasayburnlane.com.

And if you've enjoyed any of my books, in any format, please do leave a review online. Reviews help other readers to find my books.

Acknowledgements

Thank you to George Fitzsimons, nun consultant and Rome guide. Thank you to Diana Ford for bridge advice. As always, any errors are my own.

Thank you to my fantastic editor Alison Jack and terrific cover designer Donna Rogers. You're the cat's pyjamas.

Thanks to my ace beta reader team: Christina, Rosalie, Radhika, Madeleine, Jean, Emma, Michelle, Cynthia, Candice, Victoria, Deborah and Dana.

Historical note

I'd long wanted to set a book on the Kent coast, near where I live. I noticed Kingsgate Castle (now private residences) while walking the coastal path from Broadstairs to Margate, and was intrigued enough to find out more. As you can imagine, I was thrilled to discover it had been a smart hotel in the 1920s, the Kingsgate Castle Hotel, popular with golfers and theatre people. The perfect place, I decided, for Marjorie and Mrs Jameson to take a break.

Kingsgate Castle featured in several guidebooks of the time, which helped me to get a feel for the type of activities people enjoyed at smart seaside hotels. It was known for golf and tennis, with dancing and bridge in the evenings.

I also looked up the hotel in newspapers of the time and was startled to find court reports of an assault, when a retired Indian Army major did serious damage to another guest after a game of bridge got a bit heated. I couldn't resist incorporating this into the plot.

But I was keen to get Marjorie and Frankie out of the smart hotel and down to Margate, where the Dreamland pleasure park had recently opened with the brand-new scenic railway, a wooden rollercoaster which attracted swarms of visitors. The Dreamland Heritage Trust has a website full of information about the history of Dreamland, and lots of fascinating photographs.

Local history blogs were useful when I needed a theatre for Sarah and Bertie Post to perform in, and I settled on The Hippodrome at Margate, which sadly no longer exists. It was a huge, luxurious modern place in its day, doing twice-nightly music hall or repertory performances.

If you'd like to know more about my research into this book and the world of the 1920s, take a look at my blog, The Stories Behind the Story, at annasayburnlane.substack.com.

About the Author

Anna Sayburn Lane is a novelist and journalist. She writes historical cozy mysteries and contemporary thrillers.

Anna studied English and History at university, then began her career as a reporter on a London newspaper, later moving into medical journalism.

She published her first novel, *Unlawful Things*, in 2018, followed by *The Peacock Room*, *The Crimson Thread* and *Folly Ditch*. *Unlawful Things* was shortlisted for the Virago New Crime Writer award and picked as a Crime in the Spotlight choice by the Bloody Scotland crime writing festival.

In 2023 she began writing the 1920s murder mystery series of classic detective stories set in 1920s London. *Blackmail In Bloomsbury* is the first in the series, featuring apprentice detective Marjorie Swallow. *The Soho Jazz Murders, Death At Chelsea, The Riviera Mystery, Death On Fleet Street* and *Murder On The White Cliffs* continue the series.

Anna lives between London and the Kent coast.

You can connect with me on:

◐ https://annasayburnlane.com

▪ https://www.facebook.com/annasayburnlane

✎ https://annasayburnlane.substack.com

Subscribe to my newsletter:

✉ https://annasayburnlane.com/signup

Also by Anna Sayburn Lane

Step back into the roaring twenties with classic detective novels set in 1920s London. *Murder On The White Cliffs* is the sixth in the series featuring plucky apprentice detective Marjorie Swallow.

Blackmail In Bloomsbury: book 1
Everyone at the party had a secret. Someone killed to keep theirs...

When a bohemian party ends in murder, there's no shortage of suspects. Half of Bloomsbury wanted Mrs Norris dead – but who wielded the knife?

Was it the handsome but troubled artist? The vivacious young actress? Or the aristocratic lady novelist? Marjorie and Mrs Jameson must find the true killer to save an innocent man from the noose. From the garden squares of Bloomsbury to the seedy backstreets of Soho, they navigate the glamour and peril of Jazz Age London in a thrilling story of secrets and lies. Marjorie needs all her wit, pluck and charm in this perilous hunt for the killer.

This classic murder mystery will keep you guessing to the very last page. The first in the 1920s Murder Mystery series, Blackmail in Bloomsbury will delight fans of Agatha Christie and classic crime.

The Soho Jazz Murders: book 2

It's January 1923 and London feels dreary after the festivities of Christmas. So Marjorie is excited about meeting the American Ambassador's niece, a genuine 1920s flapper with a love of jazz, dancing and fun.

But their night out at Soho's infamous Harlequin Club comes to a tragic end. Soon Marjorie is working undercover as a dance hostess in the club to unmask the drugs gangs that threaten the West End. It's a perilous occupation - and there are more deaths to come.

The Soho Jazz Murders is the second in the 1920s Murder Mystery series, featuring the irresistible apprentice detective Marjorie Swallow.

Death At Chelsea: book 3

Detective duo Mrs Jameson and Marjorie Swallow are called to investigate when a famous gardener suspects that someone is sabotaging her priceless lilies, ahead of the 1923 Chelsea Flower Show.

But soon it's not just the flowers that are dying. Rival gardeners, intrepid plant hunters and King George V himself are caught up in a poisonous bouquet with its roots deep in the mountains of Tibet.

The third in the Marjorie Swallow 1920s Murder Mystery series takes readers to grand country houses, dodgy pubs serving Covent Garden flower market and – of course – all the glamour of Chelsea.

The Riviera Mystery: book 4

Ready for a trip to the French Riviera? This "sunny place for shady people" hides dark secrets. Marjorie and Mrs. Jameson embark on a dream vacation aboard the famous Blue Train, only to be swept into a whirlwind of intrigue, deception, and murder.

Invited to stay at the luxurious Villa Beau Rivage, they're surrounded by diamond merchants, film stars, and artists. But when a tragic death shatters the party's glitz, Marjorie finds herself drawn into a deadly game where no one can be trusted.

Can Marjorie and Mrs. Jameson uncover the truth? Dive into a world of 1920s glamour, mystery, and suspense.

Death On Fleet Street: book 5

When the Daily Post received a notice announcing the death of Lord Ravensbourne, something is clearly up. Not only is his lordship the owner of the Post, but he is still very much alive.

Apprentice sleuth Marjorie Swallow must find out who sent the death notice, before the threat becomes reality. But Lord Ravensbourne collects enemies like other men collect stamps. Everyone has a good reason to wish him dead.

Soon Marjorie is deep in the murky world of 1920s Fleet Street, the home of British newspapers, where backstabbing journalists will do anything for a scoop. Can she protect Lord Ravensbourne – or will the sinister prediction end up as front page news?

www.ingramcontent.com/pod-product-compliance
Lightning Source LLC
Chambersburg PA
CBHW022254290725
30340CB00015B/145